THIEF
of
DREAMS

THIEF of DREAMS

JOHN YOUNT

VIKING

VIKING
Published by the Penguin Group
Viking Penguin, a division of Penguin Books USA Inc.,
375 Hudson Street, New York, New York 10014, U.S.A.
Penguin Books Ltd, 27 Wrights Lane,
London W8 5TZ, England
Penguin Books Australia Ltd, Ringwood,
Victoria, Australia
Penguin Books Canada Ltd, 2801 John Street,
Markham, Ontario, Canada L3R 1B4
Penguin Books (N.Z.) Ltd, 182–190 Wairau Road,
Auckland 10, New Zealand

Penguin Books Ltd, Registered Offices:
Harmondsworth, Middlesex, England

First published in 1991 by Viking Penguin,
a division of Penguin Books USA Inc.

10 9 8 7 6 5 4 3 2 1

PUBLISHER'S NOTE
This is a work of fiction. Names, characters, places, and incidents
either are the product of the author's imagination or are used
fictitiously, and any resemblance to actual persons, living or
dead, events, or locales is entirely coincidental.

Grateful acknowledgment is made for permission to reprint "Futility" from *Collected
Poems of Wilfred Owen*. Copyright © 1963 by Chatto & Windus, Ltd. Reprinted by
permission of New Directions Publishing Corporation. *The Poems of Wilfred Owen* is
published in Great Britain by Chatto & Windus.

LIBRARY OF CONGRESS CATALOGING IN PUBLICATION DATA
Yount, John, 1935–
      Thief of dreams/John Yount.
         p.   cm.
      ISBN 0-670-83802-0
      I. Title.
   PS3575.O89T48   1991
   813'.54—dc20   90-50391

Printed in the United States of America
Set in Sabon
Designed by Bernard Schliefer

This one for Deborah,
in celebration of her spirit
and the long, lyrical parabola
of line she casts.

THIEF
of
DREAMS

PROLOGUE

It was 1948 and everyone watching the truck pull the house trailer across the front walk, breaking flagstones and crushing plantings, was unhappy. Worse, the trailer had to go around in front of the farmhouse where there was only twelve feet or so of reasonably level ground before the lawn sloped steeply down to the highway, and not all that ground was usable because there was a thick growth of flowering quince planted just in front of the porch.

But it wasn't just the damage the trailer was doing or the peril it was in that made the family, gathered around to watch, so worried and sad. Madeline Tally had left her husband and come home to stay with her parents, and to them as well as to James, her son, marriages were supposed to keep going like the roll of seasons or the sun coming up in the morning. Even though Madeline's husband was a rough construction man, known to take a drink, and Madeline's mother and father were quiet, steady, churchgoing, country people; still vows were vows, and anyway, they'd grown fond of him. But Harley and Bertha Marshall had taken their daughter and grandson in because they wouldn't have known how to do otherwise.

As for James, he was thirteen and understood almost everything that was in the air, even if some of what he knew, he kept in that sad, sure, nonverbal chamber of the heart where everyone keeps a great deal of what they know. He was worried about

1

his own culpability in all this trouble, and he had other worries too, not necessarily separate, about whether he had, or would ever be able to acquire, enough sense, strength, and bravery to get along in the world. So, burdened and subdued, he stood a little apart from the others, watching the trailer inching along and listening to the shrubs beginning to crack and break against its side. He could see the grim face of the driver in the rearview mirror of his truck with his jaw set like iron against the damage he was doing and against the beginning tilt of the trailer. And he could see his grandmother and two first cousins in the side yard, watching the truck and trailer creep toward them, his grandmother wringing her hands in her apron and his cousins not bothering to hide their general disapproval.

"Mercy," Grandmother Marshall said when the trailer began to lean dangerously toward the highway.

His cousins, Clara and Virginia, were fifteen and seventeen, and James wasn't completely sure just what their bad attitude was made of. A little jealousy, maybe, that his mother and he amounted to two more orphans his grandparents were taking in, as Clara and Virginia had been taken in when their parents died the year James was born. Maybe it was the damage the trailer was doing. Deep tire tracks across the lawn, crushed plantings along the walk, broken flagstones, and now the shrubs in front of the porch scraping and breaking against the side of the trailer. James figured the ugly, purple house trailer had to be a part of it, not only for the damage it was doing but because the cousins might think it would make them look like a trashy family to have it in their cow pasture. James could understand that.

When the trailer let out a deep groan and began to tip even more heavily toward the road, James decided to move over beside his mother and his aunt Lily, who were standing together on the ruined walk. He'd been down the bank from it as it inched along, and he realized suddenly that, if it did turn over, he'd have to be lucky and pretty quick to get out of its way. Poor Aunt Lily, James thought, had the most right to be unhappy, but James couldn't see anything in her face except worry over whether or not the trailer was going to make it to the cow pasture. She had never been married and never left home, and when she wasn't teaching or sewing clothes for Clara and Virginia, she was working among her flowers and plants. The yard was her pride and her hobby.

As the trailer crept past the far corner of the porch, the wheels on the uphill side of it began to leave the ground, and the hitch, or some other part of the trailer, began a terrible popping and grinding.

"Mercy," his grandmother gasped and twisted her hands into the apron she wore over her housedress.

"Goodness gracious, there it goes!" Aunt Lily said, great alarm and perfect resignation in her voice at the same time. She grabbed James's shoulders and squeezed, but the truck lurched forward, and the trailer was yanked past the corner of the porch and into the relatively flat side yard.

James's grandfather, who was the postmaster of the little one-room country post office on the other side of the driveway, had come out to watch the whole operation too, but he hadn't said a word, and when the trailer got past the corner of the porch, he turned toward the post office again. He was a tall, gaunt man with a widow's hump, which somehow didn't seem a sign of frailty or weakness, but the emblem of a private and stubborn strength. He didn't say much to anyone, and James was never sure what his grandfather might be thinking.

The trailer went through the side yard without doing any damage except for leaving tire tracks and knocking down part of a row of hollyhocks at the far edge. James's grandfather had already taken out a fence post and cut the barbed wire so the trailer could be pulled into the cow pasture. Staked out at the southern edge, the jersey watched the truck and trailer come lumbering into her lush, green province, and when the truck growled to a stop, she stretched out her neck and bawled.

"Don't you just know how she feels?" Virginia told Clara in a voice that wasn't as soft as it could have been.

"I want the two of you to help me in the kitchen," Grand-mother Marshall said. "You go on. I've got things for you to do."

With great dignity the girls turned and marched up on the front porch and into the house while James looked at his mother to see what Virginia's remark had done to her. But if she had heard it, she showed no sign. She and her sister were standing with their arms loosely about each other's waists, gazing after the trailer, identical expressions of sad resignation on their faces.

It did look pretty shabby in the cow pasture. The man had parked it maybe twenty-five feet from the yard where the pasture appeared to be nearly level, but the trailer still leaned noticeably toward the scrub growth of birch and redbud separating the pasture from the steep bank down to the highway.

"Well, Harley said if he could get a team and wagon around in front of the porch, that trailer would go too, but I surely didn't think it t'would," Grandmother Marshall said. "Mercy," she added, and shaking her head over it, she turned and, in her listing walk, followed the girls inside.

Mopping his face and neck with his handkerchief, the driver came into the yard while Aunt Lily studied the trailer with round sad eyes. "Oh Maidy," she said, "you can't live in that thing. It's tilted thirty degrees!"

"I can straighten it up all right," the driver said, giving the trailer a brief glance over his shoulder, "but lady," he said to James's mother, "if you ever take a notion to go somewhere else, don't call me. Some other fool's gonna have to pull it outta here."

"I'm sorry," Madeline Tally said. "I just didn't realize. . . . Can I do anything to help?"

"Yes," the driver said, "you could get me a tall glass of ice water." He mopped his face and gazed at the broken shrubbery in front of the porch and the great depth of the tire track where the lawn sloped down to the highway. "There was no weight on that uphill wheel at all," he said. "I've got to be a damned idiot."

"I'm sorry," Madeline Tally said, "there just wasn't anywhere else to put it."

But he was already looking at James. "Boy, you want to jump in and help?"

"Sure," James said.

"Then start gettin them jacks and blocks and a few of them short planks out of the bed of the truck. I'd like to get back to Knoxville before three in the morning."

While James unloaded the truck, the driver squatted alongside the trailer and peered beneath it. "You get cowshit on you and you can take a bath and change your clothes," he said. "You ain't got to drive all the way to Knoxville smelling like a manure spreader." He came over to the truck and scrutinized the boy as though he were trying to guess his weight or birthday. He was a smallish but rawboned man whose mouth was stained with chewing tobacco. James wouldn't have thought the driver would have had such worries since an odor of ancient sweat and tobacco already hung over him as rich as frying bacon and as rank as a skunk. "You reckon you could crawl under there and do exactly like I say?" he asked.

"Sure," James said.

But the driver was very particular and hard to please, and by the time James had jacks set under the four corners of the trailer, he was wet with sweat from crawling and wiggling about on his stomach or on his back, and the grass had begun to make his skin itch wildly. Still, most of the cowpiles were dry as sawdust and light as cardboard, and when the driver got James out from under and clear so he could begin to jack the trailer up, James only had the wild, green stench of fresh cowshit on one knee, although his hands were black from the greasy jacks and he was otherwise thoroughly filthy.

The man went from corner to corner, raising the trailer with his long jack handle, all the while setting his big carpenter's level along the rear bumper, here and there on the floor inside, and across the tongue where the gas bottles for the stove, refrigerator, and furnace were bolted. Finally the boy crawled beneath the trailer again to set blocks under the cross members, but this time the driver seemed nearly impossible to please and had James rearrange the blocks again and again, only to have him take them down altogether and dig away at the earth with a handleless garden hoe he pawed out of the bed of his truck and threw under the trailer for James to use. At the left rear corner of the trailer, no matter what James did he couldn't satisfy the man, who finally inched and wiggled underneath and did it himself. But at last, a little at a time, he lowered each jack, explaining how important it was to keep the weight distributed evenly as it came down on the blocks. When the jacks were free and he'd gone over the trailer again with his level, he winked at the boy and said, "Now that's the way to do her, son. Once, by God, up—and once, by God, down. None of this farting around all day, treating the thing like a yo-yo."

When the boy had dragged the jacks and timbers out and the man had thrown them back into the jumbled bed of his truck, he gave James his empty water glass, smudged with black fingerprints. "I'd be obliged if you'd tell your momma I'm done and ask her kindly if I could have just one more glass of ice water." He took out his red bandanna, mopped his face and neck with it, blew his nose into it, and shoved it back in his hip pocket. He considered the sun in the bright blue August sky and winked at James again. "I'll be back in Knoxville this side of midnight. Get on to the house now and fetch your momma," he said. "You may live here, but I don't."

When the driver had drunk his ice water and Madeline had counted out sixty-five dollars into his wide, dirty palm, he told James to get in the truck with him. Guessing that there was some other mysterious chore to finish, James did, but once they had scraped past the ruined shrubbery, crossed the broken flagstones of the walk, and bumped back down into the driveway, the driver stopped and withdrew the big leather wallet chained to a belt loop of his trousers. "This ain't no refund," he said; "you earned it fair and square," and he tucked two one-dollar bills into the breast pocket of the boy's T-shirt.

James looked down at it. He would have been happy to work all day for such a sum.

"Well get the hell out of my truck, boy," the driver said. "I didn't take you to raise."

Deeply embarrassed, James twisted the handle, bumped the door open with his shoulder, and got out. He was still trying to think of something to say, when, without a backward glance, the driver turned into the highway and gunned the truck off toward Tennessee.

James watched the truck out of sight while all sorts of complicated things went on inside him, some of them crossing the threshold of thought, some not. A few miles away was the town where he'd been born and had lived the first eight years of his life, and for five years, while his family had moved from city to city and state to state, he'd grieved the loss of it and of these high, cool, North Carolina mountains, thinking there was nothing so wrong that it couldn't be put right if only he could get back again. But he was a dreamer and had not yet learned that dreamers seldom considered the fine print of their desires. The truck driver was heading back toward Knoxville, where James had last seen his father, although his father had since gone to Pittsburgh, a place he'd never been and therefore could not fix in his imagination. Pittsburgh, New York, Boston, or Bogotá— one place name was about as good as another to James; his father had vanished, and he himself was here. But he'd never liked cities or the frequent moves to take up temporary residence in one trailer park or another. And if he and his mother were still living in a trailer like gypsies, the trailer was at least parked in his grandfather's cow pasture. The house where his mother had been born was right there, looking just the way it had throughout his memory and probably his mother's memory too. And even if he had not quite got back to the town where he was born, he was close enough so that the air had the same sweet smell, the sunlight came down, somehow, as it should, and the earth felt nearly the same underfoot. And if he could not weigh what had been withdrawn from him, something important had been restored. In some odd way he even felt grateful for Virginia and Clara, who seemed to think of him as a threat, as an enemy even—they were family, after all, and not strangers.

The sun was dipping behind a mountain, and the light it shed, oblique and diffused, began to settle toward evening; and everything the boy could see looked old, settled, and permanent—the few farmhouses, the fields and pastures, and the ancient mountains themselves. His grandfather's house, the little white post office, and behind it, the barn, might have grown from the earth. And although the trailer didn't belong, it was after all only a small blemish.

All at once his itching neck and arms and the sticky grease on his hands became oppressive, and he came out of his thoughts enough to start up the driveway. There was an overflow pipe from the cistern just above the house, and his grandfather kept a cake of Lava soap there to wash up from barn chores. But he hadn't taken more than a few steps when he noticed that his mother, aunt, and grandmother had gone out to look at the trailer, his aunt and grandmother, no doubt, never having seen the inside of a house trailer in all their lives. They went inside; yet, in perfect miniature, Grandmother Marshall's voice reached him: "They Lord have mercy, child, it's no bigger than a henhouse." And then, perhaps in apology: "But it's right clever, isn't it? It's as clever as it can be." He heard his aunt's voice too, but he had gotten further up the driveway, the house had come between, and he couldn't distinguish her remarks.

At the cistern he scrubbed his hands again and again with the soap, rinsing them each time in the icy water from the overflow pipe before he plucked the two dollars from his T-shirt pocket and tucked them in the pocket of his jeans. When he got the cowshit washed off the right leg of his jeans, he took off his T-shirt and scrubbed his face, neck, arms, and chest. He was covered in goosebumps when he was done, and one leg and the waist of his jeans were wet, but he felt much better. He could see his grandfather, having closed the post office, working in the vegetable garden above the house, and he thought of going up there and asking if he needed any help, but as always the uncompromising, stooped silence of the man seemed best left undisturbed.

A few nights before, when he and his mother had got down off the milk-run Trailways bus, his grandmother and aunt had hugged them and made over them; and later, even Clara and Virginia had acknowledged them by being sulky over the sleeping arrangements—Clara and Virginia would have to sleep together in Virginia's small bedroom over the living room while he and his mother took the back bedroom on the second floor, which doubled as Clara's room and Aunt Lily's sewing room. But Grandfather Marshall had treated James and his mother as if they had always been there, which was to say he gave them no more notice than he gave the rest of his family. He clumped in from doing the milking and the chores, took his supper at the head of the table in the kitchen, and then retired to his chair by the fireplace, where, after a while, his mouth—a round, nearly toothless hole between his fierce beak of a nose and his broad, stubbled chin—fell open in sleep.

Grandfather Marshall seldom acknowledged children or spoke to them except in deep, booming commands: "*You young'ns get quiet in there!*" Worst of all he had terrible nightmares and would call out in that same booming bass in his sleep, sometimes in the middle of the night as James was making the long journey to the bathroom in the downstairs rear of the house. When James was far younger and on visits, more than once his grandfather's voice would suddenly fill the dark rooms, and James would bolt from the bathroom, down the hall, through the parlor, up the stairs, and back to his bedroom, waking everyone in his panic except his grandfather, who had to be shaken out of those nightmares or he would go on groaning and calling out forever.

Grandfather Marshall had never punished him or, to his knowledge, Clara or Virginia, but James knew the girls feared him too. James's mother had told him about the terrible hidings Grandfather Marshall had given his own children even when, for all practical purposes, they were grown. Once she'd told him about a puppy her brother, James's uncle Henry, had been given when Henry was only a boy, a puppy that yelped in the dooryard at night until Grandfather Marshall had risen one night, snatched the puppy up by its hind legs, and clubbed it dead with a stick of stovewood. James's mother had offered such stories when, for one reason or another, James had thought his own father had been cruel. She had offered them with a little deprecating snort to put James and his notion of cruelty in perspective.

He watched the old man stooping among the squash and beans and tried to weigh the purpose of all that silence and privacy, but he didn't understand it, and there seemed no way to respond to it except with a distance and silence of his own. Still, he would have liked to do something, to help, to make a difference somehow.

In the next moment he spotted the stile his grandfather had built so the fence could go back up around the cow pasture and he and his mother could still get to the trailer. It was sitting in the lee of the barn and was very like a stepladder, only twice as wide and very heavily built, and he wondered if he could carry it out where it belonged, but he couldn't budge it. He couldn't even figure out a good way to take hold of it until he got a bright idea and climbed inside. Then, if he used every bit of his strength so that specks of bright light burst behind his eyes and went whizzing about, he found he could lift all four legs an inch or so off the ground and even carry the stile a few steps before he had to put it down. After he'd moved it forty feet or so and was exhausted, a quail began to call somewhere above the barn. "Bob, Bob White," the quail said in a voice that was wonderfully clear and splendid.

Living where he'd been living, he hadn't heard that pure, sweet sound in a long time. He knew enough to know it wasn't the usual birdsong—which, however beautiful, is in the business of laying claim to this bush, this tree, this volume of air and space of earth—but a beckoning by which the quail gathered themselves together. It was also the call James and his father imitated when they were out together in the woods or off fishing somewhere and had lost track of each other.

He listened until, at last, it came again; and, without any words whatever, he somehow understood that he couldn't untangle what had happened and lay out anyone's proper share of blame. He didn't know why such an understanding should have come just then, and if someone had been there and asked him, he could not have told them what he was thinking, since it wasn't truly a thought but a feeling.

Still, no one is able to hold on to grace for long, and in the very next moment his acceptance and humility seemed merely a kind of desolation in which, without help from anyone, he would have to invent himself.

MADELINE
TALLY

The pasture, wet with dew, was silver under the moon, and a little of the moonlight even strained through the small windows of the trailer where she lay. She needed sleep and yearned for it, but it wouldn't come. A little while before, she'd almost dropped off, but in that very last moment she'd seen Edward Tally against a bright blue sky, his spurs dug into the telephone pole across from her momma and poppa's house, leaning back against his safety belt. How startlingly trim and hard he'd looked in his work clothes, and his hair and eyes were black as an Indian's. She had been working as a substitute teacher, yes, and had come out to stand beside the highway in order to catch a ride with Stanley Green, who taught math and used some sort of hair oil that smelled so close and sweet, she feared someday it would make her throw up in his automobile. Yes, and Lily was late, as usual, no doubt still fussing with her hair and clothes, and if they weren't out by the road waiting to step into his car the moment he stopped, Stanley Green, prissy little man that he was, would go right on by without even so much as slowing down. So she had been stuck there with this strange man looking boldly down at her.

Absolutely everything about that day came back to her, the fresh green smell of the morning, the warm sun on her shoulders, the dress she was wearing, and even the faint odor of creosote from the telephone pole, which, no doubt, his spurs had released.

"So," he'd said, "y'all decided to get modern with the rest of us then?"

His voice had been so easy, jovial, teasing; but she didn't know him from Moody's goat, and the question, if that's what it was, seemed at best, familiar, and at worst, insulting. She knew she was blushing, but she meant to give him a look that would put him in his place, only he wasn't looking at her any longer, but at his labors, fierce wires of muscle straining in his arms and knotted in his jaw. She dropped her eyes and said nothing. She fidgeted, looked up the road to see if Stanley Green was coming and over her shoulder to see if Lily was.

"Well," he said, his voice grunting with the strain of whatever he was doing, "I expect everybody will be hooking up one of these days. Hey, there's one or two folks on the other side of Cedar Hill that's even put electricity in their barns. Got yourself a radio yet?"

She didn't know why, exactly, she couldn't bring herself to speak. Perhaps because he'd taken her by surprise, or because his hair was so black the sun made it blue, but in the next moment there was a ripping sound, almost like paper being torn, and down he came, first landing on his feet and then his rear. "Damn," he said, and while she stood mute and shocked, Lily appeared, rushing past her and across the highway to him. "My goodness! Are you hurt?" she asked, immediately trying to help him up as if there were no such thing as sex, or proper behavior, or being introduced, or flirting men, or shyness in all the world.

"I'm okay," he said with an embarrassed laugh, "I just wasn't paying attention." But if he was talking to Lily, he was grinning right over Lily's shoulder at her.

"Well you're certainly not okay," Lily told him. "Look at your arms! You've hurt yourself terribly!" And then turning around: "Maidy, what on earth is the matter with you? Help me get him into the house."

Of course Stanley Green's Chevrolet would trundle into view at just that moment. "But here's our ride," she blurted to Lily like an idiot.

"I'll make him wait," Lily said. "Now you just show this poor man up to the house so Momma can take a look at him."

Embarrassed, although not nearly as much as he should have been and not as much as she was, he unsnapped the safety belt, which seemed to have done him no good at all, and allowed himself to be escorted into their kitchen where Bertha Marshall would later remove splinters and paint him from the inside of his wrists to the inside of his elbows with iodine. Still, on the way up the driveway, he kept up his easy conversation, the bold grin never leaving his face. A few of the light poles in the valley were hard as iron, he told her, and a man had to watch himself if his climbers weren't going to strip out and make him fall. She sensed his implication and resented both the flattery and the blame. He asked her where she worked—one question she managed to answer—and he told her that some members of her family were maybe just a teeny bit more friendly than others.

All day at school she couldn't get him out of her mind. She and Lily had both been thrilled about their poppa's decision to lumber off the ridge behind the barn and use the money to wire the house. There was a light fixture in the ceiling and two receptacles in the walls of every room in their home, and she and Lily had each bought a pretty lamp for their bedrooms; and, without their parents' knowledge, they had, indeed, put a radio on layaway. Theirs was just about the last house in the valley to be without electricity, and it was all very exciting to be getting it, but somehow she couldn't even savor it any longer without Edward Tally—he had introduced himself in the kitchen, but as with Lily, he had looked at her rather than at her mother—stealing center stage. Also, when she got to school, she noticed he'd left a single spot of blood on her dress just above her knee, and off and on all day she caught herself staring at it as though it were a ruby.

It seemed all too painfully appropriate that such a vivid memory should reach her just when she was dropping off to sleep and yank her wide awake. Here she was again, a little over fourteen years later, right back home where she had first seen him, and he was just as impertinent, rude, and incapable of being ignored in her memory as he had been on that morning in 1934.

Not that she hadn't had boyfriends before he showed up; she'd been twenty-two, after all. One or two of them she'd even thought she might like, but her father had been so strict that merely the notion of his disapproval had kept her distant and cool around them, and finally, he scared most of them so badly she couldn't help finding them dull and uninteresting. She and Lily had been the last two at home, all three brothers having gone off on their own, and already she and Lily were hearing jokes about being old maids. And so Lily was. But that hadn't been it at all. There had simply been something about Edward Tally. He just wouldn't be denied. And by the end of the next day, when he and his partner had finished putting in the service and the meter, he somehow thought he had a right to come and court her. He'd even charmed and buffaloed her mother and father, so that they smiled to themselves when he came in his old open flivver and took her off on picnics, drives, and dates, even as far away as Bristol, Tennessee, and didn't get her back until midnight, when she'd always had to be in by ten. Ha, she thought bitterly, if they'd only known. If her father had only seen that he was just exactly the sort of man he'd meant to protect her from.

She couldn't help being furious and stared up at the ceiling of the trailer, fuming that she was thirty-six and not twenty-two; that she had a thirteen-year-old son to look after; that she was living in a cow pasture with not only no electricity, but no water either; that she had very little money and no prospects; that she was, in every conceivable way, worse off for having met Edward Tally.

And how disinherited and sad it made her feel that her family was keeping something back that she'd counted on. There was a strange reserve in them that went beyond anything they might say or do. She was sure they didn't mean to show it—Clara and Virginia aside, who were young and in a snotty stage—but it told her they really did have their own lives to lead, lives they had been leading in her absence for a long, long time. It was just that she hadn't known you could lose your place with family. No one, she thought, meant for it to happen. But if you went away, they had to get on with their lives without you and maybe couldn't quite admit you again because you'd lost your place with them. How were they supposed to know how unhappy you'd been, or that you'd counted on them and dreamed of them constantly?

Oh stop it, she thought. It was insane to think such thoughts when she was so tired and needed to sleep.

She turned and fluffed her pillow. If absence had cost her her place at the center of their hearts, then who was to say that being among them again couldn't earn it back, even if it had to come a little at a time? And who was to say she had no prospects? Her life wasn't over. In a few days, when she got herself together, she'd begin to look for a job, and she had enough money to buy some sort of a car; anything that would get her to work and back would do. And was she living in some dreary trailer park? No she wasn't. And was she going to be yanked about from one dirty, indifferent city to another? Or be abandoned in one strange place while Edward Tally moved on to the next without her? Absolutely not.

Don't think, she told herself. Think tomorrow. Her legs ached with tension and fatigue as if she were coming down with flu, and she stretched them and pointed her toes in order to force the ache out. In the faint, silver moonlight entering the small window of the trailer, she turned on her side, acknowledged the sound of crickets, and closed her eyes. They felt full of sand.

Oh but it was a wonder to her that she hadn't seen through Edward Tally at once. It astonished her that she'd thought him the boldest and most exciting man she'd ever met, when, in fact, he was only unsympathetic, headstrong, and selfish. Jesus, she thought, but she'd been dumb. Love. Ha. Maybe someday they'd prove that being in love was a form of insanity, but she didn't need to wait; God knows, in her own case, she'd proved it out already. "Hey, sugar," he might say when they were courting, a big, delighted smile on his face, "I've come to take you to the movies." And she'd be happy to go. "Put on your prettiest dress, sweetness, we're going to a dance over to Blowing Rock."

She couldn't deny him anything, anything at all. It was as though she had no will of her own. Only she did. It might have been down too deep to recognize, but it was there, making her moody and distracted, making her snap at her pupils in school and at Lily, and oddly, making her miss him outrageously when they weren't together, although she could see now what she truly missed and would always miss was the ability to make some mark on him, the ability to make him acknowledge her in a way he was incapable of doing. She'd known she wanted something more from him, but she hadn't herself known precisely what, and when he'd asked her to marry him, she'd thought she'd gotten what she was after at last.

How bitter it was to be so wrong. Why, he hadn't even asked her to marry him at all; he'd merely said he thought it was time they did. She remembered precisely the way he'd spoken, laying it out like some expensive dress he'd bought without bothering to find out if she liked the style or color or fabric or anything. And she'd said yes. Yes. But she'd mistaken one thing for another, mistaken his motives and her own.

And even after they'd gotten married and she was able, however feebly at first, to say she wanted this rather than that, wished to do this rather than that, he couldn't learn to take her into consideration. He could only be surprised. He could only figure he'd made a mistake in a few specific cases, or that she was in one of her moods. But the specifics never added up to a general understanding, except that he began to figure he couldn't please her no matter what he did. But he could never learn to take her into account.

One Saturday he'd driven her out to see a house in Cedar Hill, and when she'd said she liked it, he'd flashed her his big, boyish, disarming grin and told her he'd signed papers on it and made a down payment, no matter that she'd thought they couldn't begin to pay for it. And they wouldn't have been able to if she hadn't gotten busy and found herself a job and got a colored woman to come in and do a bit of cleaning and look after James. Still, those had been their best years, even though she was always tired, and they had begun to fight—or she had, since he would never fight—and there was a basic unhappiness underneath everything they did. She could make some sort of impression on the house, choose paint and wallpaper, plant flowers, arrange and rearrange the little furniture they owned, and when their meager finances allowed, even add something here and there. And of course she had James, who was so small and sweet and pliable. But then Edward Tally walked in one fine day and announced that he'd quit his job with Watauga Light and Power Company and taken a job on construction in Morganton seventy-five miles away, so he saw them only on weekends, and not all of those by far, since he started working six days a week. And sure, the overtime meant she could give up her own job if she wanted, but she didn't want. But it also meant that if he wished to see his family, he'd have to spend nearly three hours Sunday morning driving up the twisting mountain roads to Cedar Hill and the same amount of time going back Sunday night, and so, start work on Monday exhausted. When he left that job for another in Tullahoma, Tennessee, they did not see each other for months at a time.

Of course she hadn't felt she was very important to him. Who could blame her? And of course she'd complained. Who wouldn't? People married because they wanted and needed to live together. If you loved someone, you wanted to be with them; it was as plain as day to her, and she told him so. But who would have expected him to show up with an ugly purple house trailer, as though that would solve everything? As though that didn't involve leaving her home, her friends, and everyone she'd ever known. As though it didn't involve taking James out of school and away from everything he loved. Edward Tally was an inconsiderate man to the marrow of his bones, and you could teach a cat to sing quicker than you could show him that and make him see it.

She hated living in a trailer. Hated having to put on a house-coat and slippers and sometimes a raincoat to walk to the bath-

house in the middle of the night to use the toilet, or to go all
that way to take a shower or wash her hair or do the laundry.
The trailer wasn't the least bit snug, as he often claimed with
a twinkle in his eye and a grin on his face when the rain was
lashing it with a sound like gravel being thrown against its side
and the wind was fairly making it rock. And who could make
love with any joy and peace when James was only a few feet
away and nothing but a thin plywood partition like the bellows
of a concertina between them? Oh, but she'd been unhappy.
And unhappier still when he'd finally had his way and sold their
home in Cedar Hill, which they'd been renting out and which
he'd allowed them to believe they'd return to. And he hadn't
put the money back toward the better house they'd buy someday, as he'd promised, but had bought himself a fancy 1941
Packard—and would have bought a new one, no doubt, if there
had been any new cars to buy. And he'd taken to coming home
one or two nights a week definitely tipsy, with no regard for
her and the dinner she'd made. And he could see no harm in
it, as though it were only a boyish prank or a working man's
innocent due. What did he care that she'd been worried out of
her mind that he was dead on the highway or that the supper
she'd cooked him had been kept warm until it wasn't anything
more than a drab mess in her pots and pans? Earlier in their
marriage he'd only rarely done that sort of thing, but toward
the end she never knew when to count on him. And likely as
not he'd try to tell her he'd only just had a couple of beers and
the time had just slipped past him. As if she hadn't lived with
him long enough to know how much alcohol it took to put that
glazed look in his eye.

And there were nights when he didn't come home at all. At
midnight or maybe one or two in the morning she'd get a call
from one of his construction buddies she'd hardly met or never
met, and this strange voice would tell her he'd had a little too
much to drive, but they'd see to it that he got to work the next
day, and he'd be just fine. Sure, she'd see him the next afternoon
shuffling up with his hat in his hand, they would say, as though

they, too, were telling her about a schoolboy prank, as though it were funny and innocent or even, somehow, endearing.

She'd got so sick of it that sometimes she really didn't mind so much when he'd quit one job for another and leave her and James for months in one strange city while he went off to the next. They'd fought until, at last, they didn't fight anymore, or make love anymore, or even talk, so that when he said he was going to Pittsburgh, she'd said that was fine, because she and James were going home to North Carolina. With an icy calm she could feel reaching for her heart, they had discussed mechanical things like money and the trailer and the car and had left the other ninety-nine percent of what was between them go unspoken.

Oh God, she thought, let me start all over again with a clean slate, clean and blank with nothing written on it, I pray you, Jesus God Lord Almighty Christ. Please just let me sleep. But her stomach didn't feel so good, and she slid her legs to the edge of the bed and sat up very slowly, hoping she wasn't going to be sick all over everything with no water to clean it up. She'd left him, she told herself sternly. It was done. Why on earth did she have to leave him again every single night? Why did she have to list her grievances over and over, try him again and again like a judge in court?

She got up and quietly slid back the thin plywood partition that separated the bedroom from the rest of the trailer. Dimly she could make out the boy sleeping on the couch, wrapped in a sheet and a blanket. She'd given up trying to get him to let the couch down and make it up properly as a bed. When it was time to sleep, he'd snatch his pillow, sheet, and blanket from the storage compartment under the couch, fold the sheet and blanket together lengthwise, and climb inside. In the morning he'd grab them up and stow them under the couch again. It was an uncomfortable couch, even for sitting, since it was covered in stiff, green Naugahyde, with huge buttons to hold the batting in place, but when he didn't let down the back, there was scarcely room for him to lie there. She hated having him sleep on it like that, absolutely hated it, as though what they had left of dignity and self-respect might somehow be put at risk by permitting such small compromises. Other folks, it seemed to her, had a much larger margin of safety in such matters.

Quietly she opened the small gas refrigerator and poured herself a glass of milk, and, as if watching him had disturbed his sleep, he began to turn over, making small, careful adjustments even as he slept in order to keep from falling to the floor. She drank her milk, her hand shaking, the rim of the glass rattling against her teeth. "Damn you, Edward Tally," she said, not loud, but loud enough to rouse her son, who sat up on the couch and blinked at her through the dim moonlight.

"Momma?"

"Hush and go to sleep," she said. "I'm just having a little milk to settle my stomach."

JAMES
TALLY

He followed Piney Creek, sometimes wading the deep meadow grass along its cut banks watching for grasshoppers to use for bait, sometimes wading the stream. It was a pretty creek, but not a big one, usually no more than twenty feet across and nowhere over his head, but it was clear and clean and full of fish. Hog suckers lay motionless in the shallows until they were spooked. Then they'd dart away, swift as bullets, to lie absolutely motionless somewhere else. And there were hornyheads and perch and schools of minnows and, in some of the deeper pools, even a few smallmouth bass. Sometimes he'd see the bass gliding like shadows to disappear under a rock or under an overhanging bank.

He would have liked to catch some of those, but he had little chance. They preferred minnows or crayfish, and he needed to let them take the bait and run until they got ready to swallow it and he could set the hook. But that called for being able to give them line, and he only had a cane pole he'd bought for a quarter at the country store down the road. He'd tied a length of braided green line to the middle of the pole and finally to the tip, so that if some monster fish broke the tip, it would have to break the pole a second time to be free. The line, a snelled hook, and the split-shot sinkers he'd taken from his father's canvass musette bag of fishing equipment. He'd asked his mother if he could use the equipment in the bag, and she'd pawed it out of the closet in her bedroom. He didn't ask to use his father's fly rod and reel, although he might have caught a bass with that. It was a split-bamboo trout rod, and Piney Creek was too warm for trout, and anyway, his father was particular about the fly rod. Once, when his father had been away, James had borrowed it without permission, and sure enough, he'd managed to step on the tiptop and break the rubylike center of the final eye. The rod had an extra tip, but it was the principle of the thing, and his father had taken a belt to him, which James expected and figured he deserved. When Edward Tally had come home after six weeks away, the first thing James said to him was that he'd broken the fly rod. He liked to get certain things over with and behind him, but his father waited until after supper before he inspected the damage, took off his belt, and gave him the deliberate and inevitable punishment.

His father had two possessions that seemed almost magically elegant and powerful. One was a Lefever double-barreled shotgun, which smelled of gun oil and was kept in a leather leg-o'-mutton gun case; and the other was the glowing, honey-colored rod, the sections all fitting snugly around an inlet wooden spindle kept inside a canvas bag. But even under the best of circumstances, James wouldn't have pretended that his mother had authority over these possessions, and to do so just then, when she might have granted permission, would have seemed low and venal. As it was, even having his mother search through his father's clothes, shoes, and other stuff seemed to stun them both for a little while, as if Edward Tally had reached across a great distance to box their ears.

Still, his mother had gotten over it and gone off to Cedar Hill with his aunt Lily and his cousins. And barefoot and shirtless, he'd gone fishing. There was bright sunshine and the warm, green smell of grass, and the varnished odor of the stream all around him, and after an hour or so the hollow feeling in his stomach left.

He'd spent the better part of two days digging a ditch from the farmhouse to the trailer, laying the sod carefully aside and digging the water hose down deep, sure that when he filled in the ditch and replaced the grass, the waterline to the trailer would be invisible. But it wasn't so. There was a long, dirty depression across the yard and part of the pasture. But rain might wash away the loose dirt in time, and if he straddled the sunken part with the lawn mower, then the grass in it would get longer, and the yard might look okay even if it wasn't. He thought he'd try the same thing with the tire tracks. Digging in the hose for the drain was a much simpler proposition, a matter of twenty feet or so before the slope of the land would carry the sink water away toward the scrub growth and highway. His grandfather had said that would be all right. Also an electrician had come and run a line out to the trailer from the house, so they had lights and water, even if it was only cold water, which tasted strongly of the new hose.

He was disappointed in the way the yard looked, but his aunt Lily and mother and grandmother had praised him, and he figured he had the silent approval of his grandfather as well. Three nights before, when Harley Marshall had learned at the supper table that James had got the stile out to the fence by himself, he'd stopped eating to study him for a few seconds. "Bertha," he'd said to James's grandmother, "you'll want to call Irey in the morning and tell him not to come by then, for he was to help me tote it." After that, he'd given his head one nearly invisible shake and gone back to eating. But toward the end of James's first day of ditch digging when his hands had begun to creak with blisters, his grandfather had suddenly appeared with a pair of work gloves, new ones that nearly fit, which James figured he'd bought at the country store half a mile down the road. Stooped, silent, the old man had pondered the ditch, nodded his head, and tucked the pair of gloves inside the waistband of James's britches. One quick, sure movement and he was already making his unhurried way back across the yard, disappearing around the broken quince bushes by the front porch before James could even thank him.

So, everything considered, he figured he was doing pretty well, and he planned to take home enough fish to feed everyone, even his cousins, although an hour and a half had got him only five keepable hornyheads, and not one of them ten inches long. Still, each bend in the creek had a deep side where the current undercut a bank and possibilities lurked.

He kept his hornyheads strung through the gills on a forked willow branch, and when he saw a good spot ahead, he'd jab the long end of the branch in the bank to keep his fish in the water; and after swatting around in the deep grass until he had a fresh grasshopper kicking against his palm, he'd sneak to the edge of the bank, careful not even to let his shadow fall on the water, and swing the grasshopper—legs kicking and wings askew—into the current. Waiting for the telegraphed thump, thump, thump of a bite to travel the line and pole into his hands, he was free to think expansive and, it seemed to him, profound thoughts.

First he figured out his cousins, deciding that a good deal of their stiff and unfriendly behavior came from years before when each of them, in turn, had taught him what little he knew—and what little they knew too—about sex. They were embarrassed about that, he decided, and probably hoped never to see him again, or at least not until they were truly as grown-up and sophisticated as they were trying to be. He hadn't committed the actual act with either of them, although it had all been very exciting, and he would have done so if he'd known how and if they would have allowed it. He had been not quite eight and on a visit when each girl began to desire his company alone in the barn or the smokehouse or hidden away in the laurel thicket at the end of the pasture where they wanted to play husband and wife. They couldn't absolutely do it, they explained, because they were first cousins and weren't, and could never be, really married. Trying to seem just as grown-up and earnest as they were, he had pretended to understand, although he had no notion what *it* was. Still, each of them had wanted him to see and touch that soft cleft—delicate as a seashell—at the crux of them. And they wanted to see and touch him too. Likely they feared he might remember all that just a little too vividly. And he did. He didn't have much of anything else to remember along those lines. Not, anyway, if he didn't count a great many fantasies. Yet, somehow, he felt worldly and wise.

In fact, fishing down Piney Creek in the bright sun, he felt on the threshold of great things. His character, despite past disappointments, seemed perfectly redeemable and even capable of being invented out of raw material, hammered out and tempered like a new blade, just to suit him. Why not? Very little in his spirit felt inescapable except maybe a constant melancholy. He'd worked hard the past few days. Honorable blisters had broken and stiffened in his hands, and with that sort of work on his character, he didn't see why he couldn't become a fellow of such strength and integrity that no circumstance would be able to provoke cowardice, weakness, self-pity, or dishonor in him. He knew such strength of character to be possible because he had the example of Osceola, chief of the Seminole. He'd read a book about him only a few months before. Osceola was three-quarters Indian and one-quarter Scot, and that seemed an important coincidence since he, himself, had some Indian blood from his father and a lot of Scottish blood from his mother. There was no doubt that Osceola was the perfect man, the ideal blueprint to follow. He was as brave and just as anybody could want. He would not surrender or be moved about and told where he could live. He was fair with his own people and gave runaway slaves refuge in his tribe. And he never would have been captured, James was certain, if a general he'd defeated many times hadn't tricked him under a flag of truce and taken him prisoner. Even so, deceived and locked in prison, he'd shamed his jailors absolutely by sitting in one spot without speaking or eating or sleeping or attending to any bodily function until he simply dropped dead. You couldn't beat that, James thought. Nobody could beat that.

He didn't figure to be put to quite such a test any time soon, but he did have to start in at a new school in a little more than three weeks. He'd had a lot of experience changing schools, three times during the fourth grade alone, but he didn't like it. Yet this time things could be different. He could teach himself not to be so anxious and fearful, and maybe if others saw this calm, sober strength in him, they wouldn't tamper with it, and he could get by without fighting. It was possible.

He had just caught a hornyhead nearly as colorful as a rainbow and was stringing him up through the gills when he caught sight of something moving below the next bend down the creek. Elderberry bushes leaning out over the water partially hid whatever it was, but James could see it was some sort of animal. Careful to make no noise and no quick movements, he eased his stringer back in the water, set his pole aside, and began to creep on all fours through the deep grass until he could see that the animal was a raccoon, busily feeling around stones in the bottom of the creek. It looked about half-grown, but he couldn't be sure since he'd only seen a few, and none in broad daylight. He didn't know what it was after; but, its beady black eyes glittering with concentration and its elbows pumping like a woman scrubbing out clothes over a washboard, it seemed totally unaware of him.

Finally the young raccoon caught a crawfish in his finicky fingers, although he lost it and caught it again half a dozen times before, mysteriously, he began to scrub the crawfish against the top of a flat rock, which was a few inches out of the water. Maybe he's trying to kill it, James thought, but the crawfish looked at least vaguely alive when the coon began to eat it with the greedy intensity of a squirrel hulling a hickory nut.

The moment he was finished with the first, he began looking for another, his elbows pumping and that fanatical gleam back in his eyes. He caught one almost immediately, but it managed to get away from him; still, it wasn't long before he had a third to worry against a stone and eat. The next thing he pulled out from under a rock, however, wasn't a crawfish, but a snake about sixteen inches long. Even James gave a start where he lay hidden, but the young raccoon merely puzzled at it, turning it thoughtfully this way and that in his black hand, watching it writhe as though he were speculating about what it might be and how it might taste. At last, apparently unable to solve the riddle, he picked up the rock, put the angry creature back where he'd found it, and set the rock gently down again. It was an action so unexpectedly orderly, serious, and somehow droll that James held his nose and buried his face in his arms to try to keep from laughing; but he only managed to muffle it. Still, when he looked up again, the raccoon was searching the bottom of the stream as if nothing whatever had happened and had moved even closer to him than before. He lay on his belly and watched and had begun to wonder if there was any way in the world to catch the animal, when a skinny, redheaded boy came ambling up on the other side of the creek and looked casually down at it.

"I thought so," the boy said. "If you weren't in Momma's henhouse stealin eggs or up to some other meanness . . ." He sucked his badly discolored teeth and didn't bother to finish. "You're somethin, ain't you?" he said and collapsed to sit on the bank as if all his joints had suddenly come unstrung.

The raccoon seemed to acknowledge him only by frisking the bottom of the creek a little more frantically, as though he feared he might be hauled away, but James felt suddenly transformed from a skillful stalker into something much more like prey. It was a familiar feeling. For years he had been the stranger, the trespasser on unfamiliar land. No doubt this redheaded boy's father owned the spot where he lay hidden, and it was possible that no fishing was allowed, and everybody, by God, knew it except James. He wanted to stand up and take his chances, but it was hard not to stay hidden. Being hidden seemed fundamentally sneaky and ridiculous in the first place, and the longer he waited, the worse it got. Anyway it would probably scare hell out of this boy to appear right across the creek from him when he thought he was alone. You might as well leap into the most private part of someone's brain as do that, because when a fellow was alone, that part expanded to include the world. It would be a piss-poor way to introduce himself, and he kept his belly flat to the ground and his nose among the grass roots.

Many minutes later, rigid with funk and fear, he heard the boy cluck to the raccoon, and he heard splashing and other sounds, but it was a while longer before he dared raise up enough to see the soaking wet animal riding the boy's retreating shoulders and looking back directly into his, James's, eyes. "Damn!" he said, flopped down on his belly again, closed his eyes, and lay there while his jitters, like cold chills, diminished and his tension drained away into the ground. A pretty poor start on his new life, all in all, he thought, to let his emotions run off with him just as he usually did. Discipline, sadly, seemed a long way off. But after a while he got up again, collected his pole and his fish, and stood wondering if it wouldn't be safer to go back the way he had come. He decided it would, and so he went the other way instead, trying hard to own the day and the stream the way he had before.

He fished for another hour, but the sun didn't seem so warm or the odors of the grass and creek quite so satisfying. When Piney Creek joined another larger stream, the deep confluence where they met stirred an excitement in him that was strangely touched with fear, and he had to make himself stay. Almost every time he threw his line in, he took a good-sized hornyhead or a nice perch, but even his success was somehow unsettling.

When he realized he had more than enough fish to feed seven people, he was suddenly in a panic to gather his things and leave. It felt very late in the day. The sun was perhaps an hour from slipping behind the western rim of the mountains, and he knew the haunting and oblique twilight would last almost an hour after that, but he couldn't shake the feeling that he was long overdue.

Some reasonable part of him knew the feeling was ridiculous, but he could walk no more than a few yards before he had to run, and in less than a mile his knees were burning and his breath was coming in sobs. Still he kept on until his legs found a numb, stubborn strength, and his breathing, though raw, grew deeper and freer. When at last he came in sight of his grandfather's house, his chest was streaming with sweat, and he had become the very heart and soul of motion.

EDWARD
TALLY

He sat at the bar with his chin resting on his fists and a beer
between his elbows. On his right, Ironfield Cox was telling Joe
Hamby—who answered to the name of "Womb Broom" because of his wiry red mustache—that it wasn't much wonder
his wife had thrown him out since he'd probably gone home
with his mustache looking like a glazed doughnut.

"I never done it!" Joe insisted. "I washed good. It's just hard
to keep in mind what a nose a woman has got. I come waltzing
in and give her a big kiss, and the first thing she says to me is,
'I smell pussy,' and then hauls off and slaps me cross-eyed before
I can even unpucker." He took a sip of his beer and shook his
head. "I never smelled nuthin myself."

Ironfield snorted and kept his peace, and Edward Tally kept
his, as he had for most of the evening, since the married condition of these two men bore no resemblance to his own. Their
situations could shed no light on his and seemed to make his
isolation and misery worse by comparison.

He had known Cox ever since he, Edward, had started working construction, and as far as he could make out, Cox's wife
might just as well have been his sister. The two of them bore a
strong family resemblance. They were exactly the same height,
although Stella Cox probably outweighed Ironfield by fifty
pounds. If you didn't count Ironfield's perpetually red boozer's
eyes and the veins that had broken in his nose and cheeks, they

had exactly the same coloring. They both wore their glasses slipped a little down their noses, walked alike, and had many of the same mannerisms. They were both standoffish, smart, and maybe a little crazy in some way Edward could not put his finger on. Most important, they were content to be apart ten months of the year or more, since Ironfield didn't go home unless he was trying to dry out or was otherwise out of work. But finally, Edward could not, absolutely could not, imagine them in bed together making love. He could as soon imagine a coat-rack making love to a chiffonier.

As for Womb Broom, his wife was soft, dumpy, and mostly cheerful, even somehow in her anger. She had borne Joe five children and one monster, who was seventeen and stood about among his brothers and sisters like a stunned beef, his upper lip painted with snot, his fly half-unzipped, and his eyes the mirror of befuddlement. The whole family seemed a little soft and sticky. All of them, and especially Joe and Lois, were fond of touching, pinching, patting, and kissing each other; and a strange, friendly but mindless chaos seemed to reign in their house, so that at any minute the house itself might collapse around them, but in a gentle way that would harm no one and scarcely make a sound.

When Lois had thrown him out, Womb Broom had spent the night at her brother's house, where, no doubt, he and his brother-in-law had had a few beers and shaken their heads over the whole thing, unable to believe it was truly the disaster it had a right to be. And even when Broom had decided to drag up, leave Knoxville with Edward and hire on at Dunbar Electric in Pittsburgh, where Ironfield was working and had sent word they were hiring, Broom hadn't even got to the Virginia State line when he'd had to stop and call Lois; and he had called her again from Winchester, Virginia, and was now writing back and forth and calling back and forth, so that, Edward guessed, it would not be long before things were as good as ever between them.

So there was Ironfield and Stella Cox, who had some sort of standoffish, bloodless understanding that seemed unbreakable;

and there was Womb Broom and Lois, who would go on having spats like small children, but go on playing house too, and filling the world with replicas of themselves, while their tragic firstborn stood by—befuddled, helpless, gentle—and brooded over what went on around him, like a child surrounded by funhouse mirrors.

Edward listened while D'Fonzio, the owner of the bar and the rooms Edward, Joe, and Ironfield rented upstairs, gave Womb Broom advice. D'Fonzio knew a lot about trouble between husbands and wives, since a great deal of it started, one way or another, right in front of him with some man drinking up his pay or going off with a woman he wasn't married to. Sometimes the trouble got brought to him later. Like thirst. Like an empty glass. His advice to Womb Broom? "Take a little gasoline, bub, rub it on your hands and give your shirt and face a wipe. Nobody can smell anything important through gasoline." D'Fonzio did not give philosophical and moral advice. He left that sort of thing to the priest. He was a practical man. When there was a telephone call for anyone in the bar, whether the voice on the phone was male or female, he would cup the receiver in his meaty palm, ask the customer if he was there, and reply to the caller accordingly. "Nope, haven't seen him all day." Or, "You just missed him; he left about ten minutes ago." Or, "Yeah, he's right here; just a minute." Even D'Fonzio's wife, who sometimes kept bar for him, in this matter at least, did exactly as he wished. The bar was sanctuary, and that was that.

Gasoline, Edward thought bitterly, well, it just might help Womb Broom. As for himself, he could dunk himself in it like sheep dip, and it would do no good whatever. The problem between him and Madeline was deep and unreachable by any method he knew. As far as he was concerned they had more passion than Womb Broom and Lois ever dreamed of, and in some strange way were more standoffish than Ironfield and Stella.

Out of sheer desperation, Edward said, "Hey Broom, how about some eight ball?" already off his stool with his beer and on his way into the next room where two pool tables stood at right angles to one another. But he was so aggravated that he might, just as easily, have thrown a punch at someone.

"No beer on the table, boys," D'Fonzio said.

Edward set his beer on the low partition between the two rooms, snapped on the light over a table, and found himself a cue stick that didn't flop around on the felt when he rolled it. He flipped a coin, won the toss, and broke the rack with such violence that two stripes and one solid ball went down. The solids were in better position, however, and he chose them, shooting with great accuracy and violence until he had run them all and pocketed the eight ball, something he rarely did.

"Mercy," Joe said, laid a dollar on the table, which was what they always played for, and dropped fifteen cents in the small padlocked box on the partition, which was what D'Fonzio charged per rack.

Edward was only remotely aware of the curious and apprehensive attention of people in the bar, but he didn't connect it with the unusually loud smacks of his cue ball into the object balls and the jarring thunks of the object balls into the back of the pockets; but when he broke for the second game and his cue ball skipped off the rack and hit the wooden partition like a cannon shot, everyone stopped what they were doing to stare at him, D'Fonzio in particular, and he understood.

Joe won the second game, as though, when Edward tried to shoot gently, something tentative and ambiguous happened to his otherwise dead aim. Sometimes even the simplest shot defied him, and he missed the pocket by inches. He just couldn't please her, he was thinking. No matter what he did, some part of her seemed to harbor a grudge, some part of her was not pleased but resentful, so that it became spooky and dangerous to be around her. Not that there weren't good times, wonderful times, when that resentment, or whatever in God's name it was, would recede for a little while and they could have joy. Times when they made love as though they had invented it new out of the raw materials of emotion and need and flesh, so that anything he'd ever had with anyone else seemed a sad imitation and a poor copy. But those times had grown fewer and fewer, and the mistrust and resentment had grown so large that it came to haunt her face like a subtle restructuring of the bones beneath her skin. It took up residence behind her eyes. And after a while, he did not wish to come home and see it. All this he knew and could think into words.

But playing eight ball with Womb Broom—loosing four straight games and winning the fifth only because Womb Broom scratched on the eight ball and therefore beat himself—other fears tormented him that he couldn't always put into words. They seemed to haunt the chambers of his heart more than his brain, and struggling with them exhausted him. They appeared and disappeared like ghosts, sometimes before he could quite discover their proportions or begin to test their validity, and they made him feel weak and more than a little crazy. One of them seemed to insist that she, Madeline, wished, with a hopelessness equal to his own, to change him, to alter him; but that, even if she were granted such liberty and license, she would not love what she had made, because she had had to make it. She would resent him all the more. His son also haunted him, as though the boy had become a part of this terrible, hopeless, and complicated struggle, so that sometimes when he looked at him, he saw an extension of her, and sometimes he saw an extension of himself. He didn't wish it so, but there it was. And even when he knew their son was neither of them but a third person altogether, and merely a child, the boy could not be kept clear of trouble. How often had he come home from work to have her tell him that James had driven her nearly crazy, had done this or that, had been disobedient. And how often had he taken his belt to the child only to have her stop him in the midst of a punishment she'd promised James he would deliver, flying to the rescue, herself already in tears: "Oh that's too much, too hard! It's enough! Stop it! Stop it right now!" Who did she want punished after all, and what? And whose behavior did he think he was altering to suit her, since he seemed unable to alter his own? And didn't he always feel the odd man out? And what did it mean that he sometimes saw his son as a weakling, a momma's boy, inclined to tears, dejected and sensitive in ways that were oblique, feminine, and frustratingly unreachable?

"You gonna shoot or stand there and chalk your stick away to nuthin?" Womb Broom asked him.

He looked dumbly at the table and the arrangement of balls, not quite able to make sense of them or recall how the game was played.

"What the fuck are you a-gruntin and groanin about anyway?"

He didn't know he was grunting and groaning or why, except that it concerned his son in a way that burdened his heart and weakened his knees. "What am I?" he said, "stripes or solids?"

His once white T-shirt soiled over the roll of his belly and under his arms as if with faint rust, his khaki work pants dirty too and bagged at the knees, a faint and constant mist of sweat under his eyes and mingled with his mustache, Womb Broom regarded him with puzzled amusement. "You're a fuckin fish," he said. "Playin pool with you tonight is like stealin money."

"Right," Edward said and let out a long sigh of held breath that tasted of brass and ashes. "I give up." He dropped another dollar on the table and dropped a quarter in the locked box on the partition since he didn't have fifteen cents.

"But, hell," Womb Broom said, "I'm a good sport. I'll buy you a beer." He patted his soft belly fondly and grinned.

"A drink," Edward said.

"Sure," Womb Broom said. "You done lost enough for a bottle."

Settled on his bar stool again, half a double shot of whiskey warming his stomach, chased and smoothed by a swallow of his almost empty beer, Edward began to feel better. He figured he'd probably always wanted to live over a bar, maybe in a room exactly like the one he occupied with its shabby, worn furniture; a lace doily, gone gray with Pittsburgh grime, on the dresser; the Sacred Heart of Jesus hung on the wall above it to preside over his pocket change, billfold, and keys; and beneath his feet, the click of pool balls and the friendly confabulation of the bar, if he didn't happen to be down there himself.

What more could a fellow ask than to get off a hard day's work and return to bar and home, all under the same roof? They were all sinners here, all fuck-ups and misfits. There were no innocents, no wives and children to accuse and mystify them. There were no debts they owed each other that couldn't be paid. He drank off the last of his whiskey, and his eyes teared in gratitude.

JAMES
TALLY

A little more than two weeks after Lester Buck had appeared out of nowhere to fetch his raccoon, he and James were friends. Clara and Virginia seemed to think such a friendship was predictable and bitterly amusing, and so James found himself sitting at his grandmother's table listening with burning ears to the girls describe how ridiculous, peculiar, and probably feeble-minded Lester was. What was worse, James didn't feel he had the right to argue or make a fuss. Since his mother had gotten her job at Green's Department Store in Cedar Hill and begun to work late, he ate six nights a week at the house and felt like a charity case. Perhaps because they were disinterested, or maybe because they were entertained, James's grandmother and grandfather made no comment either. But his aunt Lily, who had flunked Lester in the fourth grade, had a much more generous opinion of him.

"He doesn't wear clothes that are too small for him or too big or worn-out because he's peculiar," she told her nieces. "He just doesn't have anything better." She gave each of them a significant glance, but there was no malice in it. "I shouldn't really have to explain that," she told them.

Virginia had had the most to say about how peculiar Lester always looked, and she had the decency to blush, but Clara took another tack.

"Well you weren't in the first grade with him!" she said. "You ask Miss Teasdale if he didn't jump out the window and run home every time she turned her back. In about an hour his momma would come marching him back into the classroom where he'd sit, all red-faced and snotty-nosed, and then he'd do exactly the same thing again. Miss Teasdale finally had to keep every single window shut and locked because of him, and for two weeks we nearly died of the heat. But that didn't even do any good, because the moment we were let out for recess or lunch, he'd hit the front steps running, and by the time the rest of us got outside, he'd be all the way across the playground on a beeline for home, couldn't anybody catch him!"

Grandfather Marshall laughed at that, one short laugh almost like a cough, his chin into his chest and his eyes merry.

"He never got one bit better!" Clara said, looking at Harley Marshall as though this were no laughing matter. "I'll bet he wasn't in class one full day all year. He never spoke a single word to anyone or even *looked* at anybody that I can remember. He was just a little red-faced lump, watching his chance to run, and he had to do the whole first grade over because of it. Now I call that peculiar," Clara said, suddenly staring into James's eyes.

"I don't think it's peculiar," James said, and he didn't, although he noticed that everyone at the table gave him a surprised look, as though he might have had the grace to admit the obvious—everyone, anyway, except his grandfather, who had slipped behind his wall of privacy again. What Lester had done seemed wonderfully brave and pure to him. He himself had hated first grade; it was a prison sentence, an unreasonable and arbitrary punishment he'd suffered only because he hadn't thought it possible to do otherwise.

"And I thought you were supposed to be bright," Clara said.

"Well, I'm sure I never in my life met a shier boy than Lester Buck," his aunt Lily said, "but I never found the least bit of harm in him. I don't think there is a mean bone in that child's body, and I think it's just grand that the two of you made friends."

"He's cracked," Clara said, "and being poor or shy doesn't have a thing to do with it!"

"That will be sufficient, missy," Grandmother Marshall said.

Lester was not cracked, James knew that much, but he took his grandmother's remark to include anything he might have to say on the subject too and kept his peace. Still, the silence that followed was painful and awkward, and it seemed, as well, his fault; so, trying not to be obvious, he hurried to finish his supper and asked to be excused. After he had carried his plate, glass, and silverware to the sideboard by the sink, he left by the kitchen door, grateful to be outside in the long, oblique twilight. He didn't know how he felt, but he knew he didn't want to shut himself up in the trailer, so he got no further than the stile where he sat on the top step and listened to the crickets making little shivers of sound as though they were having chills. Across the fence, milked and contented and chewing her cud, the cow added a gourdy rhythm of her own.

He didn't know how or why people became friends, but he decided at once that it had to do with the eyes, something in them held in common that each could see and recognize, even if they couldn't name it. He'd seen that Lester was all right from the beginning. Sure, the first times they'd run into each other fishing, they hadn't spoken, but they'd managed to raise their hands in greeting, and it wasn't long before they'd said a word or two, and now they were real friends. As for his old friends in Cedar Hill, twice he'd gone in with his mother, and while she worked, he'd rushed off to spend the day in the neighborhood where he'd lived; but that had only taught him just how long five years could be, at least when it came between the time when you were eight and the time when you were thirteen. Standing around in someone's yard who wasn't sure they cared to remember you wasn't much good. Oh they had been nice enough, he supposed, but the last couple of times his mother had asked, he hadn't wanted to go back to Cedar Hill. There wasn't any way it was going to earn back the investment of homesickness he'd put into it.

He heard something stir behind him, and when he looked

over his shoulder, he was surprised to see Clara coming through the dusk of the side yard.

"We're supposed to apologize," she said, "although I don't see the point since we were only trying to help you out. Anyway, Ginny said she'd do the dishes by herself if I came, so here I am."

He turned half around to face her. "Help me out?" he said.

"Sure," she said. She propped a foot on the bottom step of the stile and seemed to strike some sort of pose. "What are you doing sitting out here anyway?"

He tilted his head to one side and didn't answer, and she looked off toward the east, holding her fine-boned, somewhat haughty face in profile. As irrelevant as the thought seemed, he found himself conceding that she was pretty, and for all that it mattered, so was her sister. They were both blond and blue-eyed, and their figures often snared his attention.

"You *are* family after all," Clara said, "and there isn't any reason to let you make an ass of yourself without warning you."

"I'm an ass because Lester is my friend?" he said and laughed. He thought she might laugh too, but she didn't.

"Friends are important," she said. "He's goofy, that's all. His whole family is. He's my age, and he's two grades behind me for goodness sake. Have you ever seen him in church, or his momma or poppa? No, and you won't. They're trashy."

"No they're not," he said.

"Oh I don't like this," she said. "I don't like the way it makes me feel. Grandmother sent me out here to apologize because she thought we acted like spoiled little snots, and maybe we did. But friends are important," she said and turned back toward the house. "You do whatever you want." As she rounded the flowering quince bushes by the porch, she called back significantly: "Birds of a feather. . . ."

A sudden flash of anger warmed his temples until he realized he'd had almost the same thought before she'd come out. He just hadn't put the same complexion on it; he hadn't thought of Lester as goofy, or, by association, himself. He sat on the top step of the stile and pondered the matter until the chill of the evening drove him into the trailer where he lay on the couch, his hands behind his head.

It was true Lester Buck seemed to have no more friends than he did, although Lester had lived all his life in the same place, while he himself had just got there. But that didn't mean Lester was goofy. He had just got off on the wrong foot somehow. Maybe because he was so shy, like Aunt Lily said, or maybe just because he'd gotten use to being on the wrong foot, it had stayed with him, become, somehow or other, who he was. Or maybe people like Virginia and Clara weren't going to see him but one way, no matter that he'd gotten to be somebody else entirely. He didn't know.

He understood, however, that his association with Lester Buck didn't do him one bit of good in his cousins' eyes. It was an embarrassment to his cousins to have him and his mother living in an ugly purple trailer in their cow pasture, never mind the reasons for it, which all by themselves were sleazy and embarrassing. And then there was Lester Buck's house, which had neither bathroom nor running water nor electricity. It was the sort of house you didn't see anymore, with an open dogtrot running down the middle, a kitchen and sitting room off one side, and two sleeping rooms off the other, so that when you went from the kitchen to one of the bedrooms, you had to cross this hallway, which was roofed over but open at both ends and cluttered with tools and washtubs and lanterns and clothes hung on pegs or nails driven in the walls. The house had never seen a coat of paint and had no foundation but was merely held off the hard-packed mud of its yard by large, stacked stones under its four corners. And there was Effie, Lester's mother, her big chapped hands scrubbing out clothes over a washboard in a galvanized tub, or else boiling them in a big black iron pot out back and scooping them up with a wooden paddle and slopping them over a line until they were cool enough to wring out and hang properly. And Roy Buck, Lester's father, with his asthma and weak heart and general poor health, and that terrible scar across his face that tugged down the corner of his right eye so that tears seemed always to leak out there—a scar James's grandmother had told him came from a knife fight when Roy Buck was younger, and since it was his grandmother saying this and not Virginia or Clara, it would be the truth—and no education or job and only forty acres of steep, poor land to make a living on. And Lester himself, all bone and greenish freckles and bad teeth.

The whole thing made James's stomach hurt somehow, and he stared at the dim ceiling of the trailer for a while before he found himself remembering the first time he and Lester had really had a conversation, rather than just raising a hand and nodding and speaking and then going on to keep a respectful distance between them while they fished. He had come down to the spot where Piney Creek flowed into Sugar Creek and was cheered to see Lester already there, but he hadn't even had a chance to raise his hand in their usual formal greeting when Lester hooked a huge bass. James had never in his life had a fish on so large, and Lester didn't have it long, since, after racing all over the long deep hole where the two streams met, it surged completely out of the water on James's side and got free. He could see it afterward, no more than five feet from him, finning in the current and popping its mouth and gill covers open very wide. Finally it shook its head like someone who'd just caught a heavy punch, and for a second James could even see the red in its eye before it turned downstream and, with one, and then another, muscular twitch of its tail, glided out of sight. "Holy God," James croaked, "what a fish!"

But Lester merely blushed and without a word brought in his line and inspected his hook.

"I was looking right down on his head," James said. "I bet he weighed five pounds!"

"Maybe three," Lester allowed, and then, as if those single-word greetings they had exchanged for nearly a week amounted to a conversation that, at last, could be continued, he added, "I've done lost him bout once a week all summer. Can't do nothin with him." He turned an even deeper shade of red. "Don't have the line to give him, and he straightens my hooks out."

James went up Sugar Creek, where the water wasn't quite waist deep, and waded across. He had an extra one of his father's snelled hooks with him, and when he got on Lester's side, he worried it out of the fabric of his shirt pocket and offered it. "Try this one," he said, "it's as strong as you'd ever want."

Lester glanced at the hook. "Ain't got the money to buy it off you," he said.

"Didn't ask for any," James said. "It's way too big for hornyheads anyway."

But Lester wouldn't take it for free. He brought a matchbox out of his pocket with six or eight hooks in it that had been scraped free of rust but still looked as old as family heirlooms and told James even two or three of them wouldn't be a good trade, but James took only one. It had been a little smaller than his father's hooks, but it turned out to be so soft that even forcing it through the carapace of a grasshopper often bent it out of shape.

"They aren't trashy," James said aloud to the dim ceiling of the trailer. Lester wouldn't even take a silly hook from him without offering something in return. And he'd never been to Lester's house when Effie didn't ask him to stay to supper or inquire about his mother. And Roy always inquired about his father, whom he didn't even know, although out of some strange sense of propriety he never asked about his mother, whom he knew every bit as well as Effie did, having, like Effie, been a schoolmate. "They are not trashy," he said; they just didn't have any money or any luck.

But Lester's father wasn't off in Pittsburgh, was he? No. Roy Buck was home where he and Lester worked together worming tobacco, drenching cows, hoeing and weeding, splitting wood, and. . . . Phooey, he thought suddenly, what did that have to do with anything? The trouble with being around Virginia and Clara was that, pretty soon, you began to think like them.

He turned on his side, making up his mind to trouble himself no more about the silly attitude of his cousins. He adjusted himself comfortably on the couch. His mother would be home soon, and he found himself thinking about the '39 Ford coupe she'd bought from the Kaizer-Fraizer dealer in Cedar Hill. It was gray and had a cream-colored steering wheel and gearshift knob, which looked expensive and reminded him of mother-of-pearl, and he liked the gearshift on the floorboard rather than on the steering wheel where the later '39 models had it. He hoped she would let him drive a little, but he doubted it, even though his father had sometimes let him drive the Packard. His father was far braver in such matters than his mother.

But then, as though his mind were strolling a beach and idly picking up pebbles and shells, he wasn't thinking about the Ford coupe any longer, but about Lester's collection of wild animals. His raccoon. His pet crow, Black Jack, tethered by one foot to the fence around the barnyard, cocking one outraged eye or the other toward the kernels of corn in his, James's, palm before the beak came down like a chipping hammer. Lester's pet fox, who lived mostly under the house and, for all the brains they were supposed to have, never quit trying to chew through the six-foot length of wire that attached his collar to the simple cotton rope. He might have chewed through the rope easily, but he kept gnawing and worrying the wire as close to his neck as he could reach. All these creatures, James thought, did they take the place of friends? Lester's dog, a little black-and-white fice, was the only one of them who truly was a pet and showed any affection, or wanted any.

Until weariness stole his wits, he pondered Lester's menagerie, how the fox would tolerate no one's touch but Lester's, and even Lester was often bitten. "Just had his eyes open too long by the time I dug him outten his den," Lester explained. He'd gotten the crow before it could fly and split its tongue with his pocketknife in order to help it talk, but it still had no interest in conversation, although it would call the cows down from the field, call Lester's dog Skipper, and even call Lester himself, crying, "Lesser? Lesser?" with exactly Effie's intonation. Maybe, James thought, the raccoon had some affection for Lester, but that was an even bigger shame, since tomorrow Lester was going to have to put it down. It had been too much trouble for too long, killing laying hens, stealing eggs, spoiling the milk the

Bucks kept in their springhouse, and eating nearly every ear of sweet corn from the kitchen garden the day before the Bucks might have picked it for their own use, so that Roy had told Lester that very afternoon: "I got to get rid of that animal, son, or you do."

A moment later, when Osceola appeared to hold a silent counsel with Lester's animals, James was not surprised. Osceola was dressed in white buckskins, a single eagle feather bound to the ends of each braid of hair lying across his broad chest and down his back, and he was full of a strange, stern compassion. For their part, the animals paid serious attention. The crow blinked and stared at Osceola one eye at a time. The fox pricked its ears forward and tested the breeze with small movements of its nose. And the raccoon watched with its intelligent, glittering eyes, now and again rising off its front feet as though to listen better. When he was through with the animals, Osceola had the same strange, wordless conversation with Lester, only Lester began to shiver violently until, all at once, he wasn't Lester any longer, but a young, spike-horned buck, who suddenly snorted and leapt out of the company of those animals he had claimed as pets.

"What are you doing lying there in the dark?" James's mother asked, although he wasn't in the dark and she was in a nimbus of electric light so bright that he could not look at her. He didn't know what he was doing there. "It's nearly eleven o'clock. Why aren't you in bed?"

"I was thinking," he told her, his voice full of the burrs of sleep.

"Look at your feet!" she said. "They're black as pitch. Have you brushed your teeth?" When he shook his head groggily that he hadn't, she marched off into her bedroom to leave her purse and take off her jacket. "And what do you propose to do when your teeth rot out of your head, and how am I supposed to pay the dentist bill?" She came back into the kitchen, lit the stove, and plopped the teakettle over the eye. "Well I won't have you waking everybody in the house in the middle of the night."

She took a saucer from the cupboard, mixed salt and baking

soda in it, and set it beside him on the couch. He had swung his feet to the floor and held his head in his hands. "Scrub your teeth with that. Good and hard. Use your finger."

Still more asleep than awake, he dipped his finger in the mixture and began to rub his teeth and gums with it. It tasted horrible, and he got up to use the kitchen sink.

"No you don't, young man," she told him. "You know better than to spit in the sink. Go outside." She gave him a glass of water. "Why can't I count on you to look after yourself?" she asked as he went out the door. "I just can't be around to mother you every minute, to make sure you brush your teeth and clean . . ."

Holding the glass of water against his chest with his forearm, he shut the door on her harangue and sat down on the step of the trailer. It was cold outside. As blinded by the darkness as he had been by the light, it was a while before he could make out the saucer he was holding, if not the hand that held it; and he set his water down, dipped his finger in, and began to scrub his teeth and gums with the revolting mixture until the pressure in his bladder became unbearable, and he set the saucer aside too, and went off by the fence to relieve himself. Shivering beneath the cold glitter of the stars, he hoped she would not catch him urinating so close to the trailer. He dreaded going back inside, but after he'd rinsed his mouth until the water was gone, there was nothing else to do. Besides, it was so cold his skin had shrunk and felt way too small for him.

"Wash your face and hands and those filthy feet before you go to bed," she told him and pointed out a pan of warm water and a soapy washcloth sitting by the couch. She was in her nightgown and bathrobe, and he was aware of her studying him while he scrubbed his face and neck. When he started on his feet, the washcloth and the water in the pan turned grayish black.

"I hate to ask when you last took a bath," she said.

He said nothing, rinsed the washcloth the best he could, and got up to empty the pan of water outside.

"I'll do that," she told him. "You get ready for bed."

While she was gone he stripped down to his shorts, tipped up the couch, got out his folded sheet and blanket and his pillow, and arranged them much more neatly than usual. She was gone so long, he figured she'd walked all the way to the end of the cow pasture merely to dash out the water; and when she came back, it was true, her house slippers and the hem of her bathrobe were soaked with dew, and he felt a familiar, painful tug of guilt. "I'm sorry," he said, "I didn't mean to go to sleep. I only lay down to think a minute."

"I just expect you to look after yourself a little," she said. "You're nearly grown, and I'm working like a nigger and can't look after you every single minute. Is that too much to ask?"

"No," he said.

She went off into her bedroom and slid the thin partition shut behind her. It was as though her disappointment and anger had left an odor in his part of the trailer like spent gunpowder.

After many minutes, he said, "Good night," across the darkness; and after an undetermined length of time during which he hardly dared to breathe, she said, "Good night," in return.

MADELINE
TALLY

Anger, like a low-grade fever, stayed with her through her prayers. Still, she patiently named the members of her family and asked that they be blessed, and she asked a special blessing for herself and her son, and, out of habit or guilt or hope or some martyred effort to be fair—she didn't herself know precisely why—her husband. But when she had finished, she was astonished to find herself thinking immediately about Leslie Johnson with whom she'd had dinner for the second time that week. Leslie's starched white cuffs, his three-piece suits, and his charming manners popped into her head so easily, they had to have been there all along, hidden behind her anger at James and even behind her prayers. She'd barely known there was a Leslie Johnson when she'd been a schoolgirl because he was two years younger, and he still seemed boyish to her in spite of his prematurely gray hair. But he'd become a lawyer, for goodness sake, and was quite successful in a small-town sort of way. And since his wife had died of cancer and he was childless, he was utterly free. While she, on the other hand. . . . She lay perfectly still, looking up at the ceiling for a moment before she got abruptly out of bed, snatched back the partition, and made her way to James's couch where she knelt and gathered him into her arms.

"I'm sorry, baby," she told him. "Momma is just tired and cranky." She wished with all her heart that it were true, and she squeezed him hard as though to make it true. But a stubborn resentment had taken up residence in her and couldn't be dislodged, and it frightened her and made her sad to think she felt it in James too. But maybe she only imagined it. Maybe he was responding as well as his small boy's shocked dignity and confusion would allow.

JAMES
TALLY

James carried the little falling block, single-shot .22 rifle and a spade, and Lester carried the raccoon. Or rather, it rode his shoulders, its clever black hands sometimes braced against the slope of Lester's chest or back, sometimes holding him about the neck.

It was a long climb to the top of the ridge behind the Bucks' house, but the moment they got there, Lester tilted his shoulders so the raccoon dropped softly to the earth; and then, as though it were all one motion, he took the rifle out of James's hands, chambered a shell, and shot the raccoon just behind the eye. The rifle didn't make much noise, just a flat crack, not loud, but the raccoon went down on its side, shivering as though it were cold before it began to kick aimlessly and endlessly, it seemed, although probably only seconds passed. "There, you son of a bitch," Lester said, "I hope you're satisfied," and he sat down on the ground with his long bony hands drooping between his knees and the rifle abandoned beside him.

Somehow James hadn't believed any of this would happen. He'd showed up with the fine idea that they could take the raccoon a long way off somewhere and just leave it, but it turned out that Lester had already tried that more than once that summer, and the raccoon always got back. Even when they'd started climbing the mountain, James had been convinced something would come along to keep them from doing what they had clearly set out to do. But now he found himself staring at the tiny but irreparable hole just behind the raccoon's eye and the dark stain leaking into the earth under its head, and he sank down to the ground too.

He felt the way he did during fistfights. He always stood his ground and traded the necessary insults and shoves, but he never actually believed the fight would occur, even after it had clearly begun. Neither blows nor the taste of blood in his mouth could overcome his disbelief, and as a consequence, his anger and strength never came to his rescue because a part of him wouldn't believe it and had withdrawn beyond the reach of pain or the need for rescue.

The moment the rifle went off, it was that way. Some essential part of him simply went away, and it wouldn't come back, not even when they began to labor through the iron-hard roots of laurel and rhododendron to get a hole deep enough to bury the body. He was shocked and weak in his limbs, but another side of him had gone away somewhere and wouldn't acknowledge what they had done.

When they got down off the mountain and into the nearly grassless hard-packed earth of Lester's backyard, Effie was on the dogtrot washing clothes, but she didn't speak to them. She merely gave Lester a brief, discreet glance when he passed her to take the rifle back inside to put it away. Listlessly, James propped the spade against the fence and wandered over to the apple tree by the springhouse to get a treat for the crow.

"You boys want a little something to eat?" he heard Effie ask gently when Lester came out again.

"I reckon," Lester told her and went on to fetch the spade and put it away in the tool shed.

The crow didn't seem to want the apple. When James held it out, the crow merely glared at it as though it had no idea what an apple was, and then it hopped to his shoulder and rapped him solidly in the head, pulling out a tuft of hair. "Ouch, you bastard!" James said, brushed the bird off, and inspected the side of his head tenderly with his fingertips. He wasn't surprised to find a little blood.

"Must think you're a tree and he's a woodpecker," Lester said, sounding almost like himself. "Hold him for me."

Carefully, so as not to injure the crow's leg, which was already scarred by the hog staple bent around it, Lester pulled open the metal band, took the crow out of James's hands, and gave it a pitch in the air. "So long, Blackjack," he said, but the crow hovered uncertainly for a moment and then lit again on the rail.

"What are you up to, chile?" Effie called from the dogtrot. "Blackjack don't do no harm."

"He don't do no good neither," Lester told her. "Scat," he said and gave the bird a push, but it simply flopped its wings for balance and moved a few inches down the rail until Lester picked it up and pitched it high overhead. This time, after it had fluffed in the air a moment like a swimmer treading water, it banked over to the roof of the springhouse where it made a clumsy landing. When it had righted itself, it wiped one side and then the other of its beak against the comb of the roof, getting rid of some of James's hair, and stared at its new surroundings with what looked like pure hatred.

Lester rushed at it, waving his arms. "Shoo, get outta here!" he shouted, but a single beat of its wings lifted it into the apple tree. "Well," Lester said, looking up at it, "I reckon you ain't had much slack."

"Awwwh honey . . ." Effie said, shading her eyes with her hand and looking at Lester sadly.

"I've just growed out of it, Momma," Lester told her.

"Come on," he said to James, "less us take this next'n off a ways."

"Awwwh honey," Effie said as James followed Lester around the house, "you got no call . . . Poppa didn't mean . . ." she stammered from the front end of the dogtrot.

"I know it," Lester told her, opened his pocketknife, cut the cotton rope with a single stroke, and began to pull the fox from beneath the house.

James could hear its small, keening growls before it came into view, all four feet braced against being dragged and its bushy tail thrashing side to side like the tail of a cat.

"Ha," Lester said. "Ain't you in for a surprise though."

With Effie looking after them, they went off down the wagon road, the fox making frenzied dashes toward any sort of cover before the rope, coming taut, snatched it off its feet, but it was always up in an instant, making a mad dash in another direction. When they were out of sight of the house, they cut across the lower pasture, where, at last, Lester knelt and began to pull the fox gently toward him. "Well, well, buddyroe, easy now, well, well," he crooned, but he got bitten just the same, quicker than the eye could follow. Still, he got his left hand around its muzzle, got the collar off, and stroked the fox gently and fondly until it quit bucking and jerking. But the moment he turned it loose, it skimmed across the open ground of the pasture and into the woods. Gone. Vanished. Just like that.

After a while Lester seemed to notice, in a distant sort of way, the puncture wounds the fox's sharp teeth had left between his thumb and forefinger, and absently, he sucked them and spat, sucked them and spat, gazing across the somehow outrageously empty pasture the fox had left in its wake.

James didn't know what made him think he understood how Lester was feeling, but he was sure that, on some level or other, he did understand, and he couldn't take it another minute. "Did you know that chiggers don't bite?" he asked all at once.

Lester gave him an odd look.

"That's right," James told him. "They spit on you, and the spit is such a powerful acid, it dissolves your skin at once, and then the chigger climbs down in the hole and eats the dissolved skin. You can put clear fingernail polish over the little bastards and smother them, but you'll still itch like mad because you've got all that chigger spit down in there, plus a dead chigger. It's true," James said, looking into Lester's perplexed face, "I read it in the Sunday paper in an article about strange animal facts, or some such thing. Did you know that more people die every year from bee stings than they do of snake bite? And," he said, pointing a finger at Lester as though he were delivering an important lecture, "did you know that if an eagle were flying a mile up and could read, he could have read the headlines of that Sunday paper?"

At last Lester began to grin and shake his head. "No," he said, "I didn't know none of them things, but I'm beginning to suspicion you're a little bit crazy."

"I absolutely guarantee it," James said and pushed Lester over backwards.

"Why you . . ." Lester said, but James caught one of Lester's bare feet, as horny with callous as a horse's hoof, and spun him on his back.

"Let me git a-holt . . . durn you . . ." Lester sputtered, but James rushed him, lifting the foot as high as he could and standing Lester almost on his head before he turned loose, and Lester went over as stiffly as a chopped tree to land flat on his belly.

"Ooooff! Daaagone little . . ." Lester said and scrabbled up.

But he was awkward and slow, and for a while James was able to sidestep him, to duck under his big, grasping hands, to push him off, but finally Lester managed to catch an arm, and although James yanked him off his feet, he couldn't jerk free. Laughing, they both fell thrashing and rolling down the steep pasture until James found himself nearly paralyzed by the strength of Lester's grip.

"Jesus," he said at last, gasping with laughter and pain, "turn loose! You're killing me!"

Lester obeyed instantly, but it took a while before James could shake some feeling back into the arm Lester had grabbed. His neck, which Lester had also gotten a passing grip on, felt seriously wrenched. He'd seen Grandfather Marshall wring the neck of a chicken, and he felt Lester had stopped just short of doing the same thing.

"I never meant to hurt you none," Lester told him, looking embarrassed and ashamed.

"I believe it," James said, "otherwise I'd be dead." Lester, he'd decided long ago, was made out of something inhuman, steel wire or some such thing, since no one so thin had any right to be so strong, and horseplay with him was always painful. Mostly because he was clumsy and would half kill you by accident.

EDWARD TALLY

"Enter," Paris sang out when he knocked on her door, and he came in to find her on the love seat in her underwear, wads of cotton between her toes and all her fingers sticking out at odd angles. Her fingernails and toenails were red as blood, red as her lips, and she was waving her hands around as though shooing flies. "I'm just about ready," she said and puckered her lips for a kiss.

"Sure you are," he told her, wondering how she'd known it was him, or *if* she'd known it was him, since she always complained about the man downstairs who found endless excuses to come knocking on her door. "Mmmmmmmmh," she said, kissing him, holding his head down with her wrists, although he could still feel her waving her hands around behind his head to dry her nails.

"I just have to slip into my sundress and sandals. All the serious primping is over," she told him. "Why don't you make us a gin and tonic, sweetie, while my nails dry."

He got down glasses, poured a generous dollop of gin in each, got a lime, tonic, and ice from her refrigerator, and made the drinks. She took a sip of hers, leaving a smudge of lipstick on the rim of the glass, and when he saw it, he realized his mouth felt peculiar, somehow waxy, and he wiped it with the back of his hand. There was a streak of red from his watch to his knuckles. He wiped his mouth again.

"Awwwwh, you looked cute," she said. "I like it when you've got my lipstick on." She cocked her head and puffed out her lower lip in a pout. "Then anybody can see you belong to me."

"Since Lincoln freed the slaves, no one belongs to anyone," he told her.

"Aren't we in a nice mood," she said. "Is it because of the zoo? Do you not want to take me to the zoo?"

He wiped his mouth again. "I'm sorry," he said. "Six days a week and twelve hours a day, climbing around in the top of a steel mill putting up conduit . . ." He waved the rest of his apology away. It was a lie anyhow. He was angry, but he wasn't sure why. "You look beautiful, and I'm glad to take you to the zoo, or any damned place you'd like to go." He winked at her and took a swallow of his gin and tonic, grinning, trying his best to look happy as hell, but she eyed him suspiciously, reluctant, it seemed, to give up her pouting.

Maybe she thought it was seductive, and in some strange way it was, her lower lip puffed out, the pink buds of her nipples and the shadow of her pubic hair showing through the sheer, lacy, buff-colored underwear, which was so nearly the color of her skin she might have grown it too, merely as a decoration. One long leg was bent at the knee, her foot, cotton between the vivid toes, braced on the edge of the love seat; the other leg flopped, loose-jointed, with her heel resting on the floor. She had the slender, wonderful muscle tone of a dancer and short, kinky blond hair with a vicious part down the middle as straight as a chalk line. There was, in fact, blond hair all over her, a soft whirl of it in the small of her back and on her belly, at her temples and on her upper lip, but it was soft as down, as peach fuzz, as velvet; and it made her seem both little-girlish and somehow feline. She was all over the color of ripe wheat. Even her eyes weren't so much hazel as yellow, fringed with thick, buff eyelashes she crimped in a curler.

"God damn," he said, put his drink down on the end table—pushing aside an assortment of cutesy carnival figurines to make room for it—took her breasts in his hands, and kissed her. For her part, she moaned, opened her mouth, and cupped his crotch in both her hands.

He felt his zipper come down, and she began to speak against his mouth. "I want to give my Tallywhacker a kiss," she told him.

One way or another it was an old joke to him, but not to her. According to Paris Pergola, he had the only authentic "Tallywhacker" she'd ever met.

"And it is *my* Tallywhacker," she said against his lips, "and I don't want to hear nothing about any Abraham Lincoln."

Then he was in her mouth and she was doing those incredible things with her tongue. "Holy God," he whispered.

Later, in the bathroom, he discovered lipstick on his fly, and he dampened a washcloth, dabbed it against a bar of soap, and tried to scrub the front of his trousers clean. He couldn't quite tell if he'd been successful; certainly his fly was damp, wrinkled, and disreputable-looking, but he wasn't so sure it wasn't still a faint pink in the bargain. Like having lipstick on his mouth, having it on his fly never seemed to bother Paris one whit. Outrageous as it was, it seemed to please her. She often giggled about it as though it were some sort of ad she'd taken out. A warning to other women that he was already, by God, thoroughly spoken for? A sign to other men of the sort of lover she could be, perhaps an incentive to provoke them to try and beat Edward Tally's time with her? Whatever, she would blush and giggle to see her lipstick on his fly, but she was never scandalized by it. If he wanted to clean himself up, she never pouted, but she never helped either.

Scrubbing on his fly, he felt his dark mood returning. He washed his hands and his face and found one of her most recent decorating touches when he flipped up the toilet seat to urinate. There was a bright turquoise cover on the lid made of terry cloth, which, when he raised it, revealed two can-can dancers doing a very high kick, as well as the legend *In France They Say WEE WEE*. He stared at it and realized he didn't understand, even in the tiniest and most remote way, the sort of person who would buy such a thing. Her apartment was full of stuffed animals in an assortment of vivid colors and covered in some sort of sleazy fur that seemed to float about in the air and get up his nose like cat fur, so that he sometimes plucked his nose and snorted to get rid of it. There were Kewpie dolls everywhere and a vase by her bed, which contained, not flowers, but painted birds hung from sticks such as one might win tossing rings at a carnival. He stared at the toilet seat cover and began to shake his head. "I've gone crazy," he told himself in a small, tight voice, that nevertheless broke, "totally, fucking crazy!"

At the zoo a nervous sweat misted his armpits and rolled occasionally down his ribs, but she was happy. She dropped dimes into slender green machines and received pellets of food to feed the animals; and oohing and aahing over each exhibit and pressing his arm to her side, she dragged him from llamas to antelope, monkeys to baboons. One big male with a multicolored ass reminded him at once of the stuffed animals perched on her dressers and snuggled on her bed and reminded him, as well, of himself, although he wasn't sure just why. But at last he began to take a pleasure in her happiness and forgot that a zoo was the last place he would have chosen to spend his one day off a week.

They had dinner in a small French restaurant she knew, and never having been in such a place before, he let her order for him. He was impressed, and although he could have eaten three times as much food as he was given, he thought it the most delicious he'd ever tasted.

"How did you ever learn to handle yourself in a place like this?" he asked her. She worked the desk of a small hotel, after all, where he'd stayed for a week before he'd found cheaper lodgings a block down the street over D'Fonzio's bar; and he knew she couldn't afford such prices. Hell, he couldn't afford them either.

She giggled and leaned toward him, her eyes collecting candlelight. "I was a waitress here a couple of years ago, and I even lived with the chef for about six weeks. We had such a hot romance, I thought we were going to tie the knot," she told him and shook her head with wonder or regret, he couldn't be sure. "But it turned out he was an evil, jealous bastard who was already married, for Christ's sake, and even had kids."

He had no idea what to say. He didn't even know what he felt. Perhaps a touch of the chef's jealousy around his heart, perhaps a more general regret and sadness.

"He sent me to the hospital with a black eye and a cracked cheekbone, the prick," she told him, "and that's when I packed up and moved out, but you've got to admit he can cook."

"He still cooks here?" Edward asked in disbelief.

"Sure," she said, "he owns half interest in the place."

"And you still eat here?"

"Not very often," she told him matter-of-factly. "It costs a fortune."

Asking Paris a question was like trying to walk up a steep, icy hill and sliding back two steps for every step he took. You always lost more ground than you gained. From the first it was that way. His third night in Pittsburgh, pretending to himself that he was justifiably angry and totally, by God, independent, but, in fact, feeling forlorn as hell, he'd asked if he could buy her a drink when she got off her shift. He'd thought he recognized something in her eyes somehow equally lonely and cast out. "Where?" she'd asked him with a wry smile, "in your room?" "No," he'd told her, and nodded across the small lobby of the Hampton House toward the bar, "right here." She'd studied him for a moment, her yellow eyes suddenly quite sad he'd thought. "You're married, aren't you?" she'd said. He'd nodded that he was. "Well," she'd said with a little humorless snort of laughter, "that's all right because I am too." But her shift wasn't over until midnight, and that happened to be when the bar closed. "Another time," she'd told him. Yet at a quarter till twelve she'd called his room. "This is Paris Pergola at the desk," she'd said in a cheerful voice. "You got your pants on?" He was just enough awake to say that he did. "Good," she'd said, "you keep them on. What do you drink?" Any sour mash bourbon was fine, he'd told her. Room service would be up in fifteen minutes, she gave him to understand, which allowed him to get out of bed, wash his face, comb his hair, and get dressed, grateful, for the first time, that Womb Broom was bunking with Ironfield Cox at D'Fonzio's and he was the odd man out.

Promptly at five minutes after twelve she knocked on his door carrying a tray with two drinks for him and two for herself. And except for the conversation, it was all very proper. Maybe it was her special manner, or what he thought he saw in her eyes, the late hour, the bourbon, the fact that he had been sound asleep when she called, but talking to her was as effortless as talking to a man. No, it was easier than that, and he found himself saying things he never expected to say.

When he'd told his story, she said she thought it was just very strange how someone could be attracted by what you were, and then when they had you, set about trying to make you over into someone else. Anyway that's the way it had been with her husband. He had been a history professor who taught at Pitt, she told Edward, only he hadn't gotten his tenure, so he'd moved to some college in California.

Why hadn't she gone with him? Edward wanted to know.

She laughed at that and took a swallow of her drink. Well, she guessed she just hadn't got her tenure either, she explained.

He'd asked what in the devil "tenure" was, and she told him it meant the bastards couldn't get rid of you until you died, and while he pondered the sad drift of that remark, she went on about her husband. Oh sure, he was brilliant, she supposed— anyway she never understood half of what he said. But looking back on it, as far as she was concerned, he was pretty damned useless too. He never wanted to do anything except argue some point with somebody or read. Either that or screw like a billy goat—probably because he didn't know how to do anything else. If you asked him to change a light bulb, he was in trouble. Hell, he was forty years old and he didn't even know how to drive a car and couldn't begin to balance a checkbook. People were forever calling him on the telephone, threatening to sue him if he didn't pay his bills. And boy how that would put him on his high horse, she said and laughed. Every time he'd wind up insulting them as though the whole thing was their fault. Oh but she knew all about that, she told Edward, since he'd even tried to blame not getting his tenure on her. On the way she'd acted at two or three of the silly little faculty parties he'd taken her to.

Edward laughed with her. Well how had she acted? he'd asked.

Hell, she told him, she didn't act. She never acted. She tried to have a good time like always. She said what she thought and did what she felt like doing. She cocked her head and peered at the ceiling above his head. What was wrong with that, she wanted to know.

Nothing, he told her, nothing at all. So, he said, what did she hear from Professor Pergola these days?

She didn't hear from him. Hoped never to hear from him. Anyway his name was Whitney, but she'd stopped using that the moment they'd parted company.

So then, they were divorced?

She had divorced him in her heart and said good-bye and good riddance in the bargain, but she didn't see any good reason to pay some lawyer a lot of money to shuffle papers and fart around over it. She knew it was a mistake, and Mr. Fancy Pants knew it was a mistake. A very bad joke that had lasted eight whole months. As for herself, she was back to being Paris Pergola, thank you very much, and if the great Professor Whitney wanted some little piece of paper to say, in writing, that the marriage was over, well fine; he could hire a lawyer and pay for it. But she didn't need such nonsense because she was a free person in her heart, and that was what mattered. Anyway, she didn't even know where he lived in California, or if he was still *in* California.

Having said all that, she'd looked at him and smiled, although in the next moment the smile began to waver, and she tossed her head and took a sip of her drink in order to cover up the way her smile had begun to flicker toward something else, he guessed. But then, all at once, he realized she was crying, her face still bent over her lowered drink.

Whoa, he'd told her, don't do that; but she'd given up all

pretense, and her shoulders were shaking, and he'd gotten up and gone to her to hold her awkwardly and try to shush her. After a while she managed to say that the drinks came to five dollars if he still meant to buy them, and they'd both laughed at her telling him that at such a moment. Then she'd said she wasn't crying over any fancy-pants professor; she wouldn't have him think she was. She was crying over love in general, or marriage in general, or some damned thing she wasn't sure of herself. Then, laughing and crying at exactly the same time, she stood up and held out her hand to be paid, and he rummaged around in his pockets, remembered his billfold was on the bedside table, got the money, and paid her. Somewhere between laughing and crying, she gave him a long, fond look as though they had known each other for years, hugged him suddenly and fiercely, and was just as suddenly out the door and gone. As for him, he was not only bewildered but wide awake, and he stayed that way until it was time to pick up Womb Broom and Cox and drive across the Monongahela, where, in the hellish noise and heat of the steel mill, they put in a hard eight hours at regular pay and then four more at time and a half.

And sitting across from her in the little French restaurant, her eyes gathering candlelight, he realized he was no better off and no less confused than that first night. He never had any idea what strange thought or confession might come out of her mouth. He had no idea whether, in the next moment, she would be angry, deliriously happy, or sad; or what sort of influence, if any, he had over these moods. He'd never seen anyone like her. For certain she could be the sexiest woman he'd ever met, but she could also be cold and hard or as defenseless, vulnerable, and shy as a child. For certain she kept him off balance, kept him guessing. Sometimes he told himself she was simply crazy, or he was, or both of them.

What in hell was he doing in her company anyway? he wondered. What in hell was he doing in Pittsburgh to begin with? Away from his wife and son? What silly and unimportant thing had gone wrong? He'd thought Madeline was moody and hard to understand, but Jesus . . . Maybe the good Lord had looked down and said: *Son, I think it's time to show you some real, by God, moody. I'm going to dip you in the undiluted essence of mysterious womanhood, so you'll know when you've got it good and when you've got a right to complain.* Madeline, after all, was pretty steady, now that he thought back on her. She'd loved him because, well, since she was a normal, everyday sort of woman, she had to love some man or other; she just didn't have to approve of them. And as long as he understood that and tried to behave himself and act more or less the way she wanted him to and took care to hide the side of himself that most aggravated her, well then, they could have a decent life. Anyway he could get used to it. Anyway he, by God, missed it and missed her.

"So," Paris said, "why so quiet?"

JAMES
TALLY

If anyone knew how to be the new boy at school, he figured it ought to have been him, but he didn't seem to be getting any better at it. Sitting in Mrs. Arents's eighth-grade class at the end of the first week, waiting for the final bell to ring, he had the feeling that being new was like stepping on a nail or sticking your hand in the fire; it just didn't get easier, no matter how many times you did it.

This time, in fact, he'd gotten off to a worse start than usual. Good intentions aside, on the first day, before he'd had a chance to do anything to help or harm himself, Mrs. Arents had done him in. She was quite old and frail and seemed to live in a world that had nothing to do with the one he lived in. She taught a class of "young ladies" and "young gentlemen," not the class that filled the room. And so, when she'd called his name on the roll and he'd answered, she'd made a little speech to that ghost class of hers. He was not only a stranger in their midst, she'd told them, but also the nephew of Miss Marshall, who had guided them through fourth grade, and therefore they should make a very special effort to make him feel welcome. By the time she'd finished, the entire surface of his body was full of the pinpricks of embarrassment, and he could hardly see. But he'd been aware of everyone looking at him; of a frozen, goofy expression on his face; and of one boy in particular leaning way back in his seat at the end of the first row to stare at him contemptuously. "What a pissant!" the boy said at last, and a flutter of laughter ran through the class, but apparently Mrs. Arents heard none of it. No one in her ghost class would have said such a thing, so she merely finished calling the roll. Then, with her eyes focused somewhere over their heads and a dreamy expression on her withered face, she began to tell them about the virtues of an education and of keeping a tidy mind and a tidy body.

James feared his father was right when he said that the only way to start in at a new school was to keep an eye on the biggest, toughest kid in the class until he said or did something James didn't like, and then, right then, without wasting a second, James was to knock him on his ass. "It'll be a lot easier than you think," his father told him, "because he won't be expecting it." Good advice, no doubt, but James didn't like to fight. It scared him. It was painful. And worst of all, it was embarrassing and deeply sad. But he couldn't tell his father that; he could only say lamely that he wasn't good at fighting. Edward Tally believed, however, that if James would only take his advice, there would be few, if any, fights to worry about. But what if he couldn't knock the fellow down? James had wanted to know. Or what if he knocked him down, but then he got up again and beat the crap out of him? His father had laughed at the possibility and shaken his head wisely. If James hit him as hard as he could, the bastard would go down, his father declared. But even if he didn't, James would have put so much surprise and fear into him, there wouldn't be any fight; he'd bet on that. But say the little prick did get up and beat the crap out of James, all James had to do then was hit him again just as hard as he could the very next time he got out of line; and pretty soon, his father promised, the little son of a bitch would either be James's friend, or he would at least decide trying to bully him just wasn't worth all the trouble.

Good advice, no doubt, James thought, even though his father seemed to offer him an easy victory one minute and then pull it back the next, like a carrot on a stick. It would have been a lot better to get a guarantee, but the principle of the thing seemed correct and a wonderfully simple philosophy to live by. Yet now, sitting at his desk and staring sadly out the window, the advice seemed sound only for somebody James was not.

In all his life he'd never hit anyone as hard as he could. It was a serious failing, but there it was. Also, what was he supposed to do: get up when Earl Carpenter called him a pissant and knock him out of his seat right in the classroom? He wondered if that would get Mrs. Arents's attention. Not much else seemed to.

A sweet, sad husk of another age, Mrs. Arents sat behind her desk, looking pleased with herself for having given her phantom class of young ladies and gentlemen a poem to read. He had already read it twice, but surely to God there wouldn't be enough time left to talk about it. Still, who could tell? If Mrs. Arents couldn't stop the passage of time altogether, she could certainly make ten minutes seem like an hour and a day seem like a week. Yet he admitted he'd be happy to live in her world if he could, or even in his father's, for that matter. But the sad fact was, he was trapped in his own.

He hadn't knocked Earl Carpenter out of his seat, and he hadn't done the next best thing, which would have been to knock him down at the first recess and say with an icy stare and steely voice: "That's for calling me a pissant, you pissant!" If he'd done that, his problems might be over now. Anyway they might be if he'd punched Earl every time he'd had a reason, all week long. But he hadn't, and now Earl Carpenter had seen into his heart and wouldn't be fooled by any temporary show of bravery. His best bet now was that Earl would simply forget about him, Earl and the ignorant twins, Tim and Tom Lanich, who followed the prick around like shadows. It was possible Earl would forget about him; besides, he mostly only called him names and punched him on the shoulders so they stayed bruised and sore. Once, the third day of school, Earl had shoved his head down on the drinking fountain and split his lip and chipped a front tooth, but he hadn't done a whole lot more than that. It was usually the twins who were likely to trip or shove or otherwise torment him in order to amuse Earl. Still, no serious damage had been done, mostly, he figured, because he hadn't ever fought back or even traded words with them. But he hadn't cried either, though his eyes had filled once or twice because the situation was so unfair and somehow shameful. It embarrassed him just to look at Earl, who was fifteen and had already thickened up like a man and even had to shave; or anyway, on days when he didn't, the blond stubble on his proud, cruel face glinted in the sun. He wasn't sure why the sight of Earl Carpenter affected him so strongly. But something important and otherwise beautiful about the world seemed tarnished and disgraced by Earl's presence in it. He appeared to be human, just like anybody else, but he had no pity, and only cruelty seemed to amuse him. By comparison the twins were just ordinary, everyday assholes.

"Class," Mrs. Arents said in her thin, cheerful voice, "I think you will have had time to read and consider Wilfred Owen's touching poem by now. Would anyone like to read it aloud?" She cocked her head this way and that like a tiny bird. When her eyes met James's, he looked down quickly at his textbook and frowned. "Well then," she said with her usual jaunty resignation and cleared her throat importantly. " 'Futility,' by Wilfred Owen."

> Move him in the sun—
> Gently its touch awoke him once,
> At home, whispering of fields unsown.
> Always it woke him, even in France,
> Until this morning and this snow.
> If anything might rouse him now
> The kind old sun will know.
>
> Think how it wakes the seeds—
> Woke, once, the clays of a cold star.
> Are limbs, so dear-achieved, are sides,
> Full-nerved—still warm—too hard to stir?
> Was it for this the clay grew tall?
> —O what made fatuous sunbeams toil
> To break earth's sleep at all?

touch him in hopes that the sun will bring him back to life."
He didn't want to look up, not at her or anyone, so he kept
staring down at the poem, hoping she would go on to someone
else.

"Why did you say the dead person was a soldier, James?"
Mrs. Arents asked.

"I don't know," he answered. "That was stupid. Maybe it
was because of France, or the snow? I don't know why I
said it."

"Oh but it wasn't stupid," Mrs. Arents said. "Wilfred Owen
is very famous for his poems about soldiers and the horrors of
the battlefield."

"I didn't know," James said. "It was just a stupid guess."

"Go on to the second stanza, if you please, James."

He did not please. It made his stomach hurt. "Well," he said,
holding his head miserably between his hands, "the poet says
the sun can wake the seeds and once gave life to, you know,
the cold earth, so he wants to know why, when there's already
a person there who is still warm, why it wouldn't be a lot easier
to make him alive again. I mean, if the sun started with nothing
but clay and made it finally into something as tall and complicated as a man, the poet wants to know why it would bother,
if the man was only going to die; I mean, the poet doesn't
understand why the sunbeams went to all the trouble in the first
place." His head between his hands, as though between the jaws
of a vice, James waited for her to go on to someone else, waited
for the bell to ring, or something, anything, to come along and
release him.

"Would you tell the class what 'fatuous' means, please?" she
asked.

"I can't," he said. "I don't know what it means. I just left it
out when I read that line."

"And 'futility'?"

"I think it means hopeless," he said.

"That's very close. It really means useless, and 'fatuous' means
unconscious or silly. But you did beautifully with the poem,
kind sir, and I'm sure we're all impressed and grateful."

"I sure-the-fuck-am," Earl said under his breath just as the bell began ringing as long and loud as a fire alarm.

While the class shuffled noisily into the hall, James sat at his desk with his head down, and when at last he took a deep breath and looked up, the room was empty except for Mrs. Arents, who in her shaky, ineffectual way was trying to tidy her desk; and Lester, who was waiting patiently by the door. James gathered his books. She told them to be sure and have a lovely weekend. And he and Lester left by the rear of the building, since both of them knew without having to discuss it, that Earl and the twins rode the first bus and would be waiting out front.

Without speaking, they crossed the ballfield and the trestle over the creek, following an abandoned, narrow-gauge railroad track toward Lester's house. After a quarter of a mile they left the faded cinders and rotten ties to go cross-country, Lester spreading the strands of a barbed-wire fence for James to climb through and James returning the courtesy.

Lester was worn down by his own brand of misery, and James knew it. In the eighth grade or no, Lester could scarcely read or write, and he would accept no help from James. He meant only to endure this last year until he was sixteen and could quit school forever, just as he had endured every year since he'd given up jumping out of windows. He'd simply made up his mind, long ago, that school and books were not for him, that he could not and would not learn those things that were taught in a classroom, and neither James nor anyone else could convince him otherwise. He was determined to wait it out like some exquisite torture.

Sometimes James nearly envied him, if only because he'd taught himself to be almost invisible. Anyway his classmates didn't seem to see him. He never spoke to them, or acknowledged them, or asked anything from them; and somehow, over the years, he'd taught them to look beyond him or around him just as they might have looked past a fence post or a tree. Never mind that she'd called on him that day, even Mrs. Arents wasn't immune to his magic. Already she seldom asked him a question, and when she did forget and call his name, something peculiar seemed to happen to her, as though she realized she'd called on an empty seat, and she never pressed it. The trick was all the more remarkable because Lester looked even sillier than Virginia and Clara had claimed. On his own ground or out fishing or doing chores, he looked okay, but at school his clothes were suddenly so ill-fitting and ragged, he resembled a clown. Roy had made the whole thing worse by buying a huge pair of reddish-yellow, high-top work shoes for Lester to grow into that seemed almost to glow and emitted an outrageous odor of leather James could smell all the way across the classroom. But Effie's haircut was the cruelest joke of all. Lester had been woolly-headed all summer, and James hadn't been prepared to find him looking like a bottle brush, cropped on top and shaved from the tops of his ears down, straight around his head. It took talent, mystifying talent, James thought, to be inconspicuous, almost invisible, when you looked like Lester.

When they came to the fence around Roy's land, James spread the strands of barbed wire first so Lester could slip through. On the other side they climbed up on a granite outcropping and sat down as they had done every day that week, looking silently out across the valley, each of them locked in his own particular brand of trouble. They would part here, Lester going off to the right athwart the grade of the mountain and James going straight up the valley toward his grandmother's table and the trailer. Still, they sat together for a long time, not saying anything but merely thinking and smelling the sweet scent of ragweed and ripening apples and all that went into the faint but real perfume of the approaching fall.

It had been unseasonably and steadily cool, and on the mountaintops there was already a little color, which would spread and get richer and deeper until, by the first week of October, it would have come creeping down into the valleys. Almost every night had been in the thirties, and on the second of September there had been enough frost to singe the leaves of his grandfather's squash, even if it had left almost everything else in the garden untouched. When he had time to notice this sweet, sad change of season, it was almost enough to break James's heart, although he couldn't have said why.

"Want to do something tomorrow?" he asked at last and without looking at Lester.

"Tomorrow afternoon, I expect," Lester said, gazing off in the distance himself, "got to help Poppa grade tobacco in the mornin."

"Well," James said after another long pause, "I'd better get going I guess," and he slid off the face of the outcropping to the ground.

"See you, buddy," Lester said.

"See you," James said.

It was just that his summer had been stolen from him, he thought after he'd walked a while. That was why the fall seemed unusually sad. He had borne the unhappiness between his mother and father and therefore merely existed through the summer, and so it had slipped away. It seemed to him he'd spent most of his time sitting up in a huge, grimy catalpa tree on the edge of the trailer park in Knoxville, watching traffic slip under the blue haze of its exhaust, either west into the city or east toward the country. After supper he nearly always climbed into the ancient, half-dead catalpa and stayed until it was time to go in and try not to notice the deadly silence his parents maintained between them like the aftermath of a gunshot. Oh, he'd gotten to go to a movie now and then, and sometimes his troubles seemed kind enough to wait for him outside while he went in where magic could happen, his spirit could still rejoice and even note the earmarks and mannerisms of the hero's courage, as though for future use. And once his father and his mother and he, all three, spent a grand spectacle of an evening at the Barnum & Bailey Circus. But if there had been more to June, July, and part of August than that, then he couldn't remember it. Somehow both the beginning and the end of summer had come when he'd gotten to his grandparents' house, and he'd had only a small taste before his mother was buying him school clothes at Green's Department Store, he was getting a haircut in the barber shop down the street, and a heartbeat later, he was in Mrs. Arents's eighth-grade classroom. So. No wonder the cool air and smell of fall saddened him, he thought. No wonder his stomach seemed to hurt.

But as he climbed over a fence and came up out of the ditch into the road, some chamber of his heart seemed to insist that the grief was deeper than that, deeper than the loss of summer or even being trapped in eighth grade with the likes of Earl Carpenter and the Lanich twins.

He came in sight of his grandparents' house just as Virginia and Clara climbed down from the school bus. It was the one he was supposed to ride, since the grammar school and high school were separated only by a small dirt parking lot and used the same buses; but he'd never once ridden it. His cousins didn't seem to see him. Waving to someone on the bus and looking wonderfully normal and happy, they climbed the flagstone walk and flounced into the house. He wondered if he'd ever know, or could even learn, what they seemed born knowing. Somehow, he doubted it.

When he had let himself into the small, stale trailer and changed out of his school clothes, as his mother insisted he do the moment he got home, he went out to the huge pile of wood by the barn and loaded his arms. It was his great pleasure to carry wood, and he liked even better to split kindling—at least once his grandfather had grown to trust him not to ruin the blades of the double-bitted ax—and he always had to take care not to split too much of it. Beside his grandmother's cook stove, there was a small box for kindling and a larger one for stove-wood. He filled the large one first, which took him three trips. "Lordy, chile, that's a gracious plenty," his grandmother said, which pleased him. Then, since it had grown so cool and his grandfather built a fire in the living room fireplace each evening, he filled the huge wood cradle by the hearth, which took him five trips and got him sweaty. But then it was that time of day he loved best, when the smell of wood seemed strongest, and the shadows had grown long, and the air had grown sharp and crisp. While the sweat at his temples dried, he chose pieces of maple with the straightest grain and split them neatly into kindling, his left hand, which held the wood, daring the right, which held the ax. And his spirits began to lift, as they always did, as though by his labor he could earn a place in his grandparents' household and be real family and not someone they merely tolerated. Lately he had even begun to enjoy dinnertime. He'd always thought his grandmother was the world's best cook, but the main thing was that his cousins were back in school and so interested in telling stories about their teachers and friends, they barely noticed him.

Whatever, by the time he'd carried in the last of the kindling and washed up for supper, almost all his sadness had drained away. Still, they had only just pulled up to the table and begun to pass around bowls and platters when the telephone rang two longs and three shorts, which meant it was for them and not one of the other parties on their line; and before Clara could set down a bowl of potatoes, Virginia was up, had snatched the heavy black receiver from its hook and shouted: "Virginia Marshall speaking!" Since the local telephone company was small and poor and used terribly outdated equipment—if you wanted to make a call, you had to crank the old black contraption to get an operator and then yell to be heard—there was no such thing as privacy, and everyone at the table listened openly.

"What?" Virginia shouted into the mouthpiece. "Who?" she yelled. But then her face lost all its anticipation, and she shouted: "I'll put Grandmother on!" and held the receiver out to Grandmother Marshall. "It's Uncle Edward," she said with an embarrassed glance at James.

A current made of equal parts hope and fear ran through his stomach while his grandmother talked, repeating over and over again the bare circumstances of his mother's employment and the times when she might be found at home. "This Sunday morning would be the best time," she said. "Yes, this Sunday morning!" she said in a loud but remarkably kind voice. "But James is here!" she shouted. "I say, James is right here!" And suddenly she was holding the receiver out to him and saying, "Come on, son, quickly, it's your poppa."

At first he couldn't seem to hear anything but a great hum and crackle, but finally, submerged under that, he recognized snatches of his father's voice, deep and nasal and touched with the constant humor and sadness that always seemed to color it. Although the noise of long distance kept him from understanding most of what his father said and sometimes broke off pieces of words he did understand, he knew his father was telling him about streetcars and parks and telling him that something else wasn't so bad either. He had hoped his father was going to say he was coming home, but he knew from the familiar tone of salesmanship that his father was up to another matter entirely, which both thrilled him and frightened him completely. He heard his father say quite clearly that he missed them, and then the noise on the line closed in again like a fire popping and crackling. For a while he couldn't make out anything, and then he realized he was being asked a question.

"What?" he shouted, but he couldn't hear. "What?" he shouted again, and this time he heard two words: ". . . doin, son?"

"I'm doing fine," he yelled.

Of the next question the only word he heard for sure was "school."

"School's good!" he shouted.

Into a roar of static his father managed to slip four words: ". . . Sunday . . . tell . . . love her."

"I will," James shouted. "I will!"

He understood nothing of what his father said after that, except that it sounded final. "Good-bye," he shouted, and as though beneath the sound of heavy rain, he heard the reply.

MADELINE
TALLY

"It's just, you know, the *continuity* you miss. Is that the right word?" Madeline said.

Holding his hands together as though in prayer, Leslie touched his lips with his fingertips and gave her the slightest nod, his eyes looking straight into hers in a way that made her uncomfortable or at least unsure of herself.

"As though continuity were the whole purpose of it all, no matter what the marriage is like," she said and took her eyes away from his—which were just a little too intense and intimate to suit her—and tried to glance casually around the restaurant as though the matter under discussion weren't really so important, as though it were actually quite trivial. She laughed briefly. "I'm sure my parents would agree that continuity is the whole point. And I feel like I'm committing a mortal sin. It scares me, as though I'm harming everyone's future in a way that can't be mended—mine, James's, my parents, yours. . . ." She looked at him again and found that his eyes were just the way she had left them.

"Are you sure you don't dread talking to him in the morning because you still love him?" he asked and gave her an indulgent smile across the dome of his fingertips.

"Don't be silly," she said. "What reason has he ever given me to love him?"

"That wasn't my question," he said. "What reason did he give you to marry him? You did marry him after all."

"Well," she said and laughed miserably, "that was probably because he was just about the only young man my poppa didn't scare away."

Leslie looked up at the ceiling. "Jesus, but you confirm a man's worst nightmares sometimes, do you know that?"

"I don't understand," she said. "You'll have to explain."

"I don't think I care to," Leslie said. "I'd rather order dessert. The pecan pie here is very good."

"I don't know why I married him. Maybe because I was a young girl and didn't know anything. Maybe I was crazy. I don't know."

"I just hope you don't look back on what's happening now and say the same thing," Leslie said.

The thought had never occurred to her, at least not exactly in those terms. She felt what she felt. Sorrow. Resentment. Betrayal. Although she wasn't sure whether Edward Tally had betrayed her or she had betrayed herself, she knew her marriage had been one long series of unhappy situations. And of course she felt a great sadness, not only for all the years lost, but because she was going to have to look like a bad and selfish person, an evil woman, just for trying to put her life in order, just for trying to find a little bit of the happiness everyone else seemed to take for granted. But she wasn't likely to look back and think she'd been crazy. If anything she would look back and recognize the painful days when she'd first been able to see things with some clarity.

"I know exactly what he's going to do," she said. "Tomorrow when he calls he's going to pretend that we've both been acting foolish, but he'll really mean I have. Oh, he'll admit he hasn't been treating me the way he should have, and he'll promise to do better. But he won't really change. He'll act just the way he's always acted because he doesn't see anything wrong with it. He'll expect me to come to Pittsburgh where nothing is familiar and I don't know a soul, and he'll stick me somewhere to cook and clean and make things nice for him, and pretty soon, maybe he'll come home and maybe he won't. No. I don't love him, and I want a divorce.

"Do you know what's funny?" she asked and tried to laugh, although her eyes welled up. "I don't think I ever did love him, but I wanted him to love me. If I could have made him do that, I might have been able to love him back." She knew her face was doing something between laughing and crying and probably looked peculiar. "But he couldn't even see me. Does that make any sense?" she asked him. "Why are you looking at me like that? I want a divorce, that's all."

Leslie held his hands up, palms toward her, as though she were pointing a gun at him. "I can't tell you if it makes sense, but I can tell you that you don't have any grounds for divorce."

"How can you say that?" she asked him. "It isn't any good, and I'm miserably unhappy."

"Darling," he said, leaning across the table toward her and speaking in the sort of voice that let her know she was being too loud and probably had been being too loud for a long time, "the law does not recognize unhappiness as grounds for divorce."

Her chin crinkled, and through blurred vision she saw that, indeed, other people in the dining room were looking at her and still others seemed arrested with forks halfway to their mouths or coffee cups poised before their lips as though they were listening. She was, she realized, behaving badly, but she couldn't seem to help it. It seemed absolutely predictable, somehow, that her unhappiness counted for nothing in the eyes of the law. But something, she was sure, could be made to serve, whether real or imagined. "Well, then what grounds are there?" she asked in a small, ragged voice.

"Maidy . . ." he said, using the nickname only her family and the oldest of her friends from high school ever used; he patted her thigh secretly beneath the table to comfort her. "Maidy, now's not the best time. . . ."

It was too much and she bent her head and wept, but after

a few moments, she dried her eyes on her napkin and sat up straight, determined to get control of herself. "I need to know," she said.

He looked off across the restaurant and sighed unhappily. "Desertion," he said.

"He's in Pittsburgh."

"But he sends money and he wants you with him."

"What about infidelity?" she said. "I can't prove it, but I know it. Somehow I know it."

"Adultery, yes," he said and nodded. "But it really wouldn't matter if you could prove it, and prove it a dozen times over with a dozen different women, not if he wanted to fight it. Not unless he'd actually set up housekeeping with another woman and refused to give her up. No judge I know would grant you a divorce because he's sowed some wild oats."

"That's outrageous," she said. "I don't believe you!"

Leslie shrugged and tried to smile at her. "I'm a lawyer, darling, it's what I do. I know the laws in this state."

"What other grounds are there?" she said, feeling her chin start to tremble again but fighting to stop it and stop the tears she could feel rising.

"Cruelty," he said. "But not showing up for dinner on time, coming home drunk or not coming home at all, buying a house without asking your opinion, or quitting his job and taking another one somewhere else—those things wouldn't count for much." He shrugged again, helplessly. "He would have to do physical violence to you, and frankly, he'd have to do it repeatedly. A broken nose, black eyes, a broken jaw, the sort of injuries a doctor could verify."

"Go on," she said.

"If he were insane and in an institution, or a convicted felon in prison, you might be able to get a divorce, and you might not. Women have been denied divorces in such cases. Sometimes the court seemed to feel there was reasonable hope the husbands would get well, or be released. Sometimes it seemed to hold that marriages are 'for better or for worse,' and this sort of thing falls under . . ." he made a helpless gesture with his hands,

" 'worse.' Sometimes the court, I guess, pitied the insane husband or the felon more than it pitied the wife."

He shifted uncomfortably in his chair. "Look," he said, "in most cases, maybe not all, but in most cases it's just as hard for a man to divorce his wife. It's just that, well, it's the end of the week and you're tired and I'm tired, and you've got that call coming tomorrow, and we'd do better to talk about all this another time." He looked at her, smiled hopefully, and even laughed a little. "If he disappeared for seven years, and no one saw him or heard from him, we could have him declared legally dead," he told her and cocked his head to one side as though he were inviting her to laugh with him. "You wouldn't have your divorce, but you'd be a widow in the eyes of the law."

But she didn't feel like laughing. "You're saying it's impossible to end this marriage? Is that what you're telling me?"

"Jesus, Maidy, no, not exactly," he said. "What I'm telling you is that, in this state, you just don't have any legal grounds for divorce, not a one, not if Edward wants to fight it." Leslie raised his eyebrows and cocked his head, letting his eyes slide away from her face. "If he decides he doesn't want to be married either, and you're both willing to perjure yourselves, then, sure, I can get you free. At least after you've been here long enough to establish this as your legal domicile."

"I think I want to go home now," she said.

"Look," Leslie said, "this should have been a nice evening." He caught one of her hands and held it, even though for a second she tried to tug it free. "I know how difficult all this must be for you, but I promise there's a solution. It's just that, no matter how much you mean to me, I just can't snap my fingers and get you out of your marriage. I swear, Maidy, the best solutions happen outside the courtroom, and if you can make Edward realize that, this won't . . ."

She pulled her hand away, rose, and left him at the table. She didn't look into any of the faces of the other diners, but she felt some of them searching her own, and she meant for her expression to give them nothing whatever.

Once inside the ladies' room, she thought she'd cry, had even planned on it, but she didn't. She felt so drained there didn't seem enough left of her to cry; instead, she found herself staring at her reflection in a long makeup mirror, staring into her own eyes as though for some understanding, but they seemed as blank and depthless as the eyes of a doll. If Edward wanted a divorce, she was thinking, then she could get one; if not, then not. So. The end of her marriage, if it came, would be just like the rest of it. What Edward wanted to happen would happen, and that, as they say, was that.

Many moments later she found herself still standing before the mirror. Strangely numb and almost tranquil, she set her purse on the marble counter and turned to a sink where she ran cool water into her hands and bathed her face, which felt feverish. She took her time with her makeup, and when she had finished, she entered the dining room where Leslie was drinking coffee and looking worried and unhappy. He rose to greet her.

"I've taken care of the bill," he said, "so we can leave this minute if you want, or we can stay, and you can have some coffee and dessert."

"I'm sorry," she told him. "I was upset. I know I've ruined our time together, and you didn't deserve that."

He waved away her apology. "Lots of people expect the law to fix things, but it seldom does." He smiled weakly. "It's just that I'm not usually in love with them."

She nodded soberly, distantly, as though she hadn't even heard him. "But I think I would like to go home," she said. "I'm very tired."

Leslie helped her into her coat, and outside under the stars, he helped her into his car, but she was aware of these things only in the most remote and abstract sort of way. For most of the ride from Blowing Rock to Cedar Hill it was this way, as though she were too exhausted even to think; but after a while she found herself looking at Leslie's profile and wondering—in a strangely dispassionate sort of way—what it would be like to be married to such a gentle, reasonable, and successful man, to have the nice things he could give her simply as a matter of course, to be treated with consideration. She'd had such thoughts before, but never with so little emotion.

Before she quite realized where they were, he had slipped into the parking space beside her small gray coupe and given her hand a squeeze and her forehead a chaste, gentle kiss. She watched him pass in front of his car to help her out as if she'd never quite seen him before. Why he'd never really even made a pass at her, she realized, not really. Only once had he even kissed her on the lips, and although she hadn't resisted exactly, she hadn't responded either. She hadn't quite had time to gauge her feelings, as she recalled, before he'd begun to dissemble and apologize.

"Let me know how it goes tomorrow," he said when he'd guided her to her little coupe, "just don't—"

She put her arms about his neck, kissed him, and slowly, deliberately, tilted her pelvis into his body. If he was surprised, and she knew he must be, he couldn't have been more surprised than she was. She couldn't believe she'd done such a thing, and what she was thinking, she didn't know herself. When, at last, she withdrew, she laid her palm against his cheek, searched his eyes for a moment, and then she was in her car and the motor was running and she was backing up. Leslie was standing just where she'd left him, apparently struck dumb and unable to speak; and she was almost out of town before she realized her vagina was wet.

She was not quite sane, she knew that much. From the moment she'd left Leslie at the table back at the restaurant, she had not been herself and seemed to look at whoever she had become from a great distance and with cool disinterest, as though she were watching a sleepwalker. But no, she'd felt a kind of wonder and sadness too, as though her life were over, say, and she were only a spirit, a ghost, looking back on it with nothing more than washed-out and ghostly emotion.

Strangely calm, as though she couldn't be held in the least responsible for her behavior, she drove down the mountain, oddly bemused, surprised, and perplexed by turns. It wasn't until she pulled into the driveway behind her sister's car that she seemed to reach a deeper understanding. Well no wonder she didn't feel responsible, she thought, since she'd just been given to understand that she had no power, no control whatever, which was just about the same thing as having no will, since there wasn't any way to express it. Except . . .

She sat staring at the dark, hulking shape of her sister's car in front of her, the dark shape of the house and post office, the surrounding trees and shrubs looming darkly in the faint light of the new moon and distant stars. Such a small arena for choice and will. . . . It seemed so new to her. Was she a stupid woman? Did other women always know? Had they made peace? Had her mother always . . . It was sobering, but in some way she did not quite understand, both sad and freeing.

A little at a time she seemed to come to herself as though descending stairs from her thoughts into her physical body. She was bitterly cold, and she got out of her car, crossed the lawn, climbed the stile, and shaking head to foot, let herself into the trailer, which was mercifully warm. James had the little gas furnace going, and, rolled into his blanket on the couch, he scarcely stirred when she came in. He had left on the small, dim lamp beside her bed, and she went into her bedroom and got undressed, feeling strangely fascinated with herself, as if she hadn't yet got all the way back inside Madeline Tally and maybe never would. When she came out again in her gown and robe to brush her teeth and run a basin of water to wash her face, even James was new and different to her. Sunk into sleep on his uncomfortable couch, he seemed more than merely her son, but himself too, whoever in the world that might be. She supposed she'd always known that, but never quite so clearly as she saw it now. And in the next moment she seemed to understand that she had never been merely a wife, or before that, merely a daughter. Funny, but she hadn't seemed quite able to understand that before. She wasn't just Edward's wife, whom he could disappoint and make angry and sad; she was herself. Whoever in God's world that might be.

What a strange, lonely sort of dignity there was in this knowledge, comforting when she thought of Edward, or any man, since it kept some part of her separate and intact. But looking at James asleep on the couch, she knew that what was true for her was also true for him. She had never before understood how modest a claim motherhood really was. He wasn't, after all, an extension of her, anymore than she was an extension of Edward Tally or Bertha Marshall. Somehow, from this day forward, she would have to earn motherhood, and her claim on her son seemed all the more precious for being so tenuous. In another mood she might have gathered him in her arms to tell him she loved him, waking him in the process, confusing him. But this night she would let him sleep.

She felt tender and wise. Looking back on what she had been, she was surprised that losing her virginity, say, hadn't taught her more. Or bearing a child. But those things seemed only to have happened to her; and, if not altogether without her consent, then as though she had been mindlessly following some blueprint laid down long ages before she was born. It was as though, at the restaurant, she'd watched herself all but cease to exist. Still, what little of her remained had acted shamelessly and on a whim and brought her wisdom. Oh it had looked like a humble package at first, but nature abhorred a vacuum, and it had filled her up. It had opened her eyes and brought her comfort. Just now it was a gentle thing, and if she could hang on to it, she could keep herself inviolate. And maybe she could not rule the world, but she knew, at last, that she could rule herself, and if she did not wish to be gentle, she could rule a man or two. Yes she could, she thought, and blushed.

Once again she came back to herself. She brushed her teeth and washed her face, and exhausted as she was, she realized she did not wish to yield up her consciousness to sleep for fear these new feelings, so hard won, would vanish. But she gave James one last, fond look and took herself off to bed. She didn't think she'd be able to sleep in any case, but the very next thing she knew, it was daylight, and James, dressed for Sunday school, was standing in the doorway saying, "Momma? Momma? Everybody's ready for church. They said I should get you up, so you can stay by the phone."

"All right," she told him. Still half-asleep, she heard him go out of the trailer, and in the next moment she began to realize how sick she was.

Forty-five minutes later, having vomited in the trailer sink and again by the fence—hanging on to the stile until her stomach was empty even if the retching went on and on and on—she sat in the empty kitchen of the farmhouse, rocking herself gently back and forth in the straight-backed kitchen chair. The telephone had been ringing as she'd come up the flagstones to the back door, but she'd been unable to get to it before it stopped. It was their ring all right, two longs and three shorts, but since she'd gotten inside, the phone had rung only once, and that had not been their ring. Her eyes hot and alien in their sockets and her joints aching with fever, she waited for it to ring again.

How damned ironic it was to wake up sick. She'd thought she was being so profound last night, but maybe she'd just been feverish. And maybe she'd just gotten sick to punish herself for thinking the way she had. Even though she knew there was nothing left in her stomach, the powerful urge to throw up remained, and even the smallest joints of her toes ached. She hugged herself and rocked. Her new wisdom had lost some of its sparkle, and she was no longer sure exactly how she was supposed to put it into practice. In fact, it didn't even seem new, but rather silly and old and obvious. Maybe the only thing new was her way of seeing it, her attitude. She could have seduced Leslie if she'd wanted to, and she might have wanted to if she'd only caught up to herself in time. And who was to say she wouldn't?

She moaned and rocked. The clock over her momma's cook stove told her they would be out of Sunday school and filing into church now for the regular service. She did not want her family around when she talked to Edward. She didn't want them to hear what she had to say. She wasn't even sure she wanted

Edward to hear it, as though it were too personal even for his ears.

Please let him call before they come home, she thought, but a second later when the phone began to ring, sick as she was, the sound of it went through her like electricity.

Before it started through its ringing sequence a second time, she'd shouted "Hello" into a confabulation of static, buzzing, and the faint, tinny conversation of two strangers.

"Hey, sugar? Is that you?" Edward's voice asked, broken but understandable and riding over the Lilliputian voices on the line.

She did not wish to answer to "sugar." It started the whole conversation off on the wrong foot, but there was nothing for it, and she shouted "Yes" into the mouthpiece. He wanted to know how she was, and she told him she was just fine. He wanted to know how James was, and she told him James was happy. In the interstice between Edward's remarks and hers, a tiny conversation, clear as rain, declared that Millie had had a car wreck and broken some ribs and her wrist.

"I've had a lot of time to think things over, sugar," Edward told her, and even though static blotted out some of what he said, she understood him perfectly. "This is just a piss-poor way to live," he told her. "It don't make sense. It's unnatural. I love you, honey, and I miss you."

How could he sound so cheerful, as though he'd just untangled a terrible snarl by pulling on an obvious thread? She was certain she'd heard him laugh.

"I want my family back. Working like a dog don't make any sense otherwise," he said.

It was awful what the sound of his voice did to her. It was so familiar, like home, but a barren home with a cold hearth. It was like getting the Christmas spirit in February after a season that had been all wrong and false and perfunctory. Still, his voice sounded like home.

He was waiting for her to say something, she knew. But she was so sick she ached all over. He had talked so much. Been so pleased with himself. But she couldn't say anything. Instead, through the buzz and crackle of long distance, she heard the Lilliputian conversation going on and on: *Tobacco wasn't so good, but they Lord have mercy, you should have seen the crop of apples, never seen such an awful mess of apples, split that big tree out by the barn clean to the roots.* As though it had a sound as well, she could hear Edward's need to hear her speak, his anticipation of her forgiveness, her joy at what he had decided. And she could hear it turn into something else, bitterness maybe, even before he spoke again. "Dammit, Madeline, this is nonsense. What the hell do you want me to say? You can't be happy either. . . ."

"I am!" she shouted. "I am happy!"

Edward didn't say anything, and neither did the tiny voices that had spoken of Millie's accident and tobacco and apple crops, as though she had shouted them down also.

"I want a divorce," she told him, and for a long time all she heard was a long sigh of static.

"That's horseshit, Madeline, and you know it," Edward said at last.

"I've spoken to a lawyer, and I want you to give me a divorce," she told him, her voice full of the burrs and awkward notes of weeping.

So sick she thought she might faint, holding the receiver to her ear and her hand over the mouthpiece so he couldn't hear her crying, she waited. If the floor had opened up beneath her feet and swallowed her, she wouldn't have been surprised. If her heart had turned literally to ice and ceased to beat, she wouldn't have been surprised.

"If that's the goddamned way you want it," Edward said, and in the next moment the noise of long distance, all the complicated confabulation of it, simply vanished.

JAMES
TALLY

When he came home from church, the trailer smelled faintly of Lysol and vomit and was smotheringly hot.

"Momma?" he said when he discovered her in bed with her face turned to the wall.

"Keep away," she told him in a shaky voice, "I've got the flu."

He was taken aback. All through Sunday school and church he'd tried to imagine what she and his father would be saying to each other. Finally he'd decided that she would be falsely cheerful when he came home. Yes, and then she'd sit him down on the couch and try to convince him that living in Pittsburgh wouldn't be so bad. But he hadn't expected this at all. He looked at her pale face and the damp tendrils of hair stuck to her cheek.

"Can I do something?" he asked at last.

She turned to face him then, her eyes huge and dark and full of something he'd seen in them many times before. "Everything's going to be all right," she told him in her shaky voice. "I'm just a little sick."

He knew she had talked to his father. He saw it in her eyes. And he knew that nothing was all right.

"I need to rest now," she said and turned her face to the wall again.

He went up to the house and told them she was sick, and Lily came down to check on her and came back to say that she had the flu and couldn't hold anything on her stomach, so they ate Sunday dinner without her. After dinner he went down and changed his clothes as quietly as he could without knowing if she was asleep or awake, and went out to mope around the barn for a little while before he took the new slingshot he'd made from its hiding place and a handful of round, smooth pebbles he'd collected from the creek and walked up the ridge behind the barn. It had grown raw and misty, and it was very quiet, and all at once he began to feel seriously guilty about the slingshot.

It was the best he'd ever owned. The prongs were mountain laurel, hard as iron, and absolutely even; and the rubbers were made of a prewar inner tube that Lester was lucky enough to own, the kind of lively red rubber no one could find anymore. But the pouch had come from the tongue of one of his father's worn-out work shoes discovered in the closet behind the fishing equipment.

Anyway he had judged the shoes to be worn-out and had not asked his mother if he could cut out one of the tongues for fear she would forbid it. The tongue had made just the soft, strong pouch he'd known it would. He'd also known it was a transgression that might earn him a whipping. But after seeing what was in his mother's eyes, the matter seemed more serious. The pit of his stomach told him there was bad trouble, and although he wanted to believe he couldn't possibly have contributed to it—no one except himself even knew about the shoes—sometimes he feared there was an unseen, magical, and totally just plane on which the world truly operated. And on that plane what he had done might not be trivial but grave.

He'd had the vague intention to hunt, to look for a rabbit hiding in the brush, or maybe a squirrel or a dove perched on some branch, and so, give his slingshot its final true test. If he'd gotten game, hungry or not, he'd have dressed it out, built a fire, cooked, and eaten what he'd killed. But he no longer felt like it or wanted to creep around in the cold quiet woods, which had grown gauzy with fog and rain. His mother might need him. Maybe she was even feeling better, and they could listen to radio programs together. Maybe he could tell her what he'd done.

But when he got back to the trailer, Aunt Lily was in the bedroom, and the partition was mostly closed, so he turned the radio on just loud enough to cover their conversation. It was a tense and familiar role, and he'd played it often while his mother and father held their fierce, hushed arguments and fights. He knew exactly what was expected of him. He was supposed to disappear if he could, and if not, he was supposed to distract himself and pretend what was going on was none of his business and didn't affect him. Never mind that it did. Never mind that it was sometimes even about him. He tried to listen to the radio but couldn't quite do it. He tried not to listen to his mother and her sister, but he couldn't quite shut them out either. Twice he was sure he'd heard his mother weeping and his aunt trying to calm and comfort her. But after a while he wasn't listening to the radio or them; he was occupying a tense and haunted middle ground in which mutilating his father's shoe, not standing up to Earl Carpenter, picking away at his father's canvas musette bag of fishing equipment until it was all but empty, and other crimes and misdemeanors accused and convicted him, so that whatever trouble was coming to him and his mother was just. He had earned it.

After a while his aunt Lily came out of his mother's bedroom, smiling at him with great generosity. He thought her eyes, magnified behind her glasses, were the kindest he'd ever seen, and something about them seemed even younger than Clara's or Virginia's eyes. He wondered if that was because she had never been married, but that made no sense. Neither had Clara or Virginia.

"You come on up to the house with me," she told him. "I want to give you a chamber pot to bring back to your momma." When they got outside, she put her arm about his shoulders and hugged him. "Don't worry," she said, "just let her get some rest and some sleep."

His mother didn't go to work either Monday or Tuesday, although she was up and dressed when he came home Tuesday, and from the way she looked at him, he knew it was coming. The time for saying things to each other that were beside the point was over, and it was coming.

They sat together on the couch. She took both his hands in both of hers—hers were icy cold—and she looked into his eyes for a long time, and then she told him she was asking his father for a divorce. Curiously it seemed to be information he already had and simply hadn't acknowledged. It was as though he'd been expecting something worse, although he couldn't imagine what that might be. She looked in his eyes and squeezed his hands and told him he probably didn't understand, but he understood well enough; it was just that his mind had seemed to go blank somehow, so that, for some strange reason, he saw a field with stubble sticking up through a thin covering of snow. She kept talking, but he wasn't listening. He was occupied with the field of snow, which smelled like dust, like iron.

Afterward they sat on the couch, and she looked at him, finally hugging him longer than he wanted to be hugged, until, at last, he told her that he needed to change his clothes and do his chores. Out at the barn, he carried in wood and split kindling; and somehow the slingshot, the hooks and sinkers, and even Earl Carpenter seemed meaningless considerations.

EDWARD
TALLY

Monday, after work, they sat over their drinks at D'Fonzio's bar, looking straight ahead. It was as though, when Madeline had asked him for a divorce, she had put all comfortable understandings and arrangements, all contracts, treaties, and cease-fires between men and women in question and at risk. He wished he hadn't even mentioned it to them since he had no intention of being an object of their, by God, pity. It was only that he'd just gotten things sorted out in his own mind, and he'd been shocked to discover she hadn't come to a similar conclusion. He couldn't believe that she'd gone the other way, that she wanted a divorce. Not that she hadn't showed him many times before that he knew no more about her than a billy goat. So he oughtn't to have been surprised. But he was. He was still shocked although some anger had begun to creep in and some hurt. And how was it that neither Stella Cox nor Lois Hamby had asked the assholes on either side of him for divorces? Was that fair? Did that make any sense whatever? Not a goddamned bit, he assured himself.

Just then, out of nowhere, as if he'd read Edward's mind, Ironfield Cox turned his whiskey-cooked eyes on him and said, "You're better off."

Edward nodded his head for almost a full minute as though he were palsied. "Probably," he said.

"Ahhh she don't mean it," Womb Broom said. "They don't

never actually mean it." He took a drink of his beer and blotted his mustache with the back of the hand that held the mug. He spilled only a little. "Anyhow a man needs a wife and family to sort of hold him down. Where the hell would I be if it wasn't for Lois?"

"Right about where you are," Ironfield said, staring straight in front of himself.

"What do you mean by that, you stiff-assed bastard?" Womb Broom said.

Ironfield's scalded, emotionless eyes considered Womb Broom over his glasses, which had slipped a little toward the tip of his nose. "I mean two stools down from me and one stool down from Ed." He set his empty shot glass out in front of him where D'Fonzio would see it and do something about it. It never took Ironfield Cox long to train a bartender to understand sign language. When he wanted a refill, he set his empty glass out in front of him just so; when he was through drinking, he turned it upside down.

D'Fonzio filled the glass with rye whiskey, and Ironfield took a careful sip, reducing the contents by no more than a quarter. "I've never met the lady more than twice," he said, "but there's a kind of woman who will never let anything go, or give a man any peace, and if you'll pardon me, Madeline strikes me as just that type."

"A man don't need peace, goddammit!" Womb Broom said. "Not the way you mean. It ain't good for him. He'll only ruin hisself with it. He needs a wife to help him curb his worst nature, and he needs a place to call home."

Ironfield made no reply. His high, thin head held very straight and the flesh above his shirt collar as red as if he'd recently suffered first-degree burns, he stared straight ahead at nothing. After a while he licked his lips slowly as though to savor the whiskey and took another careful sip.

Edward was so angry his ears were ringing, first with Ironfield's high-handed assessment of things, and then with Womb Broom's foolishness. Trouble was, he couldn't think of a comeback in either case, but he could have sat on a hotplate longer than he could sit on a stool between them, and snatching a careless wad of bills and change out of his pocket, he smacked it down on the bar and got up. "I need some air," he said.

"Don't let her get to you, ole son," Ironfield said, gazing placidly straight before him.

"That's right," Womb Broom agreed.

But he had already bucked open the brass bar of D'Fonzio's door and stepped into the street.

Dirty sky. Chilly. Half the time you couldn't tell whether it was sunny or cloudy with the steel mills belching all that smoke and soot. Hell, a man could get filthy just standing on a street corner doing nothing. Already it felt and looked like winter, and many of the cars had their lights on, although, if the sky and air hadn't been so tarnished, there would have been almost another hour of daylight.

A streetcar clanged and ground by with a heavy whirr of steel wheels and glassed-in volume of gold light and preoccupied, anonymous passengers. Above and behind, the trolley gave chase, sparking along its heavy, jointed wire.

Cars of every make and model negotiated the streets. People on the sidewalks. On the other side four teenage boys, loud and cocksure, went around a corner and out of sight, streaming past an old Italian woman in a winter coat and a scarf, who had a long, unsliced loaf of bread sticking half out of her shopping bag. On his side, he passed a soldier in uniform and his girl or his wife, both gazing through the window of a furniture store; a stooped old man in a vested suit, who looked like a pawn-broker, or maybe a tailor, or perhaps someone who repaired watches; a woman in bright slacks with heavy thighs and a broad ass, who looked as if she might be going bowling; and finally two black men lounging at the corner, one in a pearl-gray fedora, the other with his head tied up elaborately with a red bandanna, both talking and nodding, the one with the bandanna appearing to calculate something, drawing invisible figures in the rusty palm of his hand with the tip of his finger, while the man in the fedora nodded and nodded.

Goddamn, but he loved the city. He loved being surrounded

by people he didn't know and would never know. He loved all the energy, hubbub, all the possibilities. He loved the very goddamned tainted air he breathed. Truth be told, he'd take it any time over clean country air. Shit on the country where a single hot summer day could be so dead it would petrify and last forever, and the only thing a man could do was work—that and get to know the few people around better than anyone ought to know anyone. He craved freedom, by God, and change and possibility.

So how come Madeline—who meant to deny him all those things—how come she was able to stab him through the heart? Why wasn't it a relief, for Christ's sake? What the hell was wrong with him anyway? Was it pride? Would it have helped if he'd been the one to ask her? But he wouldn't have. Couldn't have.

Christ he was cold. He should have gone up to his room and grabbed a jacket. Should have taken the car. He felt absolutely baffled. Freedom was only sweet if it didn't expand into empty infinity. If it didn't open up like a bottomless void at your feet. If it wasn't limited, it wasn't freedom. If you didn't have to fight to gain a little of it, it wasn't sweet. Hell, it didn't even exist unless you knew for certain that you were essentially and finally, not free at all. Oh God, but he wanted Madeline for his wife and James for his son, and the bosom of his family to be there somewhere. He wanted them to look after and take care of. He wanted somewhere to belong and people to love and to love him, even if he wasn't always with them. Jesus Christ but he missed them horribly.

So why was he on his way to Paris Pergola's? Since yesterday, never mind the state he was in, tucked in his memory was the knowledge that she was on the day shift beginning today. He jammed his hands in his pockets and pressed his arms against his sides. Ordinarily he wouldn't have been the least bit chilled. Heat got to him but never the cold, not, at least, unless he was sick, or unless something in his heart had gone awry.

He wanted his wife and his boy, so he was on his way to see

Paris. He was a crazy man. A fool. Some brand of asshole he couldn't begin to name. And how could he feel so misjudged and misunderstood? How could he feel like a basically good and decent man? Maybe, he decided, every asshole in the world felt like a decent man who was misunderstood.

MADELINE TALLY

Looming up suddenly in the middle of Madeline's sickness, Bertha Marshall said: "That Leslie Johnson fellow's up to the house and wants to know if he can look in on you."

"Oh!" Madeline said, struggling to surface from what seemed an endless, painful, but exquisitely private dream. She blinked at her mother standing at the foot of her bed.

In the next moment she realized that her hair was greasy and plastered to her head with fever and that she stank. "No, Momma!" she said. "You can't let him come down here!" She knew she never wanted him in her shoddy little trailer. Not even if she were perfectly well and utterly clean.

Holding disapproval and forbearance in perfect balance, Bertha Marshall smoothed her hands over her apron, gave her head a single nod, and turned away; but she was gone only a few minutes before she returned with an enormous bouquet of flowers. "He left these," she said and began to sweep soiled, wadded tissues from the built-in bedside table into her apron pocket, so she could put the flowers down. "I didn't have nuthin proper that was big enough to hold em."

Bertha Marshall and Madeline stared at the profusion of roses and cosmos, daisies and dahlias, and other flowers they couldn't name, all arranged in a number ten juice can with spots of glue still visible down its side where the paper had been removed; and neither of them seemed capable of a single sensible remark.

"Well," her mother said after a while, "do you need anything, child?"

"No Momma," Madeline said.

Leslie didn't return Tuesday, but he called, wanting to know if there was anything he could do. She didn't talk to him. She didn't dare. There were things she had to do that had to be done before she lived another day, and certainly before she talked to Leslie.

Telling James she'd asked for a divorce made him turn so pale his lips looked blue. But he didn't say anything, and he didn't cry. He just listened and looked at her with his dark eyes, as though he'd known all along and was just waiting to have it spoken. Somehow telling him was like telling her own heart, as though she hadn't quite known what she was proposing until she heard what she was saying and saw the blood seem to drain out of him, so that his lips and even his fingernails began to look as if they'd been stained with pale blue ink. It was, she felt, the most intimate thing she had ever done and the most horrible. With all her heart she vowed she'd be the best mother she could be in order to make it up to him, even as she knew, absolutely, that she could never make it up. As for him, he looked at her and listened and allowed himself to be held, and then he told her in a small steady voice that he had to change his clothes and do his chores.

When he left the trailer, all that he had not said seemed to grow enormous and very cold and seemed to haunt the caverns of her heart. But she had done it, and in the awful silence that remained, she found she still had some strength. Maybe it was only a thimbleful, and maybe it felt surrounded by shame and fear, but it was there, asking to be spent. She would tell her mother and father, she decided, at once.

If telling James had been as awful and intimate as informing her own heart, telling her mother and father was like notifying God.

"I need to talk to you and Poppa," she told her mother, who was cutting out biscuits on the counter with movements as precise as a machine.

"Chile, you know Harley don't shut the post office till four o'clock, and I ain't got a minute to spare," she said, flinging down a handful of flour on the counter, dusting her rolling pin with it, gathering up scraps of biscuit dough, pounding them together, and rolling them out again without even looking at Madeline. She had, after all, seven mouths to feed. Not that it ever soured her temper or bothered her in the least. She had been doing more or less the same thing for as long as Madeline could remember, for longer than she had been alive to remember, Madeline thought with shame.

"Momma," she said, "I've got to tell you and Poppa something if it kills me."

"No you don't," Bertha Marshall said, cutting out biscuits with precise, mechanical twists of her wrist and without even looking up.

"Come with me to the post office. I've got to talk."

"I don't have a minute to spare," Bertha Marshall said, but she had stopped working and was leaning forward with both hands braced on the counter.

"Momma, please," Madeline said.

Without looking at her but with her eyes brimming, her mother walked past her and out the kitchen door as though she were taking the first steps of a long journey. Madeline followed her down the flagstone walk to the little white post office across the dirt driveway. Her mother didn't even acknowledge Ida Triplett, who had just come out of the post office with a package. "Why Bertha?" Ida said with a broad, friendly smile, "how nice to see you."

Up the wooden steps and through the door Bertha Marshall went, making the little bell atop the door jingle and making Madeline, who followed behind, feel like a small child, scolded in public.

Inside, her mother stopped stock still and fixed her eyes just below the counter at nothing. She looked very strange standing there with smudges of flour to her elbows, her hands not rolled into her apron as usual, but curled into fists held rigidly at her sides. Harley Marshall clearly didn't know what to make of her. He was in his traditional post office uniform: a green plastic eyeshade held on his head by an elastic band and two sleeve garters, which he wore just below his elbows around his forearms. "Why woman?" he said, "what ails ye?"

Bertha said not a word.

He opened his mouth to say something else but closed it again in confusion, his big nose and broad chin coming close to meeting without the intervening superstructure of teeth to hold them apart. Since his wife wasn't talking, he turned to Madeline, who had stopped just inside the threshold with every cell in her body electrified and her mouth dry. "What's this here?" he asked her, his eyes turning hard either to brace himself for bad news or with a ready-made anger to greet it, she couldn't tell which.

"Momma," she began. "Poppa . . ." For a second she thought she would surely faint, but that tiny thimbleful of strength insisted, having come thus far, she had to go on no matter the damage it would cause. "I just told James, and I've got to tell you too. Last Sunday . . ." She tried to find some moisture in her mouth to go on, but there wasn't any, and her tongue seemed to click. "Last Sunday, I told Edward I just couldn't stand our marriage anymore, and I had to have a divorce. He agreed to give me one."

"Oh can't you try just a little longer, chile?" her mother said, not looking at anyone or anything but staring just the same.

"Momma," Madeline said, "that's all I've ever done. That's all I've done since we first married."

"I've never heard of such nonsense!" her father said with deep color rising into his face. "You told your husband you had to have a divorce?"

"Oh, baby, can't you try a little more?" her mother pleaded.

"What crimes did he commit?" her father asked. "What terrible things did he do?"

Somehow she'd thought that was obvious. Always moving from place to place. Living in nasty little trailer parks. Coming home drunk or not coming home at all. And worst of all and behind it all, never, never taking her into consideration. But somehow she could say none of that. It was humiliating. And she knew suddenly that it wouldn't sound right. It wouldn't sound serious enough. Not the way it felt to her. "I'm unhappy," she whispered at last.

"Horseshit!" her father said. "Who told you life was supposed to be happy? You've forgot your upbringing, young'n. You've forgot the Bible and your vows. 'What God has joined together let' . . ."

"Hush up," Bertha Marshall said. "Hush your mouth!"

Bertha seemed to shock not only her husband but herself into silence, and for a long moment no one seemed to breathe. But at last Madeline whispered, "I'm sorry. Momma . . . Poppa . . . I'm just so sorry."

JAMES
TALLY

It was just that he felt numb, as though inside his head and inside his heart there were cavernous spaces where his feelings were supposed to be. He searched for acceptable emotions, acceptable thoughts to put in all that emptiness. He decided it wasn't so much his actual father he missed as the idea of having a father. The whole idea of fatherhood. Anyway he hadn't been a good son to the father he'd had. When had he ever even been able to follow his advice? So.

And he'd betrayed, no less, the advice he had given himself. He was, after all, nothing whatever like Osceola. But he was free to invent himself, was he not? Now more than ever. There was no one else around to help him do it.

MADELINE TALLY

Wednesday, feeling fragile but also somehow purified and rare, she went back to work, and Leslie was there on the dot of twelve to take her to lunch, looking as pale and haggard as if he himself had been ill. And fifteen minutes before quitting time, she spotted him from her glassed-in office on the second-floor balcony, wandering around the men's department, fingering shirts and ties he would never think of buying.

That evening he took her to the Gateway Restaurant in Cedar Hill, where she told him how awful it had been to talk to Edward and how awful to tell James and her mother and father, and she nearly talked herself into sadness again. But Leslie's hand kept seeking hers across the table, and his eyes never left her face, and all at once she understood that this sadness belonged to the old life she had given up and must not be carried, like a keepsake, into her new one. It was such a compelling thought that, after a while, she was able to retrieve the frail, purified new person she had been that morning and notice the lovely man doting on her. Slowly she found herself able to give his hand hopeful, answering squeezes and to look into his eyes and be healed by them.

After dinner. After dark. Snug in his car. She allowed him to hold her close and kiss her.

"Maidy," he said, his voice wonderfully hoarse, "come home with me. Do. Just for a little while."

She could do that, she realized. This frail new person she was could do as he proposed, and it was easy to look at him as long and fondly as he was looking at her. She gathered herself as close to him as possible and kissed him. But at last she wagged her forehead gently against his cheek and whispered against his flesh, "No, not just yet."

Perhaps she said it precisely because she might, so easily, have gone, or because he so much wanted her to, or perhaps she said it only because she could. She didn't know exactly, but she knew it gratified the new person she was. And when, at last, she got home, she felt virtuous for wanting to make love to Leslie, for telling Edward she wanted a divorce, for having her talk with James and her parents, for surviving three awful days of illness, and for knowing that she might make love to a man, not her husband, at a time of her own choosing.

James was huddled in a corner of the sofa, reading, when she entered the warm, close trailer.

"Hi babe," she said, almost cheerfully. "Homework?"

"No," he said, "it's about Chief Joseph and the Nez Percé Indians."

"Ahh," she said, caught a tuft of his unruly hair, and gave it a playful tug. "Time you paid another visit to the barber, young man." He didn't answer or look up, but he seemed more distant than rude.

After she'd changed into her gown and bathrobe, she got a sudden inspiration and melted butter, cut strips of bread to dip into it, got out cinnamon and brown sugar, and, because she knew he loved them, put a tray of cinnamon sticks in the oven. Once or twice, while she worked, she caught his curious, puzzled eyes on her.

"I only made a dozen, and I've got a terrible craving, so you'd better be quick," she told him and winked, but he only gave her a little scrap of a smile before he returned his attention to his book. Nevertheless, while the trailer filled with warm, sweet spice, she stole glances at him as he read and thought his expression had grown softer and younger.

When the cinnamon sticks were done, she arranged them on

a platter and took them over and plopped down beside him on the couch. "Dig in," she told him, but when he reached out, she poked him playfully in the ribs, and he jerked his hand back empty.

"Hey!" he said, although something in her face made him giggle.

She glanced at her wristwatch. "You want to turn the radio on?" she said. "It's nearly time for *Boston Blackie*." So he put his book aside, and they listened to the radio and ate cinnamon sticks, and she felt very snug and sly. She didn't want the cinnamon sticks, but she ate two of them and then waited patiently until he reached for the very last one before she attacked. "So what makes you think you can have the last one?" she cried, tickling him furiously while he struggled to protect his ribs, sputtering, "Stop . . . I give . . . Stop . . . you're crazy . . . Stop . . . Stop!" And finally she did stop, but not before they were exhausted and the platter was upside down on the floor. Even then, she snatched up the final cinnamon stick and gobbled half of it, although she didn't want it in the least, and mashed the other half against his lips until he opened his mouth and took it. For minutes, weak and flushed, they laughed at each other and caught their breath until, at last, she pinched his cheek and hugged him and told him good night.

And strangely, the good mood that went to bed with her was even stronger when she rose, and it followed her to work, where, all day, problems seemed to fall neatly into their solutions. Mistakes on receipts and sales slips jumped out at her and identified themselves, and putting the books in order had never been half so easy. For almost the first time in her life, she felt bright and capable. And for the first time in years she felt pretty, so much so that she caught herself nearly gloating when, once or twice during the morning, she spied her image flashing across a fitting mirror.

So she was in a wonderful mood when Leslie called at eleven-thirty to say he couldn't take her to lunch.

"I've got a damned meeting with the county court clerk," he said miserably.

"That's all right," she told him.

"I can't get out of it," he said.

"Don't worry," she said.

"I'm so sorry, honey," he said. "I'll try not to . . ."

"Hey," she said, "we'll have a lovely dinner instead."

"You're not upset?" he asked her, but before she could answer, he took another tack. "Dammit, I look forward to our lunches!"

She laughed into the mouthpiece. "You're so sweet," she told him. "I look forward to them too, but you just be here at quitting time, and you won't be in any trouble."

He laughed then himself, his relief wafting through the phone like the first breath of spring. "I've got to go," he said. "I'm late already."

When she put the phone back in its cradle, she found she was happy at the prospect of having lunch with the salesladies, or better yet, by herself. Moments later, filled with wonder, her hand still on the telephone, she realized that no matter how smart and successful Leslie was, no matter how sophisticated and assured, he was also vulnerable. It seemed to her that she'd never really noticed anyone else's vulnerability before, as though her own jeopardy, helplessness, and unhappiness were so great, she'd never had a chance at any other perspective. Still later another thought came to her touched with a delicious sense of guilt: love could make a fool of anyone, not merely her, but Leslie too. It was an alien and wonderful thought, and she savored it for the way it bound her to the rest of humanity and for the way it promised at least as much power as it threatened to take away.

She had a marvelous lunch, preferring, at last, to eat by herself. She felt a little too inspired and energetic to eat with any of the salesladies. She didn't wish to listen to their everyday conversations about the expense of children's braces or whether to buy drapes for the dining room or paper the hall, or any of the ordinary, passionless discussions she had once envied precisely because they were so dull and safe, and therefore, seemed the hallmarks of full lives and happy marriages. Anyway, God only knew what she might have blurted in the state she was in, feeling, as she did, full of wonderful secrets and power.

And after work, at dinner with Leslie, it seemed to her she got a glimpse of the way life really ought to be. There was no animosity between them. None. For the first time in a long while, food tasted the way it should, and now and again she found herself giggling.

"Do you remember the time Lonnie Crocket put the garter snake in Mrs. Dunbar's purse?" Leslie asked and laughed.

She did remember very well. Lonnie and Leslie had been in the tenth grade when she was in the twelfth; and, during lunch, Lonnie had managed to sneak a pretty big garter snake in Mrs. Dunbar's purse, wisely figuring someone in the twelfth grade would be blamed. It had been in the spring, and Mrs. Dunbar was troubled with hay fever, and every so often she would yank a handkerchief from her purse, give her nose a blow and a wipe, and go on with the lesson. The strange thing was that, when she came out with the twenty-inch garter snake, there seemed to be a moment when even the most basic, primordial instinct failed and she had no idea what it was. Who would expect to find such a thing in one's purse after all? Even Dolly Clarke, who sat in the front row, screamed before Mrs. Dunbar, although not as long or as piercingly as when Mrs. Dunbar's puzzlement became, in the next heartbeat, profound and hysterical recognition. The poor, good woman left a puddle between her desk and the blackboard and a fetid cloud that seemed to hang at the front of the classroom for the rest of the afternoon, while first a substitute from one of the other grades and finally the principal came in to harangue and threaten them.

All through dinner the two of them remembered pranks and high school love affairs and hay rides and church picnics, and it was all so easy and comfortable that they lingered over every course. Although finally, they found they were talking less and spending more time giving each other long, fond, open appraisals over raised coffee cups and idle forks until Madeline dropped her eyes and said, "You know, I really would like to see your house . . . to see where you live . . . just so I can imagine you in it."

Maybe he was too pleased to reply. She didn't know. Maybe he couldn't think of anything appropriate to say, but she sensed as much as saw him nod. Quite suddenly they both turned shy and took more time over their coffee than was necessary.

The house stood halfway up the mountain above Cedar Hill on a twisted residential street, so that the grand living room and dining room and the master bedroom looked down on the lighted streets of Cedar Hill with what seemed a benign but distinctly proprietary air. The house was made of stone; had wide, pegged, oak floors, stained a rich, warm color; and two full baths, which seemed wonderfully extravagant. It also had three large bedrooms, the most beautiful kitchen she'd ever seen, and a study with glassed-in bookshelves on either side of a huge granite fireplace and hearth. Everything was in excellent taste and neat—he had a cleaning lady twice a week—but somehow sterile too and without the warmth a woman's constant presence and touch might have given it. Leslie's wife had died while the house was being built, and she'd never lived in it.

"She got to fuss some at the builders, though, while it was going up," Leslie said.

"Ahhh," Madeline said, truly and profoundly saddened, even as she was pleased that she might become the first, and not the second, mistress of this dwelling.

In the living room once more, she could see a wan reflection of herself in the dark windows surrounded by the faint image of Leslie's furniture and appointments, all shot through with the lights of the town below. She wished to look as though she belonged, but she wasn't so sure she did, nor did her reflection quite please her the way it had earlier in the day when she'd caught glimpses of herself in the fitting mirrors. She looked ghostly with the lights of Cedar Hill shining through her. In any case, she suspected Leslie knew as well as she did that she hadn't come merely to look at his house, and suddenly that knowledge seemed to charge the atmosphere around her with uncertainty and make her palms misty. She thought of Edward, but she made herself turn toward Leslie and put her arms about his neck. "Oh Leslie," she said, realizing she had almost, out of the instinctual weight of years, spoken another name. "Oh Leslie, I love you," she insisted and kissed him. She held him as close as she possibly could, and after many long moments, when his lips almost left hers, she still didn't release him. So they stood kissing for a long time until he began to pet her and she could feel him rising, and she began to shiver and tremble, head to toe. At last he pulled back and led her away.

In his bedroom, divested of her clothes, she was shocked to realize that she felt less shy than she'd ever felt around her husband. Not once in her previous life could she remember being naked without feeling the cooling touch of shame and the need to cover up. Nor had she ever allowed herself to admire a naked man, except in the most surreptitious little peeks and glances. It was as if Leslie were the first naked man she had truly ever seen. He was slender and handsome, she thought, although he didn't look especially strong. Still, although his arms and legs were thin, they were well proportioned, and his chest and belly were thick with springy hair as silver as the hair on his head—odd, since the hair on his arms and legs and around his genitals was still mostly black. He was really quite remarkable, his nipples like dark badges among all that hair, and the curve of his penis and the orbs of his testicles, almost beautiful, almost endearing.

Oh but he was gentle and tender, his mouth upon her mouth, her eyes, her breasts and nipples. And his hands, how could they be so wise and gentle and tantalizingly slow, and where had he learned all this, and when? Had he been some nasty little boy hiding out in the barn with those pretty little dark-eyed cousins of his? How many women had he known before his wife? Since? But she had grown delirious for him to caress each new part of her. There was no spot he might wish to touch and woo that she would not gladly surrender. She would do anything he asked, she knew she would, because she was totally dotty. She knew she was. She had never in her life been so thrilled.

And when, at last, he entered her, for the space of a heartbeat she lost consciousness. Gentle and wonderful he was, and on and on he went. On and on and on. But when she certainly would have reached climax, haunting the most remote boundary of thought, was Edward. She would not admit him, but she couldn't banish the effort it took to keep him at bay, and so the moment escaped her. For some time then, the sensations, which had been so delicious, turned raw and almost painful, and the whole situation seemed ludicrous. But Leslie would not stop, and finally, as though from the wrong side, as though the whole matter had been turned wrong side out, she reached orgasm, somehow as horrid as it was wonderful.

JAMES
TALLY

When the trouble started, James was crossing the playground toward the sycamore tree where Lester was already eating his baked sweet potato, a sweet potato being the only thing Lester had had in his lunch bag all week, except when they were small and he'd had two of them; and when James thought about it later, he figured it had all happened because he'd been so deep in his own thoughts. He was about fifty feet from Lester when he heard, or maybe just felt, a presence close by; and in the next second a jarring blow to his shoulder made him stagger.

"Whaddaya say pissant?" Earl said. "Gettin any gravel for yer goose?"

His arm felt half-paralyzed, and he had a crick in his neck from the impact of Earl's bony knuckles against the point of his shoulder, but he kept walking, not even looking around, as though he'd merely stumbled or been shoved by a sudden gust of wind, although Lester and the sycamore were blurred from the moisture that pain had dashed across his eyes.

"Hey," Earl insisted, "answer me, boy! You gettin any poontang? Any frogjaw?" And he grasped James's shoulder to turn him around.

Whatever the reason, when he was forced to look into Earl's proud, cruel face, he said, "Get away from me," in a voice he didn't even recognize, and when Earl opened his mouth to speak, the heels of James's hands shot out all by themselves, hit Earl in the chest, and knocked him backwards.

"Why you little shit!" Earl said and did exactly the same thing to James, only James's feet left the ground and he landed on his back with the base of his skull slamming into the hard-packed earth of the ballfield with such force that he seemed to go blind and maybe a little crazy too, since he was up and swinging wildly before he knew it. He hit Earl once on the forehead, once in the neck, and once in the ribs before Earl's fist hammered into his eye and knocked him down again. It was such a hard, bone-against-bone blow that it didn't even hurt, exactly; instead it provided a numbing burst of color, and he hardly felt himself hitting the ground. But this time, just as he had scrambled up to his hands and knees, Earl landed on him, got an arm twisted behind his back, grabbed the hair of his head, and slammed his face into the earth, which bloodied his nose and got his mouth full of dirt. In a rage of frustration and anger, he thrashed and struggled, but Earl cursed him and rode him, forcing his face into the ground by the hair of his head.

"Get off'n him and let him up," James heard a calm, familiar voice say but Earl pushed his face into the dirt and said, "What's it to you, fester fuck?"

James gathered himself to struggle again, but his arm got twisted so far behind his back, the pain was crippling, although in the next moment, as if by magic, Earl's weight disappeared. For a few seconds James lay where he was, trying to bring his right arm from behind his back. Aching and reluctant, his arm obeyed him, and he sat up and, suddenly very dizzy, spat again and again to rid his mouth of dirt and blood. Earl Carpenter, James was surprised to see, was also sitting on the ballfield a dozen feet away. "Don't bother him no more," Lester was saying. "You done aggravated him enough."

A strange, delighted sneer on his handsome face, Earl got up and dusted off the seat of his britches. He shook his head, as though sadly, and grinned. "You gonna get it now," he told Lester. "I'm gonna stomp a mudhole in yore ass."

But as Lester and Earl came together, Earl's constant shadows,

Tom and Tim Lanich, moved in James's way, and he couldn't see what was happening. "Knock his head off, Earl!" Tom said.

"Kick his ass! Kick his ass!" Tim demanded just as a small boy from a lower grade brushed past James's shoulder and shouted: "There's a fight! Hey, Troy! Hey, Cecil! There's a fight!" And before James could even get up, a dozen people had gathered; and by the time his arms managed to steady him enough so that he could get his feet under him and stand, a whole cluster of people had gathered eagerly around.

His knees didn't feel as if they were going to hold him up, but they did, although they burned with weakness and threatened to buckle. Still, he clutched and fumbled at those in front of him until he came in sight of Lester, who was holding his fists clownishly out before him as though he were John L. Sullivan or some such old-time fighter posing for a picture, except that his lips were so puffed and broken they looked almost wrong side out, and his nose was already streaming blood. James couldn't believe so much damage had been done in so short a time. But it was easy to see that Lester didn't know the first thing about fighting. He pawed the air with his oversized fists in front of an enemy half a head shorter and at least twenty pounds heavier, while Earl, completely unmarked, moved easily out of the way and smirked; until, almost too fast for the eye to follow, he was somehow inside Lester's pawing fists and match-thin arms and had hit him one, two, three times; and Lester became all arms and legs, waving and kicking out for balance. But he didn't fall, and in a moment there he was again, serious, wordless, striking his clownish pose and pawing the air in front of Earl's face.

"Knock his head off, Earl," one of the Lanich twins shouted, and then other people began to shout, and all of them for Earl. They had to be fooling themselves, hoping that, if they cheered for Earl, he might begin to think of them as friends and be less cruel, or maybe they just couldn't bring themselves to cheer for someone so ridiculous as Lester; James didn't know and couldn't say. But for himself, he felt empty and sick in his stomach, and whether from the sudden passing of his inexplicable anger, or from fear, or for some other mysterious reason, there was no strength in his body, and the crowd jostled him this way and that. "Hey, kick his ass, Earl!" someone shouted, and as though on command, Earl stepped in and punched Lester squarely in the eye.

Lester went reeling backwards, arms flailing, and might have fallen if he hadn't managed to catch Earl's shirtfront, so that the two of them went around and around in a violent dance with Earl yanking Lester about as though Lester had no weight at all and punching him frantically to break free. But their legs only got tangled, and they both went down where they thrashed and rolled and struggled for a long time before Earl managed to escape somehow and stand up, although his shirt was torn and, probably more through Lester's clumsiness than anything, there was a thin trickle of blood crawling out of Earl's nose and a lump under one of his eyes.

Lester got up too, his arms looking as thin as twigs and his big chapped fists slowly churning the air in front of him again.

"Say you're whipped, fester fuck, and I'll let you off," Earl said.

But Lester didn't say anything at all. He just pawed the air, all at once launching a terrific roundhouse swing that whistled a good six inches from Earl's face, as though all those childish, pawing blows would have set Earl up, somehow, for a knockout; except that it was Lester, not Earl, who fell merely from the violence of his own effort. While he was trying to get up, Earl rushed in and shoved him backwards, and he fell again. "Say you're whipped," Earl demanded.

But Lester wasn't talking. He got on his feet again, his face showing no emotion, as if he weren't at all bloody, and his lips weren't swollen wrong side out, and his left eye wasn't puffing shut. As if he didn't even know that his silly style of fighting wasn't working. He came at Earl as though he were doing just fine.

Tears breaking in his throat and trembling head to foot, James forced himself inside the circle only to have Tim Lanich grab him by the collar and yank so that he stumbled back and down, his head knocking against Tim's knees just before the whole body of onlookers moved forward, and Tim and someone else fell over him and scrambled up and went on because the fight had started up again and moved a little away, drawing everyone with it.

And then people were coming from everywhere, until Lester and Earl had collected almost everyone on the playground, even some of the high school students from across the way, and James found himself cut off and shut out. He wanted no part of it, but it was monstrous and shameful that the fight wasn't his anymore when he'd started it. He wanted to run as far away as possible, only he found himself pawing and fumbling at the crowd in order to get through, his ears ringing as if a shotgun had been fired just over his head.

But people shook him off. The crowd changed shape and seemed to thicken in front of him just when he was making progress, and for minutes he couldn't even catch a glimpse of what was happening. He couldn't believe that Earl hadn't been allowed to strut off in victory long ago. Even when things were equal, fights lasted only a minute or two. Maybe five if there was a lot of circling and name calling, but this one had gone on for twenty minutes or longer, when Earl had every advantage and every right to win, and it was unnatural that Lester couldn't be made to acknowledge it. It was so unnatural and outrageous that it had put something strange in Earl's eyes when James got close enough to see them. There weren't any new marks on him, but he'd gotten dirty and sweaty and tired, and he'd begun to back away from Lester's childish blows.

"Say you're whipped," he would croak from time to time, but that only seemed to make Lester launch one of his outrageous, whistling swings. Maybe he would fall with it and maybe not, but he was always up again, looking absolutely certain that, sooner or later, he was going to hit Earl with one of them and knock him to Kingdom Come. Maybe Earl had begun to worry about that too.

But it didn't happen. All at once coach Chic Dailey from the high school was there and had shouldered himself through the crowd and caught Lester against his chest.

"Whoa, son," he said, because Lester was still trying to fumble toward Earl. "Whoa now, take her easy."

"He smart-mouthed me!" Earl said to the coach's back. "And he tore my shirt that ain't even a week old!"

For a moment more Coach Dailey held Lester against his chest, which had already gotten nearly as bloody as Lester's own, and then he held him at arm's length to look at him. His eyes narrowed, the muscles at his jaw rippled, and he started to say something but seemed to catch himself. "One of you young'ns run and get Hagerman for me and Miss Ivey," he said, and although he spoke to no one in particular, four people sprinted toward the school.

"The stupid shit jumped me, that's all," Earl said. "Ain't nobody pushes me around."

Chic Dailey turned enough to face him. He had one hand on the nape of Lester's neck, holding Lester's head in close as though to protect the damage that had been done, but the other hand was pointing at Earl, the forefinger extended like the barrel of a gun. "You're missing a good chance to keep your mouth shut, boy," the coach said. "I've known about you for a long time, and I already been told what went on here."

For minutes then, as though they were at the site of an automobile accident, everyone stood around as if they didn't quite want to be there, but somehow couldn't walk away either. It was as though they had to wait for Miss Ivey, who taught home economics and doubled as the school nurse, or Mr. Hagerman, who was the principal, to arrive and bring matters to a close, make pronouncements, make sense. At least that was what James was hoping for.

But when Miss Ivey arrived, she only raised Lester's face and looked at it, shook her head, and said, "My, oh my." She was a big woman, Miss Ivey, bigger than most men, and maybe she couldn't ever be pretty, but she seemed all the more gentle because of it.

"You'll want to look at that young'n too," Dailey told her and nodded toward James, somehow knowing miraculously exactly who and where he was.

And Miss Ivey came and looked at him, touching his face with soft, practiced fingers. "Mercy," she said, "mercy, mercy. You boys come along with me this instant."

But before they could move, Hagerman arrived, his gray, vested suit the color of iron and looking just as stiff except around his thighs where it was an accordion of wrinkles. The students automatically gave him space, and any mutterings and whisperings going on among them ceased while he looked first at Lester and then at Earl and finally at James. He was a short man with a proud paunch and a face that was never seen to smile. From Virginia and Clara, James had learned that he had a big wooden paddle in his office with holes drilled in it which left bright red rings on the buttocks, and he paddled the smaller children with it; but as the boys among them reached a certain size or age when they might have offered resistance—and he seemed to know without fail when this was—he no longer whipped them. He sent them home.

"I can't have this kind of shenanigan at my school, and I won't have it," he told them. "When Miss Ivey gets finished with the three of you, I want you off school grounds, and I don't want you here the rest of this week or next." He gave each of them another long look. "Monday a week, you can come to my office, and we'll have a talk."

"Two's enough for Miss Ivey to clean up. I'll take this one to the high school first-aid room," Chic Dailey said and grasped Earl's elbow, only Earl pulled free.

"I ain't hurt," he said.

"Well, you two young'ns come on with me then," Miss Ivey said to James and Lester.

"If you're not hurt, young man, I want you off school grounds right now," the principal told Earl.

"I got to catch the bus home!" Earl said.

"I'll tell the driver to pick you up on the highway," Hagerman said and pointed out the spot. Turning to the others then as though they were also somehow mysteriously at fault, he said, "And it's time the rest of you went on about your business."

But it was all so beside the point, James felt the whole world was out of focus, and when he followed Lester and Miss Ivey toward the school, he jarred himself when he walked, as if he no longer even quite knew where the ground was, and the feeling wouldn't leave him.

"Oh, you boys," Miss Ivey sighed as she tended them in her little first-aid room, cleaning and dabbing and applying antiseptic. "Mercy, mercy, you boys," she'd say and shake her head as if she knew exactly who and what they were, as if they had acted just as she'd known all along they would. But none of it made any sense to James, and it was a long time later, while he and Lester were walking down the railroad bed, that something seemed to wake him, and the world he knew, the true and legitimate world he recognized, came rushing back from wherever it had gone.

Perhaps they were struck too dumb to speak, but they had been walking together, just as always, as if an ordinary school day had passed with its ordinary woe, and there was nothing to be said about it, when whatever it was—the warm, earnest sun on his back, maybe, or the insistent and cumulative effect of birdsong—woke him, and he stopped in his tracks and looked about. "I don't believe it!" he said all at once.

Had he really shoved Earl Carpenter and tried to fight him? And Lester, who was perfectly innocent and didn't know the first thing about fighting, how did he get sucked in to rescue him so that he had to struggle on and on as though he couldn't quit, as though Earl were another impossibly painful school assignment to be endured? And how could that seem so ordinary and expected to Miss Ivey? And what sort of blind formula for justice was Hagerman following? It seemed impossible that any of it could have happened. But sure enough his left eye had begun to ache in a dull, far-off sort of way, and he could glimpse his own cheek under it. Also his upper lip was as tight and sore as if he'd been stung by a bee. And Lester—who had stopped walking too—James could hardly stand to look at Lester. Yet with his broken lips and his left eye swelled shut and weeping pink tears, Lester seemed to ponder the mystery too and find it more believable.

"I'm sorry," James said. "It was my fault."

After a moment Lester said, "Nawh. Don't talk crazy." With his shirtsleeve he wiped away the pink serum leaking from the slit of his eye. "Earl Carpenter's been ridin' you since you got here," he said. "'Tweren't nary fault of yours."

"You shouldn't have got beat up though," James said.

Lester made a soft sound, almost like laughing. "Couldn't seem to help it," he said.

"But, God, why didn't you quit?" James said. "Why didn't you just quit?"

Lester looked at the ground and shook his head slightly; and after a minute, he shook it again. "I reckon I didn't like the way he asked me."

"I'm going home with you to tell your folks what happened," James said.

"You don't need to do that," Lester said.

"I'm going to," James said.

Lester nodded, but then, for all the bruised color in his face, he looked suddenly gray, and he took a few feeble steps to the cut bank along the railroad and sat down. "I don't feel so good," he whispered.

James went over and sat beside him, and neither of them spoke for a long time. Lester let his head drop back against the dirt bank and closed his eyes, breathing through his open mouth almost as if he were winded, although his breaths were shaky and not very deep. He was sweating too, but after a few minutes he opened his eyes again, and at last he sat up, although his color was still strange.

"Are you all right?" James asked.

As though puzzled, Lester shook his head. "Feel puny," he said. He stayed where he was for a while, letting his breath whistle out. "Better now," he said.

He got up then, but slowly, and James got up with him, and

they went on, although Lester had to stop to rest once more before they got to his house.

Effie was taking clothes in from the line when they came into the backyard, but the moment she got a look at Lester, her eyes went wide. "Child! What in the world . . . !" she said, and then her eyes took in James too.

"I was gettin beat up, and he took my part," James blurted. "It was all my fault."

"Now Momma," Lester said, "hit ain't nuthin." He tried his best to give her an easy smile, only the new contours of his face turned the effort into something without a name. "It's nuthin broke," he told her. "I just ain't real handy at fightin."

"Awwwh, honey," she said, her back beginning to bow over the clothes she held as though they were an enormous weight, and her eyes still wide, but with pity now, more than surprise.

"I'm a little tired," Lester said, "but if you'd let me lie down, I'll be as good as gold by supper."

"Awwwwh, baby," Effie said.

"Hey boys!" Roy shouted, appearing suddenly from the barn, but no one answered him.

Lester had already stepped up on the dogtrot and was letting himself into his room, so by the time Roy came up, he already knew something was wrong; and the moment he saw James, he not only knew what it was, but seemed to make some sort of peace with it. "Had you a fight, I see," he remarked as though he were neither amused nor angry, but merely stating a fact, just as he might have said: "I see you got yourself a haircut."

"We didn't fight each other, Mr. Buck," James told him.

Something about Roy Buck's countenance changed then, as though he nodded without moving his head or smiled without moving his lips. "Well that's good," he said.

"Lester's awful hurt," Effie put in. "I ort to look—"

But Roy Buck patted the air softly to hush her, as though to say that Lester should be allowed his privacy just then. "You don't look just brand new, yourself," he said to James, which somehow made him see how very little he was hurt compared to Lester. Almost instantly his eyes filled because Lester had taken the beating meant for him and taken ten times more of it than James ever would have, if only because Lester meant to turn it into a victory. And so he told them everything—how the fight had started and Lester had rescued him and wouldn't give up, how Hagerman had forbidden all three of them to go to school, and how Lester had had to rest on the way home—while Effie put her arm around him and squeezed him against her breast and against the stiff clothes that smelled of lye soap and sunlight, and Roy nodded and nodded.

EDWARD
TALLY

He pulled the Packard up to the curb, turned off the ignition, and stared through the windshield down the street of row houses. But he didn't know he was staring until sometime later when he caught himself at it. After he had forbidden himself to think of Madeline and James, his mind often seemed to go altogether blank, and he would discover himself gazing dry-eyed and numb into space. Not even glancing up to Paris's third-floor windows, he got out of the car and opened the trunk where he'd hidden the enormous pink elephant from Womb Broom and Ironfield since he wouldn't have been able to tolerate the slightest teasing about it. Paris had two days off before she went on the night shift and was fixing his supper for the first time ever, but he knew he'd bought the elephant for strange and possibly perverse reasons he himself didn't understand. It was a ridiculous-looking thing, google-eyed, cotton-candy pink, and as big as a hog, so she was sure to like it. He tucked it under his arm, gathered up a fifth of Canadian whiskey, and slammed the trunk lid with his elbow. Across the sidewalk he went and, after some difficulty getting through the door, up the narrow, creaking stairs, the elephant pressing against the wall, pushing him off balance, and making him stumble as though it were another person trying to jostle past him. Madness. If he wasn't thinking about Madeline, how come he could feel her with him every single moment? Nitwit, he told himself, asshole, don't

125

think of anything that ever happened to you. Think of the future. No. Not good. No good at all. Paris, he told himself, think of Paris, and he struggled toward the third-floor landing, he and the elephant like two fat men trying to get through a narrow doorway at exactly the same time.

Just yesterday Ironfield and Womb Broom had gotten their one and only glimpse of Paris, waving and throwing kisses from the sidewalk in front of her hotel as the three of them drove past on their way home from work. "Mercy," Womb Broom said, although he disapproved. It was all right for a man to be unfaithful only if everything was fine between him and his wife. If not, then being unfaithful was evil and destructive and menacing to all things sacred.

But Ironfield's scalded eyes had studied Paris only a second. "Mercy, shit!" he said. "If that sweet-looking bitch had as many dicks sticking out of her as she's had stuck in her, we'd all take her for a goddamned porcupine."

On the next-to-the-last step, he barely stubbed his toe, but it was enough to make him stumble headlong against her door. He rested a moment, sweat crawling, like secret misery, out of his sideburns. Don't think at all, he told himself and knocked on the door with his forehead before he bothered to get his feet under him. It didn't feel bad.

"Is that you, cutie?" Paris called. "You get in here. I've missed you awful."

He tried to open the door with the hand that held the whiskey but nearly dropped the bottle. He couldn't even reach the doorknob with his left hand. The enormous elephant wouldn't allow it.

Stymied. Helpless.

At last he thought to pass the whiskey to his left—a simple solution, since his arm held the elephant quite nicely all by itself. With a perfectly free hand he opened the door and wedged himself and the elephant through. "Hey," he said to her heart-shaped ass, since the other end of her was peering into the oven, "look what followed me home." He set the whiskey on a table and held the elephant out by its trunk—his other arm held wide to embrace her.

"Oh, how precious!" she said, but anger immediately swept her face, and she took the elephant and slapped his arm away in the same motion. "That's cruel. You'll hurt him!" Rocking the elephant side to side with her mouth against its neck, she crooned, "Poor baby, poor baby, Momma won't let him do it anymore."

He thought briefly of explaining that it was only a stuffed toy. "Their trunks are very strong," he said at last. "You can't hurt an elephant's trunk."

Paris appeared to consider the matter. She held the elephant out at arm's length, cocked her head, pursed her lips. "Little pink ones you can," she said. "Oh you're so sweet," she told it, "you can just sit right here and watch me fix your daddy's dinner," and she set it atop the kitchen table where it took nearly all available space. "I made a pork roast and applesauce," she told Edward. "Doesn't that sound southern? And after I feed you, I'm going to screw you until you die."

"Thank you," he said.

"Thank you?" She frowned and studied him. "Thank you? What's wrong with you anyway?"

"Nothing," he insisted. "I'm tired as hell, and I want a drink and a shower, that's all."

She looked at him doubtfully.

"Really," he said. He held out his arms again, and hesitantly, her head cocked a little to one side, she came into them; but he held her gently and stroked the small of her back and her bottom until the stiffness went out of her and she seemed to relax a little.

"You scare me sometimes. I don't want you buying me a beautiful elephant and then pulling some cheap shit. You're not planning something like that, are you?"

"Hey," he said, red-faced, laughing, squeezing her, "all I want is a drink and a shower, supper, a wild fuck, and a terrific blow job."

She giggled and dug a thumb in his ribs, which made him flinch and release her. "So go get cleaned up," she told him.

In her carnival of a bathroom he felt somewhat better. The plumbing rumbled and spat, and it was difficult to move around or even find enough room to stand, since the sides and floor of her bathtub were dangerous with razors, eyelash curlers, emery boards, bottles of shampoo, creams, bath oils, and a great clutter of beauty aids he couldn't begin to identify. But at last he found himself a cake of soap shaped like a rose and worked up a greasy, lavender lather. He was okay, he told himself. He was just fine. So what if his heart felt full of holes? So what if he was crazy? It was only another way to be.

The elephant was no longer in the middle of the table when he got out of the shower; it was seated on a chair at the end with a napkin tied around its neck. And Paris was no longer in slacks, but in a sheer, filmy, wine-colored nightgown; and she had laid his pajamas out on the bed. He put them on and took a whiskey and soda from her when he sat down at the table.

"There," she said, "isn't this nice?" And they touched glasses and had a drink.

But he had to have a second long swallow in order to rid his throat of roast pork, which was so dry and stringy it went down like steel wool. He ate some applesauce and took a forkful of something bronze on the left side of his plate. It was in various-size lumps and very hard to chew, and he rolled it around in his mouth like gravel, hoping it would soften before he had to risk his teeth on it again. "What's this, honey?" he asked and tapped the mysterious bronze substance on his plate with his fork. It sounded as if he'd tapped the shell of a turtle.

She looked at him a long time, her big yellow eyes going wet. "Did I ever tell you I was a good cook?" she asked him. "Did I ever claim I was some sweet little thing who could make you southern-fried chicken and biscuits and pineapple upside-down cake? Did I?" she demanded. "It's stuffing, goddamn it!"

"I only wondered what it was," he said earnestly. "I never said it wasn't good."

"It's shit," she told him, and with a single motion swept her plate from the table. Hit by debris, the elephant rocked briefly on its chair but remained upright, a blob of applesauce exactly where it should have been on the napkin tied about its neck. She stood up to make a swipe at his plate too, but he managed to catch her hand. Everything was happening so fast, he seemed to have missed the exact moment when tears had begun to pop from her eyes.

"Whoa! Jesus Christ, don't cry!" he said and struggled around the table without letting her go until he could gather her in, contentious, dangerous elbows and knees and all. "Whoa, hey, whoa, whoa now," he told her. "I want that dinner you made for me."

After a lull and a second explosive little struggle, she seemed to settle into weeping while he held her and explained over and over that he was only a hungry working man who was just grateful as hell that she'd fixed him something to eat, and all he wanted was to by God eat it.

"Really?" she asked him at last.

"Absolutely," he told her.

She was still for a long time, her forehead resting against his chest. "Let me go to the bathroom and fix my face," she said in a very small, tired voice.

Nervously, carefully, he released her, although he kept his hands in space on either side of her shoulders like a man who had just balanced something but didn't trust it not to fall. But she did go into the bathroom, and after he'd cleaned up what she'd flung on the floor—dishes in the sink and food in the garbage—he learned how to eat what she'd cooked for him, and it wasn't so bad. If he chewed the pork for a while, a healthy bite of applesauce would allow him to swallow it pretty well. The stuffing was another matter. Still, by the time she was back at the table with her makeup renewed, he'd learned to take a bite of stuffing, followed by a discreet sip of whiskey, let matters steep and marinate for a moment, and then begin to grind the stuffing down to its chewy center. He was so convincing that after a while the suspicious look on her face began to fade, and she sat across from him with her elbows on the table and her chin held between her palms and watched him eat with something close to enchantment.

"I wish I'd had time to make a dessert," she told him. "Would you like some coffee or anything?"

"Sure," he said, "and another drink."

He meant to clean his plate no matter what, and when, finally, he tucked the last shred of roast and nugget of dressing in his mouth and saturated it with whiskey, he looked up at her and found—wonder of wonders—that her eyes were both full of light and jumping with mischief.

"Googh," he told her, trying to keep the whiskey behind his lips.

He chewed, and they looked at each other, and because he was a sadder, smarter fellow than he'd ever been before, he saw the sorrow hiding in her eyes as well. It dwelt in some aspect of them he couldn't quite identify, but he knew he saw it, just as he knew all the happiness and mischief were only a momentary, giddy overlay. He knew all this without thinking it into words, just as he knew that, like him, Paris was a crazy person. She'd just been crazy longer. Maybe she had more talent and tolerance for it, or maybe she'd just had more practice, since, for sure and certain, he wasn't the first son of a bitch she'd run into. He chewed and smiled at her, his eyes watering, but the smile she returned was dazzling, and in the next moment she was around the table, had caught the front of his pajamas, and was towing him toward the bedroom, his pajama bottoms stretched a foot from his belly.

In another second she had shucked him out of them and herself out of her gown, they were on the bed, and she was in search of whatever it was she always seemed to need but could never quite reach or satisfy. He didn't know when, exactly, he'd begun to realize that he didn't have so big a role in all of this, that finally, Miss Paris Pergola was somehow, strangely and sadly, all but alone and unattended. But she whimpered and moaned and labored, sometimes turning childlike and languid and frail, only in the next moment to begin to brutalize herself upon him until he feared she would split herself in two, pound him into jelly, and reduce the bed to splinters. Or she might take him in her mouth with such piston violence, it was painful, and she'd gag, and the corners of her lips would begin to crack open, which only seemed to make her go at it all the harder.

At last, when she had exhausted both of them, she laid her misty cheek against his chest and gathered herself close to his side. "Oh Eddie," she told him, surprising him, somehow, that she knew his name, "I love you so much. Wasn't that grand?"

"Yes," he said, but he felt so miserable that he willed the breath to go out of him and willed his black heart to cease and desist. Still his breath came and went and his heart thumped as though on purpose to spite him, lifting her blond head to the sill of his vision with each beat. Gently he stroked her head, her silky shoulder and flank, while his heart subsided but kept its painful, subterranean rhythm.

"Will you hold me all night?" she asked.

"Shhhh," he told her and petted her hair.

How had she gotten herself so screwed up? How had he? Madeline? Or was he the only one? One thing for certain, even with Paris right beside him, he felt as grieved and lonely as if he were the last human being left in all the earth. He wasn't going to make it, he knew that much. Before long he wouldn't be just crazy; he'd be insane or a hopeless drunk or dead. Maybe all three. How could Madeline take so much of him with her that there wasn't enough left to run on? How had she grown into him like that? He lay still and pondered it while the light failed and there was nothing to brighten the bedroom but a faint glow, like a moonbeam, seeping in from some small light in the kitchen. After a while Paris began to breathe deeply, then to snore softly like a cat purring, and then to grind her teeth, just as she always did.

What kind of man was he and what kind of horseshit was this, that such a thing could happen? It seemed to him he'd never depended on Madeline for his happiness before. A lot of it had absolutely nothing to do with her. A hell of a lot of it was in spite of her, goddamn it. How could she take even that with her when she left? And his son. Irritated or impatient or proud or shamed or pleased or whatever James had made him feel by turns, he was his own flesh and blood, and Jesus . . .

It was horrible. Embarrassing. Humiliating. But being without them was a torture he could never have guessed at. He loved them, and there was no way to deny or duck it. Knowing that, the only thing to do was the last thing he would have expected of himself.

Gently, carefully, a little at a time, he eased himself from beneath her head.

Bottom. He had hit the absolute and total bottom. No pride, no dignity, no nothing. But for the first time in weeks, he felt the possibility of hope. In the dim light diffusing into the room from the kitchen, he found his shoes and pants but couldn't locate his shirt. His underwear he didn't care about. Holding his clothes to his pale groin, he looked at Paris until his eyes teared. "Oh doll," he whispered, but something closed off his throat. Like a thief, he slipped into the kitchen and out the door, not even stopping to put on his pants and shoes until he was on the landing.

Outside it was so cold his skin shrunk immediately along his arms and across his chest. Did he only imagine, sweet Jesus, he saw her pale face at the window as he started the Packard and eased away from the curb?

He parked by a fireplug in front of D'Fonzio's, and as he hurried, bare-shanked and shirtless, across the sidewalk, a voice from up the dim sidewalk remarked: "What happened, bub, her husband get back?" His anger flared like a match but went out just as quickly, and he was up the stairs to his room two steps at a time. He snatched on a long-sleeved shirt, flung clothes into a pair of cheap suitcases, and swept whatever else was his—razor, toothbrush, boots, ties, dirty underwear, it didn't matter—into a laundry bag. When he'd carried it all to the foot of the stairs and dropped it, he pushed through the door to the bar.

"You'll need a taxi in the morning," he said to Womb Broom and Ironfield, slouched on their accustomed stools. "I'm dragging up."

"Goddamn!" Womb Broom said. "Friday's payday. If you're going home, wait till the eagle shits, and I'll go with you."

"I don't have time," Edward said.

"Goddamn, you could let a man finish his drink and think a minute!"

But he was already half out of the room. If Ironfield said anything, he hadn't heard it; but as he gathered up his things and the door closed behind him, he heard one last, surprised, disbelieving, and exasperated "Well, goddamn!" from Womb Broom.

Outside again, he snatched open the rear door of the Packard and threw his two suitcases and the laundry bag inside, but when he slammed it and started around to get in the driver's side, there was laughter.

"Shit, that lady's husband must be fuckin ferocious. Look at him go!" someone said.

"Hey, think a minute, bub. She may not give him your address," another remarked.

But he had started the engine and backed up over the sidewalk toward them. He saw bodies dodging but didn't know if they were men or boys. They seemed both good-size and very agile. There was a part of him that wanted to maim and be maimed, but he didn't have time for that either. "Crazy bastard!" "Mother-fuck!" they shouted. But he slammed the Packard into low, squealed off the sidewalk, and fishtailed into the street.

Hours later, far down the Pennsylvania Turnpike, doubt tried to cool the joy and clarity he felt at getting Madeline and James back. Suppose, no matter how contrite he was and no matter how much he insisted he'd changed, she wouldn't take him back. And how much had he changed except in his own mind? But that was everything, it seemed to him. And it would make all the difference. She'd see that. She couldn't help but see it, and they'd be a happy family again, happier than they'd ever been because he knew now where true happiness was and what it was made of.

He drove through a corner of Maryland and West Virginia and then down the endless Shenandoah, the dark mass of the

MADELINE TALLY

A few inches below the top of her windshield, the harvest moon sailed through the clouds above her as she drove down the mountain from Cedar Hill, and it made her realize she still hadn't gotten past the thrill of driving herself around in her own car, small and old and plain as it was. At least it was all hers, the only substantial, grown-up thing that had ever been hers alone. She laughed suddenly and softly. Now if she herself could only manage to feel substantial and grown-up for more than a few minutes at a time, she'd be getting somewhere. Still, it was both good and important to get up in the morning and drive herself to work and away from her family. And it was just as good to drive herself home and away from Leslie's house in the evenings.

This evening after dinner and lovemaking at Leslie's, it seemed particularly important that she'd been able to leave when she wished in her own car. The last two times she'd been to his house, she'd driven there and parked in his driveway so that she wouldn't have to feel dependent on his charity or his whim—although she'd never had reason to mistrust either—for a ride back to Cedar Hill and her car.

Still, she wasn't sure how she felt about his final gesture. Without her permission he'd fished her car keys out of her purse and held up a key of his own. "To the front door," he'd said, smiling and slipping the key on her ring.

She gave it a glance where it hung from her ignition in the dull light from her dash, and it seemed a little menacing.

At the foot of the mountain the valley spread out under such a bright moon, she could have driven without her headlights. Farmhouses and fields were lovely, and although the highway was wider than it had been when she was a girl, it followed the original roadbed, and very little of the scenery had changed. But she had changed.

When she pulled into her father's driveway and parked behind her sister's car, on a sudden impulse she took Leslie's key from her ring and shut it in the glove pocket before she got out. The air was cold and still held the spice and sweetness of fall, but there was a bite in it that made her think of winter. It wasn't dew stinging her through the open toes of her shoes, but frost. No wonder the fields and farmhouses had given back so much moonlight on the way home. She had a sudden vision of walking a path through the shoveled snow out to the beggarly trailer, and she thought again of Leslie's key.

But with the waiting period, the sheriff in Pittsburgh having to serve Edward with papers, the uncertainty of what Edward might do, all the necessary and inescapable proceedings, it could take a year. It could take two.

Recently Leslie had mentioned driving her to the airport in Asheville and putting her on a plane to Reno, Nevada, where, in only six weeks she could have her divorce. Was he serious? She didn't quite know, couldn't quite be sure. But to go to Reno like some movie star—he might just as well have suggested that she take a ship to India and become a snake charmer.

Slowly, carefully, so as not to slip, she crossed the frosted stile into the cow pasture.

The divorce would be all she could take even in familiar surroundings with her family about to help her remember who she was. But to fly on an airplane, which she'd never once done; to go to Nevada, where she'd never been; and to live there for six weeks in order to get a divorce? To do such things would be to lose herself completely. She knew that much. If she behaved in such a way, she'd never again know who she was.

By the time she got the door to the trailer open and stepped inside, her toes felt frozen and she'd twisted her ankle on the uneven ground of the cow pasture, which was no damned place for high heels, she told herself. But the trailer was warm; James had left her dim little bedside lamp on; and was, head and all, covered in his blanket and sound asleep. She patted his rump before she began to undress and wash her face and brush her teeth.

In bed at last, she realized how tired she was, not only in body but in mind. She was, she decided, a relatively new person and so, naturally, a little anxious and unsure. It was only normal, and comforting herself with that thought, she fell asleep almost at once.

In the morning she was surprised to see that James didn't appear to have moved, but she set about making breakfast, thinking he'd rouse any minute. Yet he kept himself turned away and completely covered. Finally she smacked him lightly on the rump. "Hey," she said and laughed, "roll out, sleepyhead, or you'll be late for school."

She poured his orange juice, fixed his cereal, and even put the milk in it for him, but although she'd seen him shift, he'd made no significant move toward getting up. "Hey, rise and shine, young man, right now!" she said. "You know the pressure on the bathroom. Your cousins, and me, and Lily, and . . ."

When at last he turned his misshapen face to her, she caught her breath and took an involuntary step backwards. "What on earth . . . !"

"I can't go to school today," he told her, his chin crinkling for a moment as though he might cry, but he seemed to master it. "I can't go tomorrow or next week either," he said.

"Just what happened?" she said.

James looked at the floor, cleared his throat softly, and then cleared it again. His left eye was half-closed, and his nose and mouth were so swollen, she wouldn't have known him. "A fight," he said.

"I blame your father for this," she said suddenly and bitterly. "I do! Why do you have to fight? *Why?*"

James looked at the floor and made no answer. At last he raised his shoulders and croaked, "I didn't want to."

For a moment Madeline was rigid with anger. Somehow Edward, James, and all males everywhere seemed maddeningly defective and bent on making her pay for their craziness. She looked at James who still had his shoulders raised as though her question had no answer, but wouldn't release him all the same, as though not being able to answer it had paralyzed him.

"I didn't want to fight," he said in a broken voice. "From the first day of school, I didn't want . . ." He stopped and wagged his head miserably between his hunched shoulders. "Girls don't understand," he said. "You don't know. There isn't any way you can know. . . . I couldn't . . . Lester had to save me . . . and he couldn't, but he . . . and now . . ." He shook his head and ceased, as though despairing of a voice that jumped from tenor to baritone to tenor again and was so disgustingly full of the garbage of emotion.

"Oh baby, I'm sorry," she said and went to him to kneel and hold him. "I'm so sorry," she told him, petting his back and neck, to soothe the stiffness out of him. But it wouldn't yield. "I didn't mean to be cross," she told him, trying to look into his discolored, swollen face, into his eyes; but he hid from her. He was just a child, she realized, and so small, so very small to be beaten so, and she was his mother. She felt totally culpable, and at the same time, unfairly put upon; and as she held and petted him, tears for both of them and for something larger and without a name began to start. She rocked him and crooned to him and crooned to herself; and, at last, James went limp and began to cry with her. He tried to talk, but for a long, long time she understood very little of what he said, except that he never, ever, wanted to go back to school again as long as he lived.

She had no idea how much time had passed until Lily came in for keys to move the little coupe in order to get to school. She was with them only a moment, but she was so casual and loving and almost cheerful that when she left, Madeline felt better. Even James seemed to take some sort of cue from his aunt, as though, if Lily could treat the matter so amiably, then maybe it wasn't the black disaster, the end of the world, he'd thought. Or maybe he'd just cried himself tranquil because Madeline was able, at last, to get some sense from him about what had happened and how long it had been going on.

"Why didn't you tell me about this Earl Carpenter weeks ago, sweetie?" she said, but James merely shrugged. "Why didn't somebody call me at work yesterday, for God's sake?"

"Aunt Lily was going to," James told her, "but Grandpaw said he didn't think I was going to die, and she could wait until quitting time to call and not bother you while you were working. Only the phone got busy, and you'd already gone when she got the store."

Madeline's next question died away in her throat.

"She didn't know where to try after that," James told her. "I think she called the Gateway Restaurant, maybe."

For reasons she couldn't admit, even to herself, her eyes started to fill again, but she quickly wiped them and got control of herself. "Well," she said. "Why don't I fix us a real good breakfast, run you by the doctor's office in Cedar Hill to see if it's really you under there, and then"—she cocked her head and winked at him—"force you to go to a movie?"

She took his chin gently and kissed him on the forehead. "I'll call Green's and tell them I won't be in until noon."

"Ugh," she said, picking up his bowl of cereal and making a face, "it's turned to glue! Makes you wonder what it does in your stomach," she said and laughed. "I'll fix us some bacon and eggs."

"I have to see Lester," James said.

JAMES
TALLY

The terrible thing was, although he'd been determined not to let her make him cry, he felt better. He didn't even feel betrayed by her mothering or his tears, not yet anyway.

"I'm about to pee my pants," she said, rushing suddenly from the trailer. "I'll be right back, but I've got to call the store too."

Washed out and frail, he sat where he was, thinking how easy and sweet it would be to give up and be forever what he'd been for the last half hour. He would love to go to a movie and watch something make-believe, something that couldn't come down from the screen and touch him or demand anything from him. And he would like to go to the doctor, just for the attention; except he knew he wasn't hurt. How great it would be, though, to go and be told he was very ill and didn't have long to live, three or four years, say. That was a thinkable amount of time, not at all like a lifetime; and it would change all his obligations. He could merely be gentle and wise and sympathetic. Who would expect more?

He could stay home. Read a lot. Sometimes he could listen to radio shows. Sometimes, if he felt well enough, he could be taken to movies or maybe for rides in the car. He thought it would be nice if he had to be in a wheelchair. But maybe it would be better if he only had to use canes. He had a vision of himself, pale, thin as a string, taking sad, slow, heroic strolls. Since there would be absolutely no harm in him, he wouldn't have to fear any. No one, not even Earl Carpenter and the Lanich twins, would dare do him injury, and he would be required to injure no one. Ill health and approaching death would be his only enemies, but only he would know that they were truly advocates because they would free him, bless him with peace at last, and he would bless everyone else. His mother. His father. Lester Buck. Everyone.

It was a vision of such sad happiness that he yearned for it, basked in it. If it wasn't perfection, it was for sure as close as the likes of him could come.

After a little while he realized the pressure in his own bladder had reached the threshold of pain, and he eased himself off the couch as though he really were very ill and almost unable to walk. At the open door he looked for his mother but didn't see her and slipped down the steps and around to the tongue of the trailer in order to put something between him and her approach, and there, took a long, delicious, shivering piss.

EDWARD
TALLY

He was exhausted but wide awake, and all his senses were rubbed raw and keen by the time he entered the remote keep of the mountains and valleys where, for years, he'd climbed poles and pulled cable for Watauga Light and Power Company. Every turn of the road, every bridge, stream, dwelling, barn, field, and fence row was familiar, down to what looked like the selfsame haystacks and shocks of corn. Even the ragweed in the ditches was just as he remembered, and, bruised by man or animal or merely the wind, the scent it gave up was exactly right. And there was the scent of fallen leaves, melting frost, apples, and earth. The cold, varnished smell of fall—as well as what his nose believed it smelled of fur and feather—the wild spice of squirrel and rabbit, grouse and quail from his hunting days, and of gunpowder too, which allowed him to possess them. And all this pierced him as though it were the very soul of homecoming, as though he were returning to his true religion, whose tenets were not merely Madeline and James, but all the aspects of this early morning. Why his family and this familiar ground seemed to share a single spirit, he didn't know, but it felt real and true.

He was sure Bertha Marshall had told him Madeline worked at Green's Department Store, and he couldn't think what to do except walk right in and present himself. He thought of stopping somewhere and calling first, but the idea scared him. He didn't want to give Madeline time to remember all she held against him, and so, work up her anger and defenses. Anyway, it seemed to him that if he appeared without warning, she'd somehow be able to see his love better, in a truer light. She'd have to acknowledge its power to pull him back to her across a great distance without any pale, mechanical announcement beforehand. Anyhow he didn't want to give her a chance to turn him down or to run off where he couldn't find her.

It was only a bit more than eight miles to Cedar Hill, fifteen or twenty minutes, and the closer he got, the more nervous he became. His hand shook when he fished a cigarette from his pocket and shook when he lit it. He glanced at himself in the mirror and saw that his eyes were red and he needed a shave, that his shirt was wrinkled and his hair was every which way, as though he'd just gotten out of bed. He looked like a drunkard and a bum, which he feared was just the way Madeline thought of him. He rubbed his face vigorously with his hand, as though that would help, and combed his hair with his fingers. Hell, maybe she would pity him. He'd take that. He'd take anything as long as it would make her hold still long enough to hear him out. If she would do that, then he was certain everything could be saved, that his life and hers and James's too would make sense once again.

He flipped his cigarette out the window and lit another, his last, and drove the final few miles into Cedar Hill with sweat rolling down his ribs despite the cold air pushing through the open window.

Downtown there was a parking place right in front of Green's Department Store, and he took it, although he sat behind the steering wheel for a long, long moment before he worked up the courage to go inside. He didn't see her anywhere on the main floor or on the mezzanine above. Finally, feeling very uncomfortable, he tapped a saleslady on the shoulder who was refolding a man's dress shirt. "I'm looking for Madeline Tally," he said. "Can you tell me if she works here?"

He had the feeling she gave him a quick appraisal. She seemed a little surprised and not much impressed. "I think she's not coming in until after lunch," she said brightly. "Can I give her a message?"

"I'm her husband," he said without knowing why he'd said it. It certainly wasn't a proper message, since he didn't want Madeline to know he wasn't in Pittsburgh until the moment she saw him; but somehow he wanted to set this lady straight.

"Oh," she said and gave him a different kind of glance. Although he couldn't quite read the results of this one, he could tell she was embarrassed. "Her son . . . your son wasn't feeling well, I think, and didn't go to school, and she was looking after him, so . . ." She blushed. "I didn't take the call, but I can find out for you, Mr. . . . . Tally."

"I'll just go on over," he said and blushed himself as though to keep her company.

In the car again, feeling compromised, he yanked the Packard into reverse and backed into the street without looking. Luckily no one was coming, but in glancing in the mirror long after it would have done him any good, he was struck again with how seedy he looked; and the sight of his once favorite barber shop a few doors down filled him with sudden inspiration. He had time. Plenty of time.

There was one new barber he didn't know, but otherwise nothing had changed, and being called by name and welcomed home with surprise and cheer made him feel better. He brought in a suitcase and asked to use the back room, where he could wash up and change. The black shoe shine, who was so old his brown eyes were nearly blue, brought him soap and a clean towel, and Edward stripped himself before the sink and washed Paris Pergola and Pittsburgh away, he hoped, forever.

When he got back in his car forty-five minutes later, the man who looked back at him from the rearview mirror was much more acceptable. His hair had been washed, cut, and combed. His face had been wrapped in hot towels, lathered, shaved clean, and massaged with shaving lotion. Errant hairs had been snipped from his eyebrows, nose, and ears. And finally, eyewash had made his eyes as clear as if he'd never missed a night's sleep or had a drink in all his days. "The works," Roy Harris, the owner, called it and claimed it had restored many a sinner.

MADELINE
TALLY

She'd had a well-deserved cry, a late breakfast, and a relaxed soak in the tub, so maybe it wasn't such a terrible day, but one of the good kind that drew people closer and made them stronger. Anyway that was how she'd decided to feel about it until someone knocked on the trailer door a little too loudly, and she opened it and found Edward. But in that moment of complete and utter cognition, all her thinking seemed suddenly meaningless, and everything she'd said and done in the last three months seemed null and void. He was supposed to be out of her life, a thousand miles away in another world. It was as if no time had passed since she'd seen him last and what had transpired from that day forward had only been a dream. If he existed, could she? She could not speak.

"Hello, honey," he said.

"Dad!" James said from somewhere behind her.

"Hey, squirt!" Edward said. "Your granddaddy said you'd had a little misunderstanding on the school grounds, and I see he wasn't foolin."

James came from behind her, brushing past her hip, not fast but not slow either, and was out the door and embracing his father. It wasn't something she'd ever seen him do, and it stung her.

"You came home!" James croaked, his face pressed into Edward's shirt.

Edward patted the crown of the boy's head. "We'll see, son," he said.

How dare you? she thought. What gives you the right? How dare you when we're trying to make a decent life! She felt tears coming to her eyes, but she swiped them away as quickly as they formed. "James, you run up to the house now," she said, surprising herself that she had a voice and that it sounded so even. "I'm sorry, honey."

Edward held James gently away, looked in his eyes, and nodded that it was all right, that he should do as he'd been told; and in spite of herself, Madeline wanted to slap them both for the understanding that seemed to pass between them so easily, when Edward had done nothing, nothing whatever, to earn it.

"Hey, I'll see you in a little bit, buddy," Edward said, but when he turned to her again, there was something so intimate in his eyes, she almost couldn't face it. All the years they had been married were contained in the way he was looking at her; still, she was having none of it and stared back at him steadily and evenly until his expression faded. He rubbed the back of his neck.

"So," he said, "how have you been?"

She wanted to tell him she'd been just dandy until a few minutes ago. "All right," she said.

"James has grown," he said. He laughed and shook his head. "That's some black eye and fat lip he's sporting."

She said none of the things that came to mind.

"I'd like to come in," he said.

She stepped back and allowed him to enter.

"Well," he said, glancing about as though he might tell her how nice the place looked but then realized how foolish it would sound. He sat down on the couch. "I talked to Bertha and Harley a little before I came out. They sure don't change much do they? They look real good. I even got the feeling they were glad to see me."

She said nothing.

"Jesus, honey, I drove a hell of a ways to get here."

"Why?" she said.

He looked at the floor and shook his head. "You can hold on to being mad longer and tighter than any woman I ever met," he said and laughed a short, bitter laugh.

She felt as if her life, her true life, had snapped back into focus, and the question wasn't *If he existed, could she?* The question was *Would she ever feel quite real, quite whole without him, or would she and the whole world always feel false and made up and out of kilter?* "I got over being mad a long time ago," she said. "I'm something else now. When I know what it is, I'll tell you."

"You sound mad," he said, looking at her.

She didn't know what to say, so she didn't say anything.

He smiled faintly, his eyes mild, his forehead a quandary of wrinkles. "You know, I think you've been mad at me for as long as I can remember."

"That's ridiculous," she declared, but she knew better. There was no reason to admit it because it was beside the point, and anyway, he'd earned her anger moment by moment and day by day. But it was true, she'd always been mad at him, and how odd to have married him, even so, and to have stayed with him for fourteen years. "I'm disgusted," she said, "not mad. I can't go back and live my life over, Edward Tally, but I can make a new one. I thought you understood that. I thought you agreed!"

He nodded.

Her voice turned suddenly pitiful, and her eyes welled up. "You said you'd give me a divorce. It's not right for you to be here!" She stamped her foot and hated herself at once for the impotence of the gesture. "It's not! It's not good for James and it's not good for me!"

"I love you," he said.

"Never," she said. "You never did. Don't even say it. We count! We matter! And if you love someone . . ." She glared at him, unable to go on. "Oh, don't you do it," she said in a softer voice. "Don't you dare do this."

"Just let me speak my peace," he said, looking at her in a way that carried with it all their time together, all their years of marriage, "that's all I ask."

She wanted to tell him no. She wanted to tell him that she wasn't interested, that whatever he said would only be a trap to pull her and James back into the old life they'd led. But another part of her wanted to hear what he had to say, dangerous or not, wanted his apologies and promises if only as an acknowledgment of all his wrongdoing. It would be small payment for what she had endured, but better than nothing, because, when she'd heard him out, she'd know the decision she'd already made was the only proper one, and she could tell him what he offered was too damned little and too damned late. She let him know with her expression that she'd listen, but that was all, and he seemed to understand because he wasn't able to look at her anymore.

He leaned forward, propped his elbows on his knees, and pondered the floor. "It's taken me a long time, all my life, to learn what I know now," he said at last. "Maybe it's not much. Maybe a fellow ought to know it from the start," he said, "but I didn't. I didn't know it until you asked me for a divorce." He looked up at her miserably, looked down again, and rubbed his hands together as though they were cold. "Hell," he said, "not even then, because I was mad and my pride was hurt."

His voice suddenly grew thin, as though from a blow to the throat. "Maybe I didn't even know it all until yesterday, until last night." He cleared his throat, but when he went on, his voice was just as hoarse and thin as before. "I love my family," he said. For a long time he didn't say anything more. "Without you and James," he added at last, his voice scarcely more than a hoarse whisper, "I don't have anything." He shook his head as though the knowledge still astonished him. He cleared his throat again and sat with his head hung between his shoulders, rubbing his palms together.

There was nothing to fling back in his face, she realized. No apologies. No promises. Who but a man, and an arrogant man at that, would come so far to say so little? Not a word about coming home drunk time after time, about not coming home at all, about yanking them all around the country without so much as begging their pardon, abandoning them altogether whenever and wherever he chose. But even the offenses were beside the point; it was the attitude that allowed it all to happen that incensed her. Was that all he was going to say? Was he done? He could have written a postcard.

She was suddenly out of control. She knew it but could not stop it from happening. It was as though the shock of seeing him again was just now having its full effect. She could feel it inside her like a fire consuming her from her belly to the very roots of her hair, but doing something strange and icy to her genitals, weakening her thighs and knees, making her ears ring. For a moment she thought she might faint. She had to get away from him, there wasn't any doubt of that. She looked about without knowing exactly what she was looking for until she spied her car keys and took them up, her purse, and snatched it. "I won't . . . I can't stand . . ." She could have pulled out her hair that he was in her life again, that he was right before her in the flesh. "I have to go to work!" she said and rushed out of the trailer. She felt deaf, dumb, and blind and had gotten in her car and started it before she realized his car was behind her and she couldn't get out of the driveway. She thought of blowing her horn. She thought of backing into him and trying to push him into the highway; but then she realized if she pulled up and didn't mind getting into Lily's flowers, she might be able to miss him. She did exactly that, and although she was out of control and left ugly half-moon tire tracks through the garden, she didn't hit the Packard and managed to slew her little coupe around into the highway. She didn't even think of James until she was in high gear and going as fast as her car would go, but she couldn't help that either. She couldn't do anything except what she was doing until she got her wits together.

JAMES
TALLY

He climbed the stile and went on toward the house where he'd
been sent. Although it wasn't cold, he was shivering; and the
heat from the wood cook stove in the kitchen would have felt
good, except he dreaded his grandmother. She was such a strong,
steady, dignified woman, she would be shamed and grieved by
what was going on. It wasn't likely that she'd ask him any
questions, but he didn't want to be around her or his grandfather
either. It would be painful and embarrassing. He didn't even
want his grandfather looking out the window of the post office
and catching sight of him. Trembling from excitement and fear,
he crept up on the porch and sat on its front edge by the quince
bushes, where an obtuse triangle of sunlight still reached the
floorboards and warmed them.

He hugged his knees to his chest, awed by the sight of his
father's car in the driveway. Could it really be there? Right
there? It was all milky down its sides with road film from having
brought his father such a great distance to be with them, to be
with his mother at that moment. Maybe this time it would work.

But as far back as he could remember there had been some
persistent, incomprehensible trouble between his mother and
father. Even in the good times he'd always been able to feel it
lurking just under the surface; and sooner or later, he'd hear
its edge in his mother's voice or glimpse some dark hint of it in
his father's eye. And sometimes, when the trouble broke through

152

and they fought, they fought about him, James, so he knew he had a part in it too.

All his shivering seemed to have shaken something loose inside him so that he could feel it vibrating in the center of his chest like a tuning fork. "Please," he said and began to rock himself back and forth, "please, please, please." He knew better than to think into words what he wanted. For sure it wouldn't happen if he spoke it aloud or even thought it. Something powerful seemed to haunt him just in order to see to it that what he most needed and desired never occurred, and he could feel it sniffing around him now, so he cleared his mind and rocked himself to-and-fro.

Thinking it might betray him even to be caught looking at his father's car, he wedged his chin against his knees and stared at the quince bushes. He could see a bit of his cheek puffed up into his line of vision, and he could see his own eyelashes because his eye was so swollen. His eyelashes looked as big as tree limbs, were incredibly tangled and disorganized, and seemed safe to think about. So was his lip, which felt heavy and tight and itchy as though it had been stung by a bee. But that led him to thinking about Earl and how afraid of Earl he'd been and how he hadn't followed his father's advice at all; yet he'd gotten a beating just the same. Not facing up to a bully, just as his father had warned, never worked. It made his stomach hurt to think that if he'd stood up to Earl from the beginning, he would have paid no bigger price, but he'd have been brave. So, after all, what right did he have to hope for anything?

He tried not to think of that. He rocked himself and tried not to think of anything at all, as though if he could empty his head of all thoughts, he might be insignificant enough to escape proper justice, might be invisible enough for fate to ignore. But the devastated musette bag of fishing equipment in the closet came into his mind. Sure he'd asked his mother if he could borrow some hooks and sinkers that first time, but he'd never asked again, and little by little, through carelessness and waste and by giving away what didn't belong to him, almost everything had disappeared. And in that same closet sat his father's shoes, one of their tongues brutally cut away. He'd asked no one if he could destroy the shoes because he'd already known what the answer would be, and so he was twice guilty, guilty before he'd even committed the act, which was far worse. He had no rights at all. He knew nothing was going to turn out well because he'd been pushing everything the other way, and there was no one to thank but himself.

Right then he saw his mother coming, but he wouldn't look at her. He didn't have to. At a glance, he'd seen her temper in the way she was walking. He gazed at the quince bushes, the stalks of his own eyelashes, unwilling to admit the worst, but not at all surprised by it, except in the way he was always surprised by the actual appearance of the bad news he had predicted for himself. He heard her get in her car. Heard it start. But he didn't look up, not even when the commotion of her leaving demanded it. He could feel, without having to look, the anger she'd left in her wake, and it blew right through him.

EDWARD
TALLY

For a moment he didn't quite know what had happened, but the door was standing open and she was gone. He'd seen and heard her all right, only he didn't quite take it in because he'd thought it would be different. Hell, he'd imagined she might hug him, kiss him, weep for joy, be happy—maybe because, all through the night, he'd uncovered his own true feelings, planned his confession, looked forward to setting things right, getting his family back, being a better man, an honest man at last; and he'd been so wrapped up in his confession and vision of things that it took him a few moments after she'd gone to understand what she'd said and done. She was still mad all right, madder than a hornet, and he doubted that she'd listened to a word he'd said.

He heard her start the car, racing the engine, as she always did. But he was parked behind her, and since she'd gone off half-cocked, she hadn't thought of that, and he'd have to let her out. He almost laughed, whether at himself or her, he didn't know. How could he have thought it would be so easy, as though sorting out the disposition of his own heart was the hard part and the rest would just naturally fall into place? As sad as it was, it was also comforting and a little funny. Some things a fellow could count on, and in a scary kind of way, they made him feel at home. He'd let her out, but not before he'd told her again that he loved her. Maybe he could think of something funny to say. Something to break the tension. It wasn't impossible that she would laugh. He got up and stepped out of the trailer, gently closing the door behind him. He remembered a time or two when he'd been able to convert her fury to laughter, but as he turned, already smiling at the prospect, he saw her careen the little coupe off the driveway, somehow sling it around the Packard and gun off toward Cedar Hill.

"Son of a bitch," he said.

For a moment he thought of chasing her down and having it out with her, but he thought better of it. Let her cool off, he told himself. It had been a shock for him to appear out of nowhere, and naturally it would bring back her anger. She never did well with surprises; he didn't remember ever giving her one that worked the way he'd thought it would. Okay, he told himself, all right. It was embarrassing, in front of the boy and her family and all, but the only thing to do was acknowledge it and make light of it. Buy her some flowers, say. Wait her out. Grin and tell everyone that she was still mad as the dickens. Be patient with her, until, some damned way or other, he could convince her he was a changed man.

He took a deep breath and let it whistle out through his nose. His eyes were suddenly tired, and every muscle seemed weak. Even the air in his lungs felt thin and oily, unhealthy from all the cigarettes he'd smoked. He crossed the stile, sadness and disappointment tugging at him, and went on toward the house, his hands shoved in his pockets and what he suspected was a very silly and addled grin on his face, although he figured it was probably the best expression he had to offer.

As he stepped up on the front porch, he noticed James and said, "Hey, worrywart!"

James was hugging his knees to his chest and rocking himself back and forth. He didn't look up.

"Say," Edward said, "aren't you supposed to be in school?"

The boy stopped rocking but otherwise didn't move. "Are you going back to Pittsburgh?" he asked in a grown-up, matter-of-fact voice that took Edward so by surprise, it left him nothing to say. The question seemed impertinent and absolutely to the point. He pondered the skinny child, who kept himself stubbornly turned away, and then sat down beside him. He took the pack of Luckys out of his shirt pocket, shook out a cigarette, and lit it.

"You don't smoke yet, I reckon," he said. "That's good," he remarked after a moment as though he'd gotten an answer. "I was already smoking when I was your age." He gave a little snort of laughter. "Use to pick butts up off the street. We called it shooting snipe. Don't know why. I'd smoke those and coffee grounds. Yeah, and corn silks and rabbit tobacco too. Hell, I'd even roll up newspaper with nothing in it, light the end, and smoke the news. Sometimes suck a flame down my throat, seemed like a foot," he said and laughed. "That's when we lived in Atlanta, on the edge of colored town where my Daddy sold insurance to the colored folks. Collected maybe fifty, seventy-five cents a week from them when he could." Edward looked off across the valley. Pondered the mountains. The fall colors were faded at the highest elevations; some of the trees had even lost their leaves up there; but they were still bright in the foothills. He pondered the fertile creek bottoms, the pastures and fields. "Wasn't pretty country like this."

What the hell was he babbling for? The boy already knew how grubby his childhood had been, knew all about how much trouble he'd had with his father, and how early he'd left home. Maybe he'd never told him about the smoking, but, hell. . . . So, of course, here he was again trying to make James feel better by comparison; and since James was about ten times smarter than he was, the boy had no doubt been on to him from the beginning, whereas he was just figuring it out himself. Still, dammit, what sort of comfort was there to offer? "Yessir," he said, "this is just about the prettiest country I ever saw. Do you know what *Watauga* means in Indian?"

James sat with his chin wedged against his knees, his rocking diminished to almost invisible oscillations. He did not speak.

"Well," Edward said, "I don't know for a fact, but I heard

it meant the land of many beautiful waters." He took a drag from his cigarette. "It's the rainfall that makes these mountains so pretty. Makes all the good creeks and rivers."

"You and Mother are still going to get a divorce, aren't you?" James said in his matter-of-fact voice.

"Ahhh, son," Edward said. He rubbed his eyes and the back of his neck. "You know," he said at last, "I think I've been better than my pop, but I haven't been so good with you and your mother. Maybe I just don't have another chance coming." He took a drag from his cigarette but found he didn't want it anymore and snapped it off his thumb across the quince bushes and down toward the road. The boy kept as still as held breath. Edward didn't know what to do about him, so he caught him by the neck and shook him gently as though to shake the sadness out of him. "Don't count me out though, squirt," he said.

James allowed himself to be shaken, but his mood didn't alter. "I've got to see my friend," he said.

"Don't you boys go to school once in a while?" Edward said.

"I don't have to go for a week and a half because of the fighting," James said.

"Ahhh." Edward nodded. "I guess you started this little rumpus then, huh?"

"All three of us were suspended," James told him, getting up but then standing motionless, his head hung, as if he didn't know whether or not he was free to go.

Edward laughed and got up himself. "You ought not to fight them two at a time if you can help it."

"Me and Lester fought Earl Carpenter," the boy said, looking into some intermediate space beyond his feet. "Not at the same time," James said and shrugged. "Earl had already whipped me, and Lester was only just trying to drag him off."

"Ahhh," Edward said and nodded. "Well," he added cheerfully, as though he didn't mind being abandoned a second time, "I'll give you a lift to see your buddy then."

Without looking at him, James went off into the house. "I need to tell Grandmother where I'm going," he said as he went through the door.

How incredibly urgent it had seemed all through the night that he get back to his family, explain himself, set things right. And here Madeline had gone off to work, and James was going off to see his friend. So where was he, Edward, going to go? What was he going to do with himself? Of course Harley and Bertha would put him up. Although Madeline certainly wouldn't thank them. No. And he wasn't welcome in the trailer either. Well, there was a tourist court in Cedar Hill.

A buzz of uneasiness made him check his billfold. Eighty-four dollars. A very good thing that he had cashed and not deposited his last paycheck. He could go to the bank in Cedar Hill and have his funds transferred. He had almost four hundred dollars in Allegheny Bank and Trust. Yes, and he'd call Womb Broom and tell him where Star Electric could forward his pay. He stuffed his billfold back in his hip pocket, but he didn't feel any better. He felt much worse. Completely empty and lost. Jesus, but he'd thought they would at least talk to him, listen to him, hear him out; but maybe, at last, he had ceased to matter to them. It was an awful lonesome thought, but it just might be true.

JAMES
TALLY

He told his grandmother where he was going and then went out the kitchen door and down the driveway when he knew his father was waiting on the porch. He was sulking, making his father pay a price, and he felt bad about it, but he couldn't make himself stop. He let himself in the car and sat quietly on the passenger's side until his father came down the walk and got under the steering wheel.

"You sorta sneaked around the other way on me," his father said, grinning good-naturedly.

He didn't say anything.

"Well," his father said and took the steering wheel in both hands as though making a strangely important gesture of it, "where does this buddy of yours live?"

"That way," James told him and pointed.

After they'd driven a little way, his father remarked that it was a strong friend who would jump into a fight for his buddy, but James merely looked out the window.

"What did you say his name was?" his father asked.

"Lester Buck," James said.

Out of the tail of his eye he saw his father wagging his head side to side as though puzzled. "No," Edward Tally said, "I don't reckon I know that family." He shook his head again. "Working for Watauga Light and Power Company, I figured I'd met just about everybody, one time or another."

"They don't have electricity," James said.

"Ahhh," his father said. "Well there's still some families in these mountains who don't see why they can't get along without it." He cocked his head and grinned. "Course it's hard to say they're wrong, since it wasn't so very long ago when the whole damned world had to get by without."

"They're poor," James said, keeping his face turned away. "That's why they don't have electricity or much of anything else."

Edward Tally nodded.

"Everybody makes fun of Lester because he has such sorry clothes and his mother gives him these stupid haircuts, but he's the best friend I ever had."

"I'd like to meet him," his father said.

"He got worse beat up than me," James said. All at once his eyes grew wet. "He wouldn't give up. He's terrible at fighting, but he wouldn't give up. He's not afraid of anything," James said.

His father didn't speak.

"Why can't I be like that?" James blurted. Was he going to cry now in front of his father too? What was wrong with him? The way he was behaving didn't make any sense. What did it have to do with the awful chasm between his mother and father?

"Everybody's afraid of something, son," his father said.

"Not Lester," James insisted. "Not you." He looked out the window through brimming eyes, wiping his nose on his sleeve and his eyes with the heel of his hand.

"Me and Lester too," his father said.

Not like me, James thought. All at once the landscape outside the window came into focus, and he realized they had missed a turn. "We were supposed to turn off back yonder," he said, wiping his nose on his sleeve again. His father cocked himself up on one hip, got a handkerchief out of his pocket, handed it to him, and told him to blow his nose. When they came to a farm road on the right, his father pulled in and turned around.

"It's just that folks are different," his father said. "Some fellows are afraid of heights or snakes; some are afraid of water

or being in the woods, or big cities." He took James by the
neck and gripped it, but not hard enough to hurt him. "And
you're not afraid of any of those things, squirt," he said and
laughed.

His father did not understand, but there was no explaining
it. "It's just there," James said and pointed to the wagon road,
rough and half washed out, winding up from the blacktop on
the right. He hadn't expected his father to drive it, but the car
paused only a moment before his father shifted the Packard into
low and turned up the rutted dirt track. The car bounced and
lost traction and scraped something underneath, but then it took
hold and climbed, James's side seeming to hang off the edge in
space.

The labored sound of their approach brought first Roy and
then Effie Buck out on the open dogtrot. If Roy was surprised
or curious about an automobile appearing where few had ever
been before, he didn't show it; he looked like a man who knew
who and where he was, but Effie seemed worried and frightened.
Still, James was out of the car almost before it stopped in order
to set their minds at ease.

"Why chile!" Effie said, "we didn't know who in the
world . . ."

"My dad brought me," James said, already embarrassed and
puzzling over just exactly how to make introductions when his
father got out of the car and Roy Buck came down the steps,
and the two men shook hands and called each other "Mr. Tally"
and "Mr. Buck" and seemed to share at once the same shy,
formal, but easy friendliness with each other, as though it were
all written down in a book somewhere that both men had read.

Effie stayed on the porch and did not speak, as though that
were a part of the book too, not even when Edward Tally
touched the brim of an imaginary hat and nodded to her.

"Mrs. Buck," he said, but Effie merely nodded back, very
formal and ladylike.

"Is Lester around?" James wanted to know.

"He is, son," Roy said with a gentleness that made James

uneasy, although he didn't, at first, know why, "but he's kinda puny."

James looked to Effie on the porch as though for confirmation or explanation and saw that she was caught in an agony of worry, although it was all contained in her eyes and in the way her big, mannish shoulders were hung, so that if he hadn't known her, he wouldn't have seen it. "He's in bed, honey," she told him.

"James explained to me how your boy took up for him, Mr. Buck," Edward Tally said. "If there's something we can do, we'd sure like to do it."

"Well, I've been to a neighbor's down the creek this mornin to call the doctor out, and I reckon there's not a thing to do right now but wait on him to get here." Roy turned to James and gave him a good facsimile of his usual easy grin. "Don't know why you couldn't look in on him though. Just let me take a peek and see is he awake?"

From the dogtrot Effie said that she'd just made a fresh pot of coffee and would be pleased if James's father sat with them while the boys had their visit; and James's father said he'd be glad to if it wasn't too much trouble; and the three of them went up on the dogtrot, and Roy stuck his head in Lester's room and said in his unusually gentle voice that somebody had come to see him who sure wasn't walking, and then stepped back and let James in and softly shut the door behind him. It was very dim in Lester's bedroom, and though James didn't know why, it always smelled a little like a snuff box. Out on the dogtrot he heard Effie say, "We just think the world and all of that boy of yours," but he couldn't make out his father's soft response.

"Hey," Lester said in a weak voice. He appeared to be looking out of his small window, with its old, green, wavy panes of glass. "You didn't tell me you was rich. That there's a big ole Packard."

Him? Rich? It hurt to hear it, as though he'd been treated like a stranger in a place he'd thought was home. But Lester's face, when James's eyes got used to the dim light enough to see it, made him forget everything else. James was surprised Lester could talk, his lips were so swollen and cracked; and both his eyes had swelled so tight, it was hard to believe he could see anything at all.

"How you feelin?" James said.

"Ha," Lester said in a voice that was much more whisper than laugh, "I reckon nowhere near as bad as they tell me I look."

"Your face is real bad," James said. "It must hurt like crazy."

"Nawh," Lester said, "it don't bother."

"It don't look like you can even see," James said.

"I can," Lester said. Very slowly, almost too slowly to believe, Lester shifted his position in bed. "I can see out better than you can see in," he said. "I just ain't got the strength of a fly."

James didn't know what to say.

"I'm sorta wind broke," Lester said.

"Can I get anything for you?" James said. "God, Lester, I'm sorry I started it with Earl Carpenter."

Lester moved again in bed. With infinite slowness he crossed his legs as though on purpose to look casual. "Poppa's got asthma. Figures I do too," he said. He seemed to take a rest, and James could see his eyeballs move behind the puffed eyelids in the same fashion he might have seen the eyeballs move behind the closed eyelids of someone sleeping. At last he said, "I reckon asthma ain't got much to do with Earl Carpenter."

"Do you want me to leave you alone so you can sleep?" James said.

"Nawh," Lester said. "Can't sleep noway. Feels like a mule is standing on my chest."

Someone stepped up on the dogtrot and helloed, and not much more than a moment later the doctor came through the door with his satchel and Effie on his heels with an oil lamp. Behind Effie, James glimpsed his father, who with a single motion of his head told him to come out and give the doctor some room.

James sat on the steps up to the dogtrot and scratched Lester's little fice behind the ears, while Edward Tally and Roy Buck found things to talk about that somehow acknowledged the doctor's visit and the friendship of their sons without speaking of either. It seemed a long time until the doctor came out of Lester's room with Effie on his heels as mute as a shadow.

"Well," the doctor said with a wry grin, "the lumps and bruises sure are colorful, but they don't worry me much."

He was a young man, the doctor. James thought he looked too young to be an actual doctor, at least until he began to shake his head and rub the back of his neck and sigh.

"I just didn't find any evidence of asthma. His lungs sound open and clear. No coughing or wheezing or any of that. But I'm afraid he needs to be in the hospital," the doctor said and gave Roy and Effie a long, serious look. "I've got two more calls to make down the road, and I can take him on my way back, but I'd feel better if you'd let me call the ambulance from Cedar Hill to come and fetch him."

"Lordamercy," Effie said.

"Now, Momma," Roy said.

"What is it, doctor?" Effie said. "What's wrong with my baby?"

"Mrs.," the doctor said and stroked his jaw, "it would be foolish of me to say a whole lot without us getting him to the hospital where we can have a better look at him."

"Lordamercy," Effie said.

"How about taking him in my car?" Edward asked.

The doctor gave James's father and the Packard a glance and then looked at Roy and Effie where they were standing together. "It would be lots quicker than waiting on me," he said. "And cheaper than an ambulance. And since they have got to come all the way from Cedar Hill and find this place before they can start back . . . I think I'd like that best. I'll call the hospital first thing down the road and tell them Lester's coming."

"I'd be obliged," Roy said to James's father, but Edward Tally had already waved the remark away and started toward the car. He moved his belongings from the rear seat to the trunk and backed the car closer to the house while Roy and the doctor carried Lester out between them as though he were sitting in a chair. Effie disappeared from the dogtrot, but no more than a moment after Roy and the doctor had gotten Lester into the backseat, she was back in a dark dress and with combs holding up her hair. She was also carrying a suit coat for Roy, who was otherwise wearing overalls.

"Don't jostle him any more than you can help getting down to the road," the doctor told James's father and hurried off toward the highway and his car.

When they were all in the Packard, Effie and Roy on either side of Lester in back, and he and his father in front, his father began to ease down the wagon road as though the automobile were made of glass. "Everybody all right?" Edward Tally asked when they reached the blacktop.

"Absolutely," Roy said.

But somehow, after that, conversation didn't seem possible, as if the suspense over Lester and the strangeness of the five of them being in a car together were too much to overcome, as if there were no good way to talk about those things and no way to ignore them enough to talk about anything else.

It wasn't until they got into Cedar Hill that Roy Buck said, "We surely do appreciate you carrying us to town. I hate a-puttin you to the trouble."

"No trouble to it," James's father said. He took James by the neck and shook him fondly and said, "I don't know if this boy here can get a stream from a cow or not, or if I can do much better, but if milking times come and you don't want to leave the hospital, one of us will look after the milking. I know we can't do enough damage to make a cow go dry in just one evening."

"I never give the milking a thought," Roy Buck said. "Forgot about it altogether."

"Well you don't have any business thinking about it," James's father said. "Anyhow," he said, "who's to say they won't let us take Lester on back home once they get a better look at him."

Of course the Bucks didn't have a way home, any more than they'd had a way into Cedar Hill. James looked at his father's calm, mild face in profile and realized that his father understood

Roy and Effie Buck absolutely. Neither of them would have asked for anything further, no matter how badly they might have needed it. They would not presume. Roy Buck would walk home to do his milking before he would ask Edward Tally to make a special trip; either that, or he'd let the cow go untended, streaming milk from her full udders, if Lester were too sick to leave.

Somehow his father had managed to make the whole situation lighter, so that James felt comfortable enough to turn around in his seat and ask Lester how he was feeling.

"Not too bad," Lester said, and for all his damaged face, he did look a little better and more like himself. And Roy and Effie looked somehow more at ease too, or anyway as much as they could with Roy wearing a suit coat and having the top of his work shirt buttoned in severe, tieless dignity about his neck, and Effie with her hair up in combs and wearing a dress that seemed a little too tight and maybe wanted to be black but had gone greenish like a dragonfly's wings.

For a moment James felt almost unbearably proud of all of them, his father and himself included; but a few blocks later they passed Green's Department Store, and he spied his mother's gray Ford coupe, and an entirely different mood began to come over him. Although he couldn't have said why, by the time they reached the huge granite-and-brick hospital, the five of them seemed flawed and lost and silly, as though nothing but sorrow would ever find them.

His father pulled around to the emergency entrance and stopped. "You boys sit tight while we find out what's next," he said, and with a kind of threadbare dignity, Roy and Effie entered the hospital with Edward Tally, while James looked at Lester and fretted.

"Don't worry," James said.

"I ain't," Lester said; "I'm mostly embarrassed. But it's kindly interesting too. Ain't never been in a hospital before."

"You were when you were born," James said.

"I was born at home," Lester said, but he was moving his

head slowly, aiming the puffed slits of his eyes around the car. "This is *some* automobile," he said. "How long you got to go to school to do what your daddy does?"

"He never finished high school," James said. "He took a ninety-day course someplace to learn about electricity. I forget where."

Lester nodded carefully just as a black man in a white uniform came up pushing a wheelchair, a nurse and Effie close behind him. Although Lester claimed he could walk, it didn't do him any good, and he was lifted into the wheelchair as though he were all but paralyzed. The nurse even covered him with a blanket, although it wasn't really very cold, and whisked him off into the bowels of the hospital where they couldn't follow.

Inside, however, a cheerful lady sitting behind a long white counter told them where to wait. There would be a doctor in to talk to them, she said, just as soon as they got Lester examined and properly settled.

"Folks," James's father said and blushed as though suddenly embarrassed, "I've got to run an errand or two, but I'll be back as quick as I can." He reached for Roy Buck's hand and gave it a single pump as though to seal a bargain. "If you can think of anything you need," Edward Tally said, "I'll bring it back in a jiffy."

"We don't need a single thing," Roy Buck said, "but we sure are obliged."

"Well," Edward Tally said, looking at James, "I expect the shoe's on the other foot. I wouldn't worry though," he said, taking in Effie as well as Roy, "it looks like Lester is in real good hands, and I expect they'll have him fixed up pretty quick.

"Son?" Edward Tally said to James and nodded toward the exit.

James followed him outside without having the least notion of what he might want.

"Squirt," his father said, "I'm going to have to find me a place to spend the night. That shouldn't take long, but I haven't had a whole lot of rest lately, and I'm just about to go under.

I need about an hour or so of sleep, and then, hell, I'll be as good as new."

"Okay," James said.

"You can come with me or you can stay here," his father said. "You're welcome to do either, but my ass is dragging out my tracks and I've got to lie down for a little bit."

"I'll stay," James said. "Thank you," he said, "for bringing Lester and Roy and Effie to the hospital."

"They're good folks, son," his father said. "I'm proud they think so well of you." He looked at James very seriously for a few seconds, winked, doubled up his fist, and bonked James on the head with it as though he were driving a cork in a bottle; then he turned and went off toward the Packard. "I'll be back in two hours, squirt," he said over his shoulder.

MADELINE
TALLY

Exactly as if she'd had too much coffee, her fingers dithered over the keys of her adding machine and were cold; she couldn't concentrate for more than a few seconds at a time, if that; and every fifteen or twenty minutes she had to go pee. Each time she returned to her desk, she had to reacquaint herself with her bookkeeping as though she'd never done it before, but the next moment would find her in a daze, having done nothing at all.

"Damn you, Edward Tally!" she'd whisper through clenched teeth, grip her hands to fists, and try to get back to work again. But the columns of debits and credits, the stacks of sales slips and order forms, would make no sense to her until she rediscovered the basic logic and principles of her job. And just as likely, at that very moment she'd spy one of the salesgirls looking up at her with curiosity, since Leslie Johnson had been calling for her at lunch and quitting time for better than a month; and today, one man, claiming to be her husband, had come in to ask for her midmorning, and Leslie had come in with a bouquet of flowers at noon, wanting to take her out to eat.

Maybe she should go to Reno and get a divorce after all. What did it matter that she would lose herself and never know who she was again? My God, hadn't she already done so the moment she'd begun to jump in and out of Leslie's bed? But perhaps the problem was that she'd lost herself long before.

Long, long before. The moment when she'd let Edward Tally into her life.

All at once she wanted to talk to Leslie and snatched up the phone, but when she got his office, his secretary said he was with a client. "Is this Mrs. Tally?" the secretary asked. "Yes," Madeline said. "Oh, I thought it was," the secretary replied cheerfully; "shall I have him call when he's free?" "No," Madeline said on a sudden impulse, "no, don't bother." What did she think she was going to say to him after all? What did she expect him to do for her? She wrung her hands for a moment and then on an impulse, called home. But when her mother's voice—perfectly familiar, country curious, drawn out—answered, "Helllloooh?" she didn't know why she'd called her either, no matter that the impulse had been urgent. "I just wanted to know how James was doing," she told her mother. "Madeline, is that you?" Bertha Marshall said. "Of course, Momma," she said, a little hurt by such a question. "Well, James went off with his poppa, down to the Bucks'," her mother said, as though it were perfectly normal for Edward to be home and James to go off with him.

Had the world turned against her? Was she being isolated, cut off, on purpose? "Momma, please . . ." she began, but then had no idea what she wished to say, what she meant to ask for. She gripped the phone, and her mouth and chin began to tremble. Help, of course; she needed help. It would have been at least a little comforting if her mother had recognized her voice. Leslie's secretary had done that much. "'Momma, don't let Edward stay there. For me, don't let him."

"Why chile . . ." her mother remarked with her voice full of wonder. "Well, he hasn't asked," her mother said, "but, mercy, we couldn't deny him."

"Momma, I can't lose what I've gained," Madeline said.

"What you've gained?" her mother repeated. "I guess I don't understand about that."

Was it criticism she heard? A simple statement of honest ignorance? Sadness?

"Daughter, if you don't want him here; then it's you that will have to tell him, fer it will not be your poppa or me."

"Good-bye, Momma," Madeline said and put the phone gently back in its cradle even as she heard her mother's voice saying good-bye, as though her mother's voice, too, were a physical thing she could set down. For a moment she felt so anxious and frantic that the very roots of her hair tingled, and her heart seemed to flutter. She put her face in her hands, pressed her fingertips against her closed eyes, and leaned her elbows on her desk. There wasn't anyone who could help her, she realized. In fact everyone thought she was wrong: her mother, her father, James, certainly Edward. Some part of her even suspected Leslie, as though, since she had betrayed her husband with him, he wasn't quite so sure that someday for good and sufficient reasons known only to herself, she wouldn't betray him as well.

Was it true? Was she evil and selfish? She seemed to herself to be innocent and misjudged, but in a manner she would never be able to justify or prove. Perhaps not even to God.

She pressed her eyes with her fingertips and took slow, deep breaths until she felt calmer and her heart settled down. All right, she thought. All right then. She had work to do. If she didn't get it done, it could quickly become as unmanageable as everything else around her, and she would be lost.

She had her job, which she'd gone out and got herself and could do. She had her little car, which she'd picked out and bought without asking anyone's advice, and unexciting as it was, it also conveyed her wherever she wished to go. They were small things to count, but she couldn't think of anything else right then, and they seemed to constitute some sort of begin-ning—she had a job and made money, and she wasn't, well, stranded, she supposed. She wiped her eyes and set grimly to work, as though adding up her own simple account made plain, once again, for all its false complications, the accounts of Green's Department Store.

EDWARD
TALLY

After renting his room, he knew at once he was too tired to sleep and so got back in his car and drove three miles to a ramshackle bootlegger's place he knew in Perkinsville. The bootlegger himself was serving a prison term, but his brother and nephew were doing business as before, except that they had very little bonded whiskey on hand, and what they had was cheap and vile. Edward decided to settle for a mason jar of corn liquor and took a few exploratory and fiery swallows on the way back to Cedar Hill. Propped in bed with his shoes off, he took one last drink, which seemed almost smooth. As though he were smoking a cigarette and blowing a smoke ring, he pursed his lips and let out a long sigh. "That's better," he said aloud, and, resolving to think of absolutely nothing, closed his weary eyes. The corn liquor, as it always seemed to do, created a pleasant warm spot at the crown of his head.

He had no idea what woke him, maybe a bad conscience; but when he jumped broad awake, it was nearly dark in his room. His shoes tied too hastily and too tight and his hair combed with his fingers, he hurried out to the car, glad to see that the sun had only just gone down and there was more daylight than he'd thought. But it had been a little more than four hours since he'd been at the hospital. What if Lester had been examined and released and the Bucks had been ready to leave no more than a few minutes after he'd left? It had been stupid not to let them know where he could be reached. They could have been waiting for hours. Or maybe they'd had to give up and go off to hunt themselves some difficult and unlikely and inconvenient way back home.

But when he got inside the hospital and discovered the little waiting room where they were sitting, he knew at once that there was a different and bigger problem. What he saw in their faces slowed his steps and made him forget any apology he might have made. Effie and James sat in their uncomfortable-looking chairs as if they'd gone deaf and dumb, and only Roy got up to meet him. By unspoken agreement, they walked a little way down the hospital corridor together; and, noticing a side exit, they turned as though they were of one mind, passing through two doors before they found themselves outside where benches and bushes and trees still had shape but had lost all color to the dusk.

With bewilderment in his voice, after a moment Roy said: "They claim it's his heart."

"That can't be right," Edward said. "He's just a kid."

"They say it's likely his teeth that caused it," Roy said. He was looking off into the darkness and speaking as though he weren't talking to anyone but only speaking the words aloud in an effort to understand them and believe them himself. He put one of his big square hands in his suit coat pocket, fumbled a moment, and came out with a piece of paper, which he held out to Edward. "This doctor I don't even know wrote it down for me."

Edward took the slip of paper and held it up to catch light from the entrance behind them. "Bac . . . t . . . er . . . ial En . . . do . . . car . . . d . . . i . . . tis." He gave his head a shake. "Bacterial endocarditis," he said. He'd never heard of it.

"It's like it's a poison that's come from Lester's sorry teeth that's got around his heart some way," Roy said. "They only just told us about it. We ain't got to see him yet." Roy Buck rubbed his face, spat, and ran a hand through his hair thoughtfully. "They aim to let us look in on him in a little bit, but then they expect us to go on back home."

"I'll have to get James back to his mother, anyway," Edward said. "It won't be a bit of trouble to take you and the missus home."

"Effie claims she's not going to budge, so I best not leave her," Roy said.

Edward let out a short, bitter laugh and then realized how it might sound. "Well," he said and blushed, "turns out I've got to come back to Cedar Hill tonight so if there's anything you want done or picked up, I can do it or give you a ride both ways, since I've got to make a round trip anyway."

Roy stared off into the darkness and ran one of his big hands through his hair again. "Goddamn," he said softly.

"He's young and strong," Edward said. "They'll fix him up all right."

Roy nodded, and they turned back toward the building and had only just got back to the waiting room when a nurse appeared to tell them that two of them, and only two, could visit Lester for no more than five minutes. Nervously, Roy and Effie got up.

"If Lester has a good night," the nurse told Edward and James, "you can see him tomorrow, but it's important right now not to tire him out."

"Lester's going to be all right, you just wait and see," Edward said when they were alone, but James only turned to look at him with something haunted and mysterious in his eyes. "You must be worn out and about starved too, squirt," Edward said, "but we'll get you home in a little bit."

"How come it couldn't have been me?" James said.

"Christ," Edward said, "that's a pretty dumb thing to say. There's always enough trouble to go around; nobody needs to ask for more."

"But it should have been me!" James said, his eyes suddenly wet and slick.

"Horseshit," Edward said, feeling exasperated and tired and frustrated. The boy had a lot of his mother in him. You couldn't explain anything to him once he got his mind made up. "Horseshit," he said again, but he put his arms around James and drew him close, one hand on the nape of the boy's neck, holding his forehead hard against his chest. He heard a sob and held the boy more fiercely against him, but he could tell there was no yielding to good sense in his son. The boy was stiff, gathered to resist him; and even the sob was more a bark than anything, a stubborn celebration of private grief that James wasn't about to give up. And sure enough, in the next moment the boy pushed himself away and, wiping angrily at his eyes, got up and crossed the room to look out the window, which would do him no good, since it was fully dark outside and the only thing the window could give back was his own reflection.

"They're going to take good care of Lester here, and he's going to be good as new," Edward said, but James stared out the window and didn't speak.

"I could set here, and you could take a rest and spell me tomorrow," Roy said just above a whisper, and Edward turned to see Effie standing in the corridor shaking her head. "I won't leave him," she said. "Not till they give us better than we've heard."

Effie came into the waiting room and sat down with such an inward look, it was surprising, somehow, that she could steer through doorways and find a chair. Roy followed as though he had something else he was about to say, but whatever it was, he seemed to think better of it. "All right," he said at last, "I'll ride on back and take care of things around the place. What do you need me to fetch?"

"My good sweater," Effie said as though she didn't care in the least whether he brought it or not, and the look on her face settled into something so deep, she might have been blind. They left, subdued by it, and none of them said anything all the way down the mountain.

Even when Edward stopped in front of the Marshalls' house to let James out, he felt awkward speaking aloud. "You tell your momma I'm staying at the DeMerrit Inn in Cedar Hill if she needs to reach me. And as for you, squirt," he said, "I reckon I'll see you tomorrow."

James didn't answer. Without shutting the door behind him,

he got out and went off up the driveway as though he'd just walked a hundred miles. Edward almost called him back, but stopped himself. Still, he couldn't keep a little anger and ex-asperation from rising in him as he stretched across the front seat for the door and found he couldn't reach it. He was about to kill the engine, get out, and walk around when Roy slipped in beside him.

"They're awful close, them boys," Roy remarked in a sad, mild voice, shutting the door behind him.

Even so, it took a moment before Edward realized that the poor manners of his son had been understood and excused, even if he hadn't been able to do it himself. A few hundred yards down the highway, chastened, he said, "Did they tell you what they were going to do for Lester?"

"They're a-givin him a thing called heparin, I believe they said, and sulfa . . . sulfa . . . something." Roy cleared his throat. "This heart thing he's got has been let go a long time, they told us. They fear, nearabout too long." He rubbed his chin and didn't say anything more for a while. "If they can get him stout enough, they mean to take every tooth he's got in his head. They've always give him grief," Roy said, "but who would have thought sorry teeth could ruin a boy's heart?"

"Well," Edward said, "from what I hear about Lester, he's not a quitter."

"No sir," Roy said, "he ain't that."

Again Edward urged the Packard up the wagon road, and while Roy milked, he tried to make himself useful feeding the stock or doing anything else he could find to do. But even as he busied himself, he was astonished that he wasn't with his own family. It seemed impossible that he could have felt so strongly and come so far only to . . . Well, he hadn't expected it to be easy. Still, he'd thought Madeline would forgive him. He'd expected to eat a lot of crow. He had a lot coming. But it seemed to him, at long last, that he'd come to understand something very important about himself and about his family. Yes, and he'd known Madeline would be angry, but he'd thought, finally, she would come to see that important thing too. He had supposed they would be in each other's arms by now. He'd hoped they would recognize all the silliness and stupidity that had always got in their way and kept them crosswise of one another and somehow get rid of it so that he and Madeline and James would be exactly what they ought to be and should have been all along.

He found himself watching Roy strain milk, and he came a little way out of his thoughts. "If that's your springhouse I saw below the house, I can carry the milk down and put it up while you tend to something else," he said.

"All right," Roy said, "I'm nearabout done."

"Don't forget the sweater," Edward said, hoisting the tin, insulated milk can and starting out on the dogtrot.

"Lord," Roy said, "I already had."

It wasn't that he hadn't anticipated something less than a sudden explosion of forgiveness and love, he thought, pawing at the ground a little with his feet in order not to stumble over the dark, unfamiliar earth. He'd imagined partial and tentative forgiveness too. A few weeks, maybe a month or so, while he earned his way back into his family. But hell, he'd thought his wife and son would be pulling for him, hoping it would work. He stubbed his toe on something and almost fell but caught himself and set down the milk can. But they didn't seem to want him, didn't act as though they were interested in even giving him a chance. He blew on his hands and tucked them for a moment under his armpits to warm them. It was damned cold, and the metal handles of the milk can had wicked all the warmth from his fingers.

He looked up at the stars through the smoke his breath made. Well, he thought, he would not accept it. He would wait them out. He had forgotten that he loved them for a while and had told himself foolish lies. He supposed they could do that too. But it hurt his feelings. He had left his job and come all this way to set things right. They hadn't come to Pittsburgh, after all.

He'd forgotten how damned black the night was in the country, but at last he found the springhouse, struck a match, and unhooked the door. He struck more matches to get the milk can in the trough and the door hooked again. But since Roy had kerosene lamps going in the house and he was no longer carrying the milk can, it was easier going back, although he jarred himself when he walked since the ground never seemed to be quite where his feet expected it. And what the hell was he doing here anyway? It was crazy and beside the point to be mixed up with the Bucks when he'd never even heard of them until a few hours before—his own wife wouldn't even shake his hand, never mind put her arms around him and kiss him hello; and his only son, who'd gotten him into all this in the first place, wouldn't even tell him good night for God's sake.

Easy, he told himself. Go easy. Get on back to your room. Have a drink or two. Sleep.

When Edward stepped back inside the kitchen, Roy was slipping cold biscuits with sidemeat in them into a paper bag.

"It's a little place for eats in the hospital, but there ain't much there and it's awful dear," Roy explained. He looked up suddenly. "I expect you ain't had a chance at supper neither. I can heat up a little grub?"

Edward raised a hand. "Not for me." He hadn't had breakfast or lunch, never mind supper. How strange that Paris Pergola had fixed his last meal. But he had no appetite.

Roy gathered up his wife's sweater and the food he'd packed and seemed to look around the kitchen in a daze as if he no longer quite recognized his own habitation. "Well," he said, "I can't think of nothing else."

When they passed the Marshalls' house for the second time, Madeline's car was in the driveway, and it seemed to reach out and take hold of Edward's heart. He had to see her and make her admit that she loved him. As soon as he'd dropped Roy at the hospital, that much, at least, had to be settled. It couldn't be otherwise.

But halfway up the mountain he thought better of it; he didn't dare risk it. He was suddenly so tired that he felt crazy. And he knew her temper. If she rejected him for the second time that day, he didn't know what he might do.

Still, he couldn't make himself go in when he pulled up at the hospital. Something inside him had got wound too tight, and he was shaking with impatience. But he managed to tell Roy where he was staying and repeat it twice so that Roy could reach him if he needed to.

He felt almost all right until he'd driven two blocks from the hospital, but then he suddenly began pounding the steering wheel so viciously, he was surprised it didn't break. "You son of a bitch!" he called himself, and for a moment his right front tire bounced over the curb, heading for the sidewalk until he fought the car back into the street. He stopped for a moment, breathing through his teeth. "You straighten up," he told himself. "You straighten up and fly right!"

Still a little shaky, he let himself into his room, got his jar of moonshine, plopped down in the room's one tired easy chair, and took himself a swallow. It burned his empty stomach almost as much as his throat. Wet-eyed, he blinked, took another swallow, and pursed his lips to exhale, while some remote, irrelevant, he-goat part of his brain speculated that, if he struck a match and held it close to his lips, his breath would probably ignite like the flame of a blowtorch. But the thought had no power to amuse him.

He didn't know how long it took before the blaze in his stomach became merely warmth, but when that happened, he mustered the energy to take off his shoes and lie down on the bed.

"Straighten up," he told himself. "You straighten up and fly right," he repeated between swallows of whiskey until he was able to sleep.

JAMES
TALLY

He and his mother didn't have much to say to each other, and that was fine with him. He had few thoughts he could part with. He'd told her where his father was staying and he'd told her that Lester was in the hospital, but she seemed no more interested in one than the other. She was angry, he knew that much, the cold, silent kind of anger that closed her off and made her abrupt and efficient in everything she did. It was the kind of anger that took two or three days to thaw, and then she would give somebody a long talking-to. And sometimes it would be a day after that before she could listen.

She hadn't been home long before she laid out the jeans, shirt, underwear, and socks she expected him to wear the next day—something she hadn't done in years—and told him she wanted him to go up to the house and take a good, hot bath and wash his hair and cut his fingernails. Maybe she thought because he had a black eye and a split lip he needed such direction; but more likely it was just a function of her anger. As far back as he could remember, when she was seriously mad about something, she always set to work, putting everything around her in order. She worked in alarming and dreadful silence. Usually it was Edward she was mad at, and she wouldn't speak to him at all; but probably because he himself was only a child, he could expect at least a few short commands. "Wash your face now," or, "It's time you were in bed, young man," or maybe out of the blue, "I expect you to get a haircut, first thing in the morning!" Sometimes when she was mad at him, he got the silent treatment, and his father got the few clipped remarks. But it was his father who had taught him with subtle, sometimes amused meetings of the eye, or a slight lifting of the chin, that his mother was not to be crossed, but that, finally, the world was not coming to an end—that it was merely one of those times when the male of the species needed to lie low until the storm passed. Although there were times when he, James, had done something sufficiently wrong that all male comradery got set aside, and she would deliver him to his father for a beating, at least until the sound of it, or maybe just the idea of it, got too frightening for her, and she'd come running up to rescue him again. It was all very confusing until you understood that females were simply something else altogether, creatures that needed to be tolerated and indulged but perhaps never properly understood, because, finally, they weren't men. They were very different, and for that reason they couldn't help you become a man. He knew that for sure. There was something essential not held in common. And even another man, he feared, couldn't help so much. It seemed to be a condition you had to get to by yourself, even if, after you made it, it was common ground.

Whatever, he didn't cross her. He took tomorrow's clothes up to the house to wear back from his bath and did exactly what he was told, stuffing his dirty clothes in the laundry bags beside the Marshalls' hamper so that his mother could wash them Sunday afternoon, as she always did. He comforted himself with the thought that at the dinner table, at least, his grandparents and his aunt had been sympathetic about Lester, and even Virginia and Clara seemed genuinely saddened and subdued.

When he got back to the trailer, scrubbed and clean, his mother shouted, "Stop!" the moment he opened the door. "Jump to the couch," she told him. "The floor will be dry in a little."

He tried to shut the door behind him without having it nudge him off the narrow metal lip of the threshold, but he didn't quite make it. Still, one leap put him on the stiff Naugahyde couch, which sighed and sank a little under him. She had waxed herself into the other end of the trailer and was up on her bed. He couldn't see her for the half-extended bedroom partition, but the floor between them was certainly very shiny. The trailer, he saw, was immaculate. Everything was dusted and nothing was out of place. The kitchen counter and the stove were without the slightest blemish, crumb, or stain; and the stainless-steel sink shone as if it were made of silver.

He turned on the radio, not to listen to, but to mitigate against the silence; anyway he was foolishly afraid that, otherwise, she might somehow be able to eavesdrop on his thoughts, and if she did that, she would prevent him.

After a long time, he touched the floor and found it dry enough to get up and get his pillow and blanket and shuck out of his clothes. When at last he'd sandwiched himself in his bed linen and cut off the radio and light, he was surprised that the whole trailer went dark. He hadn't realized that her light wasn't on. After many minutes, when he'd made up his mind she was asleep, she surprised him again.

"Good night, son," she said.

"Good night," he told her. But he hardly slept. He was too agitated and worried and too much inspired. From time to time during the endless night he would drowse a little, but it wasn't until almost daylight that he dropped into a sound sleep. Still, he woke, instantly alert, when she came into the kitchen to fix breakfast.

She set about making bacon and eggs and toast, and it was clear to him that her anger had diminished very little. She still had a set expression on her face, and not a single movement she made was wasted. Anyway, she never made such an elaborate breakfast during the week.

"I've got to go to the bathroom," he told her, putting his pillow and blanket away and dressing as quickly as he could.

"Don't dawdle," she said, as he went out the door; "your eggs will get cold."

Well, he didn't blame her. She had her reasons to be angry,

even if he didn't understand them. He knew they had to do with his father, but he couldn't afford to think about them. He couldn't afford to think about anything that might weaken or distract him.

The bathroom was busy. Virginia was inside, and Clara was in the hall, rattling the locked door and demanding that Virginia come out. But it didn't matter. He'd noticed that the wood box by the stove was almost empty, because he'd forgotten his chores the evening before. He went out to the barn where his piss steamed in the morning air and melted the hoar frost by the pigpen, and he split a heavy load of stovewood for his grandmother and carried it in.

When he got back to the trailer, his fingers were aching with the cold, and the tips of his ears and the end of his nose were burning with it.

"Well, your eggs are cold," his mother said.

"I got some stovewood for Grandmother," he said. "I forgot it last night."

"Sit down and eat then," she said.

Again he did as he was told. It seemed to him only proper, and it cost him nothing, although he was a bit relieved to see that she had already eaten. She tied a woolen scarf about her head, but still had her dignity, even wearing the scarf with her house slippers and robe. When she took up the large silky bag she kept her makeup and toilet things in, she stopped suddenly in his line of vision. "I'm real sorry about Lester," she said. "Hear?"

"Thank you," he said.

If she had anything else to say, she didn't say it. After a second, she merely nodded and went out the door.

For a long time he sat, gazing at nothing. His food was without taste, and he'd eaten no more than half of it when he heard her footsteps outside in the stiff, frosty grass and quickly cleaned his plate. It would have been a stronger thing to fast, only he hadn't thought of it in time. But, no matter. He would make up for that too.

While she dressed for work, he set about cleaning up the

dishes; and, again, before he quite knew where the time had gone, she was beside him, smelling of perfume, and somehow, of Green's Department Store.

"Use soap on those," she said, pecking his cheek, "and be good."

The door closed behind her and she was outside, but he could hear her steps for a moment in the stiff grass. Then he couldn't hear them. But some moments later he could hear the car start, the gravel pop and grind, a change of gears, and the fading sound of the motor. Then he could hear nothing more, and she was truly gone. And to some degree it was already started.

He finished the dishes as though that were a part of it, went out to the barn, carried in wood for the fireplace, and split more wood and carried it in for the stove until his grandmother said, "Merciful heavens, child! That's a gracious plenty!"

When he had taken the slingshot from its hiding place and got back to the trailer, he sat for a long time with a piece of paper and a pencil, trying to think what to say. It saddened him that anything at all was necessary, that he lived in a time which even required an explanation. But nothing came to him, and he decided to put the pencil aside and hope for inspiration. He got his blanket from under the couch and rolled it as small and tight as he could, only to realize—kneeling on the blanket with his knees—that he had nothing to tie it with. He almost wept at his foolishness and inadequacy. Maybe some spirit was trying to show him that he was too silly even to make a bedroll, never mind anything else. Abruptly he rose and turned his back so as not to see the blanket unfurl. Patience, he told himself. Now was no time for fear, or anger, or doubt, or any of that. He went to the closet in his mother's bedroom and got out his father's work shoes. For a moment he pondered the tongueless, disfigured one and then took the rawhide laces from both.

The shoestrings were rotten and they broke, but he knotted them and got the blanket tied. Having the slingshot with him felt right, but he turned it in his hands and considered it further. If only he'd had teaching in such matters. He had none of the knowledge he needed. No medicine. No magic or charms. But the slingshot seemed proper. Part of it was Lester's, part his father's, part his. Even the transgression was his, and he suspected it should not be left behind as though he weren't guilty. There was nothing to go by except what he felt to be true.

He needed to quit thinking. He had a book of matches, his pocketknife, the slingshot, and his blanket. He had no idea what an Indian boy might take or in what season of the year he would be asked to accept his trial. After a moment he went again to the bedroom closet and took down an old leather belt, hanging among a smattering of his father's neglected neckties. There was nothing else he needed, nor any further reason to linger.

He picked up the pencil and wrote: *I'm going off to be by myself for a while.* He meant to write more, to address it to someone, to sign it, perhaps to try and explain, but anything else he imagined writing down seemed useless. Worse, in some strange way he could not quite understand, anything further seemed to court dishonesty or boasting.

He strapped the rolled blanket down the center of his back by means of his father's belt, which he buckled across his chest. His knees burning and his stomach shaky, he let himself out of the trailer and turned south in order to keep the trailer between him and the house, at least until he reached the gully at the end of the cow pasture.

Once he'd crossed the fence and gotten to the bottom of the gully where he couldn't be seen, he turned east toward the highest of the mountains.

MADELINE
TALLY

The moment she pulled out of the driveway, an oddly powerful guilt over James tugged at her stomach. She should have been more sympathetic. It wouldn't have hurt her to inquire about Lester, to ask, at least, how he was doing. It was just that she felt so harried, so completely taken unawares. Well, she'd make it up to the child, she decided, even send Lester a card or some such thing.

Just as she made that resolution, Leslie, whom she absolutely did not want to think about, popped into her mind, and she saw again the way he'd looked when he came walking into Green's yesterday just at quitting time. He had looked so self-possessed, so distinguished and stylish, she had known in an instant what she desired and went straight up to him and said, calmly she thought: "I want you to get me one of those . . . what do you call them?"

Amused, his eyes twinkling, Leslie merely shrugged.

"Restraining orders," she said. "Yes, restraining orders."

"Why?" he said, grinning. "For what? For whom?"

"Edward, of course. And he'll just . . . I can't . . ."

"He's here?" Leslie asked. "In Cedar Hill?"

"Yes," she said, "and I won't put up with it." She hardly noticed the change in his face or that he'd taken her by the elbow to lead her out of the store; she was too busy blurting out the details of Edward's sudden, shocking appearance.

"You're his wife," he told her once they were on the sidewalk. "If he hasn't harmed or threatened you, you can't ask for a restraining order. He has every right to see you."

Why was he whispering? He released her elbow and took a step backward.

"Go get your coat," he said. "I'm sure you don't want all the salesladies to know your private affairs."

She went back in the store and got her coat and her purse as though she had only just realized she'd been drawn outside in the first place. Something wasn't quite right, but she was too concerned with Edward to be able to speculate about it, at least until she was back out on the sidewalk and got another look at Leslie's face.

"Legally, I'm afraid Edward has very little to fear from us," he told her. He made a sound something like laughter. "I wish I could say the same. He could name me as a corespondent, for example, and make things extremely difficult for me." He made the sound that was remotely like laughter again, and she realized how uncomfortable he was. "He could sue me for alienation of affection and have a case I sure wouldn't want to . . ."

The look she gave him seemed to take his voice away. She nodded very slowly and, once she understood perfectly, turned away toward her car.

"Maidy?" he said behind her. "Maidy wait . . . please."

But she was in her little coupe and backing up.

He had stepped off the sidewalk in a lame, halfhearted attempt to follow her when she stopped and held up a forefinger as though she were calling for a point of order. She got his house key from the glove pocket, rolled down the window, and held the key out to him, but he made no move to come any closer. He appeared to be looking somewhere over the roof of her car, perhaps at the sky. "Oh Maidy . . ." he said, so she dropped the key, backed into the street, and drove home.

Well, she thought, coming over the crest of the mountain into Cedar Hill in the bright morning sun, she could see Leslie's side of things after all. It simply made no difference to her, since, as far as she was concerned, he had ceased to exist.

EDWARD
TALLY

For some reason he couldn't justify, he woke up feeling rare and with the firm belief lodged in his head that someday he and Madeline would laugh about all this. Maybe he'd only had a nice dream he couldn't remember, but the more he thought of it, the more the notion seemed perfectly logical. Also he was ravenously hungry and didn't have even the slightest hangover. Good corn whiskey, he decided, was very hard to beat.

He wanted a bath and breakfast. Going slow and easy, he told himself, was the key. Madeline had never liked surprises, and yesterday morning was nothing if not a surprise. He rummaged through his belongings, looking for his shaving gear and toothbrush. She just needed time to consider things. To get used to him being around.

To his delight the bathroom at the end of the hall was unoccupied and very clean. If it was necessary, he could court her all over again. After he'd washed up and had himself some breakfast, he'd stop by the hospital and see how all the Bucks were faring. He'd pick up James so he could visit with Lester, and maybe leave Madeline a present. Flowers, say. Flowers were always terrific. With a very simple note. Nothing pushy. Maybe he wouldn't even use the word *love*, since she didn't seem ready to grant him the right. *Your husband,* that was absolutely all he'd put on the card. A wonderful touch, he thought. Perfect.

JAMES
TALLY

A little more than a mile above his grandfather's house, he crossed a highway he hadn't even known existed, and half an hour later, when he'd thought himself in wilderness, he crossed a dirt road running through dense woods. It was only wide enough for a single car, had grass down the center of it, and he had no notion where it came from or where it went, but it was still a road. So he kept walking. It had gotten a little easier since he'd admitted to himself that he was afraid.

Some part of him wanted to keep his grandfather's house and barn near enough, so that, if he needed, a very short hike would bring them in sight again. Even that seemed plenty scary enough. Still, another side of him knew better. If he really meant to leave his childhood behind and become, once and for all, the sort of person he wanted to be, the sort Osceola was, there shouldn't be compromise. Yet it was Lester as much as anything—taking that terrible beating even though he didn't know the first thing about fighting and had a damaged heart too—who kept him going. If that plane of absolute, total justice he had always sensed operating constantly and invisibly around him could be appeased, he meant to appease it. For sure Lester had accepted all sorts of pain and humiliation that wasn't his, had substituted himself and bought James clear. It was time for James Tally, he told himself, to do whatever was necessary to buy Lester clear.

So what if he was afraid? It wouldn't be honest to try and

deny it. He *should* be taking his fear with him, so that, when his test and trial were over and finished, and he had become a man in his heart, he could leave his fear behind and come home without it. He was certain it would happen, and Lester would be all right too and wouldn't die.

Nobody should suffer for the other fellow's cowardice, and maybe cowardice wasn't so hard to get over, just like he had already got over being cold. When he'd first started out, his feet and hands were very cold and the tips of his ears stung with it, but not any longer. There was even a little sweat down the center of his back where the blanket was strapped so tightly.

A hundred yards or so above the dirt road, he began to move through thickets of rhododendron and laurel, twice and three times higher than his head. Here and there, where the sun didn't reach, thin patches of snow occupied shallow depressions. They were stitched with the tracks of mice, but occasionally he saw where squirrels had passed over the snow, and once he saw what he took to be the tracks of a grouse. He was at the height of the land and might have stayed if the woods road hadn't been so near, but he feared any half measure that might put everything in jeopardy.

Through laurel, rhododendron, pine, and occasional stark and leafless hardwoods, he could see a higher mountain across a valley from him. He could not see the bottom of the valley, but he didn't see any roads or houses or cleared fields either. He didn't want to go downhill, but he made himself do it while a soft wind in the trees he hadn't noticed before seemed to breathe his name. *Jaaammes,* the wind said. *Jaaaaaammmmmesss.* To have the wind repeat his name so, turned his mouth dry and his knees weak.

When he'd gone only a little way down the steep slope, his feet slipped suddenly on pine needles, and he fell and slid over the lip of a granite outcropping and into space before he could stop himself. A dozen feet below he landed on the rolled blanket strapped to his back so hard there was no breath at all left in him. He gaped like a fish out of water but couldn't draw any air into his lungs or make a sound. His senses whirled in mad disorder at the sudden prospect of dying, and the hinges of his jaws popped. He struggled to breathe, but it was as if he no longer had lungs to fill, or as if his mouth were only a shallow pocket of stone with no entrance to them. Yet, at last, he began to make an inhuman squeaking like a windlass drawing up a heavy load. But it was a long time later before he could begin to fill his chest.

When he had his breath back, he propped himself on his elbows and found that he was dizzy but not hurt, and because he wasn't on the ridge anymore, the wind had quit calling his name. He looked behind and above him, sobered that he had fallen so far without breaking anything. Maybe some stern guiding spirit had merely taught him a lesson in order to make him pay attention. He felt chastened and lucky, and after he pondered it for a while, he decided he was grateful. Still a bit raw in the lungs and throat, he rested a little longer, got to his feet, and went on, but much more carefully than before.

EDWARD:

He held half a dozen red roses wrapped in fancy paper in one well-scrubbed hand and knocked on the trailer door with the other. He'd really wanted a dozen roses, but after he'd thumbed through the contents of his billfold, he'd had to reconsider. "Hey, squirt!" he'd called, "you in there?" When there was no answer, he tried the door.

The trailer was spotlessly clean and seemed inhabited solely by a piece of notepaper on the table. The message gave him a start until he realized it wasn't Madeline's hand. James had written it.

"Huh," he said and began looking for something to hold the roses. He didn't want to take them out of the paper, which looked so festive and official. Finally he found his favorite iced-tea glass, half filled it with water, rolled back the paper enough to stick the stems in, and pressed the card open so she would see at a glance: "Your Husband."

Back at the house he rapped gently on the kitchen door before he pushed it open to see Bertha working the dasher of a churn. "You wouldn't know where James got off to, would you?" he asked her.

"Well, he was right here just a little bit ago. He's not down to the trailer?"

He shook his head. "Huh," he said. "His buddy's doing better today, and I thought James would be anxious to see him." He scratched the back of his neck. "Looks like I'm a little out of step with everybody this morning. I guess I ought to get Roy home so he can milk, but I'll come back by."

Mild and friendly and without missing a single beat at the churn, Bertha said, "All right, and if I see that young'n before you get back, I'll just sit on him till you get here."

"Thank you," Edward said.

"You might take a look out to the barn," she said behind him as he was closing the door.

He didn't see him at the barn, but he called his name and, after a moment, cupped his hand around his mouth and twice made a bobwhite whistle.

A swift, tumbling river with a few mossy rocks sticking out of it occupied the floor of the valley. It smelled sweet and woodsy, but he needed to find a way across, and he walked a long way upstream before he found a place that looked broad and shallow. He'd wanted to get across it and stay dry, but he'd seen no blow-downs that came close to reaching across the river and no spot, either, where he could cross jumping from rock to rock. After pondering the riffles and eddies and smooth, slick spots for a while, he stripped to the waist, tied his shoes together, stuffed his socks in the toes, and used his father's belt to strap his britches, underwear, and shoes to his bedroll. Holding his belongings under his arm and already dithering with the cold, he stepped into the water.

It was frigid, and when it reached his knees, it was pushy and tried to climb him. His teeth rattled, and his legs felt stiff and numb by the time he got halfway across; still, the river didn't look as if it would get any deeper.

But somehow the very next step dunked his genitals, and while he gasped and grunted and struggled to keep from going any further, he took another step to his waist. He lost his footing and almost went down completely before he recovered. But even so, his shirt got soaked almost to the armpits, he dunked one end of his bedroll, and filled one dangling shoe with water. After that, all caution left him and he floundered toward the bank on feet and legs as senseless as if they were made of brass.

Once on shore he shucked quickly out of his shirt and undershirt and dried himself on the driest part of the blanket. Luckily his britches and underwear hadn't gotten wet; and, stiff with cold, he stumbled and hopped about, pulling them on over the diminished knob of his penis and a scrotum small and hard as a walnut. He checked for his slingshot, knife, and matches and found them all safe; but when he took up his shoes, he discovered that his dry shoe still had a sock snuggled in the toe, but the wet shoe was empty. Had he glimpsed something pale and limp floating away when he'd almost fallen? Just out of the tail of his eye? But he'd been fighting to keep from going under, and whatever it was had had no power to distract him.

He wrapped the blanket about him like a robe and went off down the bank looking for it, thinking maybe a long limb could fetch it in. But when at last he saw the sock, much further downstream than he thought it would be, it was barely afloat and in the very middle of the river. But even that disappointment didn't matter long, since when he got close enough to be certain of what he saw, the sock was riding a little sluice of water dropping down between two rocks, and at the bottom it got sucked under. The pool where the sock disappeared looked deep, and it was crazy to consider shucking out of his clothes to swim out and search for it.

He went up the river again to find his shoes and shirt. The blanket was wool, and even though it was a little wet here and there, it was warm, so he took it off only long enough to fold it once, slice its center with his pocketknife just enough to get his head through, and put it back on like a poncho. He wrung out the shirt and undershirt, wrapped them around the wet shoe, and cinched them and the blanket around his middle with his father's belt. His left shoe was dry, so he put it on. He put the dry sock on his right foot. And he felt almost okay, even a little plucky.

Lester didn't swim and wouldn't have wanted to wade such a river. He would have been impressed. And he wondered if whatever he had come here to appease, that imponderable, absolutely just spirit that constantly judged and brooded over him, wouldn't be a little impressed too. It was a notion that sneaked into his mind sideways, but he knew how inappropriate it was, and he shut it out at once.

He began to climb, feeling all right for a while; and pretty soon the hardwoods, plentiful around the river, began to give way, once again, to pine and balsam, laurel and rhododendron. At first he was warm enough just by being no longer in the river or wet, as though that had stoked the fire in him so high, mere cold air no longer had the power to chill him. But then, because he was wearing the heavy blanket and climbing steadily, he got too warm. He slowed his pace, stopped often to rest, and soon he was cold again, perhaps because he'd broken a sweat and perhaps because he'd gotten higher. When his teeth began to rattle, he stopped altogether and worked at the way the blanket was gathered at his waist, overlapping its edges as much as possible until he got the open spaces under his arms and along his ribs much smaller. He rubbed his hands together to warm them and took off his left shoe to rub his foot, which was much colder than the one with the sock.

Still he felt all right until he realized he couldn't hear the river anymore. The sound of it had followed him a long way and given him comfort, and he held his breath and listened, thinking that somewhere among the underpinnings of all this silence, he'd be able to pick up at least a murmur of it far below, but he couldn't, and it unsettled him. Oddly the river seemed a kind of milepost, the last link with anything he knew, as though without it he couldn't possibly calculate how far he'd come and how far it was home. He listened as hard as he could, but he didn't hear anything at all except the long sigh of vast and empty space.

He put his shoe back on and stood up, but his courage seemed to have slipped away. All this emptiness, these mountains and woods, did not care for him; he knew that with sudden and absolute clarity. The sun, not so far above the ridge he'd crossed earlier in the day, made him see that, even if he walked very fast, darkness would catch him long before he got home. All at once he felt very foolish, as if this ordeal—no matter how deeply he had felt about it—was to no purpose. A delusion of the silly child he was and always had been. Hadn't he deceived himself many times that he could be strong and brave and therefore earn a better life for himself, or at least not betray those he cared for? But he'd never once come up to the mark. Not once.

Even the stern guiding spirit, who always haunted and judged him, seemed to grow thin, as though it too might only be imagined, invented, dreamed up. And if that were true, then he was absolutely alone in all this empty space, and there was no remedy for anything, not for his parents, or Lester, or himself. All at once he wanted to run and had to sit down and wrap his arms about his knees and rock himself. If he started to run, he wouldn't be able to stop. He'd come too far, crossed a river, and come too far for running. But he wouldn't be able to stop.

MADELINE:

She meant to be very polite when she released him of the bother of thinking about her further, but she was surprised that Leslie didn't call to apologize and try to make up to her. She expected to be able to tell him that she understood the position he was in, which, she was sure, she absolutely did. Just as she was sure she understood, at last, the position that she herself was in. She simply hadn't really seen Leslie; she had made him up. She had mistaken three-piece suits, a grand house, and an education for something more fundamental that those things couldn't alter or even touch. Men were men after all. What was worse, she had used Leslie somehow in order to be able to deal with Edward, who had a prior and greater claim and had to be dealt with on his own. She wasn't proud of having misunderstood Leslie, but having misunderstood herself shamed her most of all.

So, late in the afternoon when Dorothy signaled to her that she had a call, she had her speech all ready and was lucky she even bothered to say hello when she plucked the phone from her desk.

"James is not with you, I reckon," her mother said matter-of-factly, as though she and her mother were standing face to face and there was absolutely no reason to identify herself.

"Of course not, Momma," she said.

"Well I didn't think so," her mother said, "but I was just kindly worried."

"Why?" Madeline said.

"Well he's gone off somewhere, and his daddy's been here three or four times today to take him over to see Lester. And . . . I don't know . . . the chile left a little note and missed his dinner."

"What did the note say, Momma?"

"According to Edward, it didn't say hardly anything. I just got to studyin about it and thinking how hard all this might be on the boy, and him so quiet; but I imagine he'll be here by suppertime. I just thought he might have caught a ride over to see you."

"Now I'm worried," Madeline said.

"Well it's foolish," her mother said. "I just got to studyin on it and got silly. He's not likely to miss his supper."

But after Madeline hung up, it nagged her for the rest of the afternoon, and finally she asked her boss for permission to leave half an hour early and drove straight home. Even so, it was fifteen minutes past five when she pulled into the driveway, and since her father, as far back as she could remember, wanted his supper at five, fear flamed up in her when she hurried through the kitchen door and saw that James wasn't at the table with the rest of them.

"Now honey," her mother said, "he'll come draggin in before long, and when he does, I for one just might paddle him good."

"Where's the note?" Madeline said.

"Well it's down to the trailer. Not a soul has touched it," her mother said as though she'd been accused of something.

But when Madeline turned and went out the kitchen door again, Clara remarked with haughty certainty: "*I* think he's run away."

It wasn't as if the thought hadn't tested her once or twice that afternoon, but she hadn't allowed such a farfetched worry to take root. Still, as she crossed the stile into the cow pasture, Clara's little pronouncement and the judgment it contained stung her, as though James had good reason after all. And when she stepped into the chilled trailer and snapped on the light, the roses and Edward's card and James's clipped little note all seemed part of the same message, as though she couldn't distinguish between them, as though together they represented some monolithic, utterly male, and finally incomprehensible obligation she could neither escape nor discharge. For a moment she couldn't seem to move, but then some stubbornly practical part of her brain that was still operative allowed her to open James's closet and discover that, yes, his clothes were still there. She pulled open his drawers and found his underwear, socks, and everything just as it should be. So. She turned the dial that set the furnace going and heard the small gas ring behind the tin louvers sputter to flame and the small electric fan begin to hum; but she attended to these matters in a daze.

I'm going off to be by myself for a while. How far, and where, was *off*? How long was *a while* supposed to be? It was the most inconsiderate message he could possibly have written, and her fear turned to anger before it cooled to fear again. Still, she didn't think he'd actually run away.

And snuggled among the lovely roses like a thorn, *Your Husband.* In spite of everything, *Your Husband.* And of course it was still true, no matter what she'd gone through, no matter how she had behaved or what her plans and desires were, no matter how deeply she had considered the matter or what she had discovered about herself. It was still legally and inescapably true, and he'd had the bad manners to remind her of it on a card snuggled among six lovely, long-stemmed roses. Oh but there was a god-awful irony in that so large she couldn't begin to find its limits. *Your Husband.* Yes and the limits didn't end with the merely legal either; it was a condition that surrounded her and encompassed her in ways not even a divorce could dissolve, and she supposed she'd known that all along too, although she'd tried her best not to know it. She'd made the mistake long ago when she'd been silly and stupid; how could it be so irredeemable?

Oh James, she thought, and all at once her life seemed so hopeless and unmanageable, she began to weep. What was wrong was so utterly incurable and she had struggled against it so hard, she cried from sheer exhaustion. What was worse, she hadn't moved one inch from the dead center of her troubles; she'd only managed to pull other people into them with her, poor James, her parents, and even Leslie, who didn't belong in her life at all.

Sunk into one end of the couch, she was crying without any end in sight when her mother knocked and, a few seconds later, let herself in.

"Did he come back?" Madeline asked.

"No, chile," her mother said, "but he will," and she sat down on the couch and took Madeline softly into her arms.

"Oh Momma," Madeline said. "I've made such a horrible mess of everything, I wouldn't blame him if he didn't."

Her mother began to rock her gently. "Shhhh, hush," she said.

"God, I've just been so *stupid*," Madeline said.

Her mother nodded against the top of her head. "I expect that's true," she said, "but you were as far back as I can remember, even when you were tiny."

Madeline found herself crying again, but in a different way, as if it were comforting to have her mother hold her and remind her that she'd always been stupid. Somehow the ruin she had brought about seemed a little less profound and complete and a little more ordinary, continuous, and maybe even forgivably human, although it seemed to hurt almost as much.

For a long time her mother rocked her and didn't say anything else, but at last she added: "To be fair, I always thought in some ways you were the brightest of my children too, but certainly the orneriest and hardest to please."

Madeline stiffened, but her mother held her in her soft embrace and began to pat her. Finally she laid her cheek against the top of Madeline's head. "I love you, chile," she told her, "but Lily wants to come and be with you, and I've left all of my chores undone." Her mother gave her one last squeeze and stood up. She appeared to have something else to say, but she and Madeline merely looked at each other, and whatever it was seemed to come to Madeline through her mother's eyes, and it was full of comfort and understanding. "You need me, chile, you just holler," her mother said.

When Lily came in, she said, "Why don't I make us some coffee?" and without waiting for an answer, she set about opening and closing cabinet doors until she found what she needed. Neither of them said anything—Lily busying herself about the tiny kitchen and Madeline sitting as still as if she were carved of stone, staring at nothing through one of the trailer windows— until the coffee was done and Lily had poured herself and Madeline a cup. "You know, you may have to stand in line to spank that little stinker when he shows up," Lily told her and set a cup of coffee in her hands.

Madeline looked at the cup as if she didn't know what it was. "I just don't know what to do," she said. "I just don't know what to do anymore."

"I think you should call Edward up," Lily told her. "It's getting dark, and it's cold, and there isn't any reason why Edward shouldn't be scratching around out there, trying to find where that child has gone off to sulk."

"I can't call him," Madeline said. "He's everything that's wrong; he's absolutely everything that's wrong with my life."

Lily's eyes, magnified by her thick glasses but lovely still, hadn't the least malice in them. She brushed the back of her fingers gently against Madeline's cheek. "You know," she said, "I never thought you understood men very well. I saw a long time ago that they were far from perfect, and just, well, decided to do without. But I *like* them, you know, for what they are. Anyway, it's my opinion that Edward is worth two or three of Leslie Johnson."

Suddenly offended as well as miserable, Madeline drew back from Lily's caress. "How could you?" she said. "You haven't a speck of experience with either one of them."

"That's true," Lily said, "but that gives me a certain objectivity, don't you think? . . . Oh lamb," Lily said, "I came down here to give you a hug and see if I couldn't make you feel better, but certainly not to speak my mind. I don't suppose you'll ever forgive me," she said, "but please try." Her eyes were large and blue green and guileless. "Whatever else you do, though, you ought to call Edward, don't you think? James is his son, too."

"Just go away," Madeline said, but when Lily turned to go, Madeline said, "no, don't, please. I'm sorry. I need you to stay with me. I just can't call him yet. I will in a little while, but don't go just now. I want you to stay."

Lily looked at her for a long moment as though she were puzzled, but she didn't leave. Instead she wordlessly opened her arms and took her sister in.

By dark he'd nearly completed a small lean-to. He'd built it close to the base of an ancient hemlock, and his pocketknife, none too sharp to begin with, was useless by the time he tried to cut some nearby spruce boughs to get him off the ground and make some sort of bedding. The two forked sticks, nearly as thick as his wrists, which stood at the front corners, and the heavy stick between them, which supported the slanting roof, had taken the edge of his knife all by themselves. The lighter, longer branches he'd slanted from the roof beam in front to the ground in back, he'd had to worry and haggle into. He'd meant to weave other, smaller branches from side to side among them to make a kind of latticework roof, but he could see that darkness was going to catch him, and he'd woven in only four of those. To cover the roof he'd used the flat, nearly fan-shaped branches of hemlock, which were slender as pencils where he cut them, but even by that time it was often easier to break them from the tree than to use his knife. By the time he was ready to gather bedding, he put the knife away altogether and broke the spruce boughs.

All his labors, from gathering the dead lower branches of nearby pine trees for firewood to building the lean-to, had been dogged and slow; and when he threw his last load of spruce boughs into his shelter, he slumped down upon them without enough spirit left to build a fire.

His hands were black and stiff with pitch. There were blisters along the thumb and forefinger of his right hand from trying to wring branches through with his dull knife. And he was all over as cold as dead flesh. But he didn't quite know any of these things. When his panic subsided at last, it took all sorts of other things with it. He had very few thoughts after that, and those he had seemed far away, like the faint glimmer of heat lightning below a dark horizon. He knew he was alone and that whatever he had hoped to appease by coming here had gone away and wouldn't return. Only if he gave up and went home would it show up to torment him—sure, and be as real as his failure. Maybe it had always been only a way to steer things that couldn't be steered, a way to earn the respect of something that didn't even exist to respect or disdain him. He thought none of these things into words, but in some remote and distracted fashion, he knew them. What he didn't know was if he stayed on out of hopelessness or fear of hopelessness, which had only turned stubborn because there was nothing else to do; they were so nearly the same, he could make no distinction between them.

But after a while it did come to him that his feet were aching with a cold so intense it reached into sinew and bone. He needed a fire, but when he started to get up he discovered that he was almost too numb and stiff with cold to move. His arms and legs didn't work very well, and his fingers merely fumbled at gathering the small twigs he needed and fumbled at the matchbox and matches. Still, he was able to strike a flame and kindle a tiny fire, and finally, to nurse it into something worthwhile. Strangely, when he began to get a little warmer, he started to shiver.

He remembered his wet shoe, undershirt, and shirt, and he arranged them by the fire to dry. A little later he took off his poncho blanket and wrapped himself in it, feet and all. The slit he'd cut for his head became two slits when he opened the blanket up to wrap about himself, and they let cold in to steal away half the warmth he was able to shiver up.

EDWARD:

He had just decided to call the Marshalls to see if James had turned up, when Madeline called him. He didn't know whether to be grateful to the boy or worried, but it didn't take him nearly as long as it should have to drive down the mountain. He wondered what in hell that kid was up to anyway, but in the next moment he found himself just as interested in exactly how Madeline had sounded over the phone. At least she didn't sound angry, but he certainly couldn't call it friendly either, or even exactly distant—hazardous, he supposed, was the way she sounded. Perhaps she hadn't even had a chance to find the roses or his card. "James hasn't come back, and I think you should be here," was almost all she'd said. He'd said, "I'm on my way," and after a moment he could call neither long nor short, she'd said, "All right," and then hung up.

When he pulled into the driveway, he didn't know whether to go up to the house or down to the trailer, but he hadn't much more than gotten out of the car when the tall, stooped figure of Madeline's father loomed briefly in the open kitchen door and then came on down the walk to meet him and offer a solemn handshake.

"I expect he'll wander in directly. He's a good boy, James,"

Harley said. "Lily and Madeline are on down at the trailer."

"Thank you," Edward said.

"You think of a way I can help, son, and I'll try to do it. He's a good boy, but just now I'm not certain you shouldn't turn him and his momma both over your knee."

"I guess I need to find him first," Edward said.

"He'll be on in," Harley said. "I'm satisfied he will."

"I better go on," Edward said and nodded good-bye, glad that it was dark since he was unaccountably blushing. Harley Marshall nodded too.

When he knocked on the trailer door and went in, the two women were sitting on the couch with something especially close and conspiratorial about them. Before anyone said a word, Lily hugged Madeline, got up and gave Edward a brief fierce hug, and let herself out.

"I feel like I just missed something," Edward said, hoping to lighten the mood, hoping, at least faintly, for good news; but he could tell before the words were out of his mouth that he wasn't going to get either one.

"The girls think that James has run away," she said.

How her eyes could acknowledge and reject him at the same time he didn't know, but they did. He saw in them all their years of marriage, but that history seemed wrapped in something nearly impenetrable.

"But Lily persuaded me that you are his father, and it's your concern as much as mine. Anyway," she said, as though jealous, "you were with him all day yesterday. What do you think?"

He wanted to say that it shouldn't take her sister to tell her who James's father was, but he didn't. The fact was, he didn't know what to think. All at once his son seemed as mysterious to him as his wife. "I'm as surprised as you are," he said at last. "What with the doctors not sure if Lester's going to make it, and those boys being so close and all, it makes no sense to me."

"Lester might die?" Madeline said.

"Well," Edward said, "he's looking a lot better today, but James sure doesn't know that. I just don't understand what in hell is wrong with that boy." But almost immediately some part of him did understand, almost.

"Lily thinks he might be somewhere close, wanting us to find him, that he just needs us to think about him, worry about him."

"Maybe," Edward said, "but, I don't know. . . . He holds himself to blame for Lester in a way that's pretty deep in his bones. I don't know. . . ."

"He didn't take any clothes," Madeline said. "He didn't take anything that I can find."

For some reason, Edward wasn't as comforted as he should have been, but he didn't want to admit it. He nodded and said nothing. There didn't seem to be any good reason for the strange brand of uneasiness he felt.

"I want you to find him," Madeline said suddenly. "I want you to find him and bring him home!"

And where the hell was he supposed to look? If the boy didn't come walking in on his own, he could be anywhere. What if he had stepped out on the highway and stuck out a thumb? Somehow he didn't think that had happened, but he couldn't *know* it. He didn't know what he actually knew, except that maybe Madeline would always ask more of him than he could hope to deliver.

"I'll find him," he said to comfort her, but in the next moment he felt such a fundamental connection between himself and his son, he believed his own promise. He *would* find him. What he would do after that, he didn't know. Maybe just face the facts and go back to Pittsburgh. As he turned to leave, he noticed the roses just exactly as he had left them, the note pressed open, the festive paper still around the stems; and finding James seemed far more likely than finding a way to make peace with this woman he had married and loved.

But by daylight the next morning, bone-tired, wearing a filthy and ragged work jacket and high-top work shoes he'd dug from the trunk of the car, he wasn't so sure. He'd tramped all over the Marshalls' property and beyond, and then gone down to the Bucks' and talked to Roy and searched his barn and buildings too, and then climbed up into the woods behind the Bucks' habitation, just as he had behind the Marshalls', calling out until his voice was hoarse and weak and the flashlight he'd taken from the glovepocket of the car had lost its beam and would hardly light his footsteps. But he kept searching, if only to give the obscure and ambiguous promptings of intuition a chance, if only to give sheer luck a chance.

Earlier, climbing the ladder into the Bucks' haymow, he felt certain James was there, but he wasn't. And much later, when he was crossing a bridge over Sugar Creek—Roy had told him how much the boys use to fish together—he felt absolutely sure James was camped on the broad sandbar underneath, and he stopped the car, walked back, and climbed down the embankment. "Son?" he'd said in a voice filled with emotion. "Son?"

He was convinced James was hidden close by, perhaps within a few feet of him. The flashlight he carried was useless by then, showing only a thin, gold worm of light behind its dim face, and he could see very little. But after a while he understood the space under the bridge was empty. Nothing was there except the cold muttering of water.

Twice during the night he'd gone back to the trailer to see if James had come home by himself, and each time Madeline had looked more pale and tortured. When he presented himself at daylight, he could tell she had been crying, and they looked at each other a long time before he said, "I'm going over to the sheriff's office in Cedar Hill, and then I'm going to talk to Lester in the hospital to see if he's got any ideas. But I'll find him."

"You need some breakfast. Sit down," she said.

Exhausted, he sat; and exhausted, he was certain, she fixed his breakfast. She even sat with him while he ate, although she only held a cup of coffee listlessly between her hands. Still, somehow, they seemed almost married to him again. At least some barrier was gone, even if it was only replaced by a sad helplessness, even if the marriage only felt contractual and thin.

"What should I do?" she asked him after a while.

"Stay here," he said. "Be by the phone. I'll find him," he told her. "Don't you worry. I'm going to find that boy."

When he'd eaten, he stood up, and she stood up too, and they considered each other for a moment before, at exactly the same time, they came together and embraced. Neither of them said anything, and the embrace was not made of what his heart desired; but he was grateful for it, and it gave him hope. Still, he thought it best to relinquish her before something went wrong or she said anything he didn't want to hear.

"I'll call you if there's any real news," he told her and opened the door to leave. "If he comes in, you can leave word at the hospital."

He hadn't slept during the night except to doze for a few minutes at a time. Once he'd heard a thumping behind his shelter, even felt it through the ground, and so he knew something heavy had approached. But, benumbed and impassive, he sat where he was until whatever it was seemed to pass on by. Twice, although he'd thought he'd gathered enough wood for the night, he'd had to roam the dark woods to gather more, coaxing his fire closer and closer to his lean-to until in those last hours before dawn it was only inches from his shins. All night he'd sat up, wrapped in his blanket, his arms around his legs and his forehead on his knees.

Just before daylight he discovered that his shirt and undershirt were dry. They were stiff and pocked with soot and small holes that sparks and popping embers had made, but they helped a great deal against the cold when he put them on. Just a little after dawn, the thumping came again in front of him, and he looked dully over his knees, seeing nothing except the dim woods, until the doe, perhaps thirty yards away, moved her head and then cocked her ears this way and that. She was looking directly at him, and spiritlessly he looked back. She took a tentative, dignified step in his direction, turned her head to watch from the side, and then abruptly began to make off, followed by two more deer he hadn't seen either; but his forehead was back on his knees long before they were gone. Still, the sun was well up before he got warm enough to lie on his side and fall asleep.

MADELINE:

Just let him be all right, please let him be all right, she thought, if only to keep down the shameful and desolate feeling that it was too late for changes because she'd long ago designed who and what she had become.

EDWARD:

When he'd shot a grouse he couldn't find, it had been his practice to drop his hat where he'd last seen the bird and then begin to circle, searching every inch of ground and widening the circle with each revolution until he found what he'd killed or wounded. Sometimes even that didn't work, but he used the trailer, where James had left his note, for a dropped hat, and began.

The sheriff had agreed to put James's description on the radio and request that anyone who had seen him call his office. And after Edward had explained the circumstances, the sheriff softened a little about not committing manpower until James had been gone forty-eight hours. Children, he said, grinning, often thought they were going to run away, but usually only hid in some friend's basement or in some safe place close by, and the only harm done was to their parents. So Edward had had to explain more than he cared to about his son, about his marriage, about Lester being James's only friend, and about the boy being sensitive and unhappy and having no place to go, until the sheriff agreed to send two deputies out to the Marshalls' as soon as they could be freed from other duties, probably sometime that afternoon.

But Lester hadn't been much help at all. He had no idea where James might have gone, although he was ready to leave the hospital to hunt for him. One of his doctors, just coming into the room at the time, agreed that he was much better, but not as well as all that. Still, Lester had none of the special information Edward was hoping for. The boys didn't have a hideout or secret place where James might be found, and James had given no hint to Lester of what he might be planning. So, although Edward talked to Lester for quite a while, trying to learn anything that might help him, he came away with little more than a strong feeling for the depth of friendship between the two boys. He was touched by the reverence Lester had for James, whom Lester thought a little peculiar only because he was so smart.

Feeling more fearful for his son than ever, he found himself driving Effie Buck home, just as he had driven Roy to the hospital that morning. As for Effie, although she had spent two nights sitting in the waiting room and was haggard and pale, now that her own son was out of danger, she seemed ready to transfer her enormous capacity for worry to James. When Roy Buck offered to help look for James, Effie agreed he should do exactly that. She would simply spend a third night at the hospital. It would be easy as pie, she'd told them. She could look in her boy's eyes and tell by the light in them and by the color in his face that he was out of danger, so she'd be able to rest no matter where she was.

But Edward had insisted otherwise, exaggerated what the sheriff's office was going to do, pretended he thought James was going to come walking in with nothing wrong with him—at least until he got the hiding that his father was going to give him. Yet everything he'd said had sounded so false and thin that by the time he'd convinced them there was no real cause for worry, he himself was more worried than ever.

And by the time he had delivered Effie, gotten back to the Marshalls', and started Madeline making phone calls to all James's former friends in Cedar Hill—something he'd promised the sheriff he'd do—there was fear deep in his bones. Lester's reverence had helped put it there almost as much as his own bluff speech to the Bucks.

Circling down through the scrub growth between the cow pasture and the trailer, he felt the fear. He wasn't finding anything at all useful. The pasture was a museum of prints Madeline, James, and the cow had made, and none of them were yesterday's. They couldn't be, since yesterday had been so cold the ground had been frozen. It was warmer today, and still only the topmost layer of earth had grown soft. It was hopeless, but he didn't know what else to do. In the scrub between the fence and the highway, there were no marks at all to read.

Yet half an hour later when his circling had grown large enough to include the fence at the southern end of the pasture, he found himself staring at two marks beyond the fence and just under the lip of the gully where the soil was loose and grainy. The first one looked like someone might have set the edge of his foot against the steep pitch. The second looked a little more like a full footprint, except it was too large for James. Unless perhaps he'd slipped, and the side of the gully was very steep. A little way down from the top, the sides of the gully were made of hardpan and showed no marks at all, and there were none up the other side, not even toward the top where the sun hadn't hit and the looser soil was still raised with frost. On his side the frost had melted, and that too, he thought, could have made the impressions larger than the feet that made them. He looked at the marks a long time, trying to be reasonable, trying to be smarter than he was, wondering if they'd truly been made yesterday or sometime before, wondering if they were footprints at all. He climbed through the fence and slid down the bank as though it had been greased.

Walking carefully to one side of center, he followed the gully a long way up the mountain before he saw anything else. But then, on the bottom edge of a little skiff of sand not much bigger than a dinner plate, he found a faint crescent. He knelt and pondered it, rubbing his chin gently against his thumb and the side of his hand. It wasn't much of a mark, but it was the perfect size and shape to have been made by the toe of a boy's shoe, and that knowledge made his eyes wet.

After a while he got up and went on, but he found nothing else. As he climbed, the gully got more and more shallow until it ceased to exist, but somehow he felt sure the boy had come this way, never mind that he'd twice been sure the night before and been wrong both times. The evidence he had, slim as it was, signified. He felt it.

The tufted grass where the gully played out had been scorched by frost and teased by the wind and bore no sign that he could read, but it didn't matter. He turned back toward the Marshalls', thinking of the state penitentiary a dozen miles away and the dogs they kept to track down escaped prisoners. He didn't know how he was going to get them, but he meant to do it, and fuck the sheriff's office if they wouldn't cooperate. It seemed important that he get them at once because he'd already lost half a day and it was making up to rain or snow. He couldn't tell which, but the heavy clouds that had begun to gather didn't look as if they were going to blow away without trouble.

MADELINE:

When the police car pulled into the driveway, she went out to meet them at once. She told them she'd had no luck with her phone calls—she hadn't expected to, although she'd called more than a dozen households in Cedar Hill, and a few of them, to her embarrassment, had trouble remembering just who James Tally was and never did seem to understand why they should have been chosen for a call—but, worse, she realized the deputies didn't know what she was talking about either. The sheriff, it was clear, hadn't bothered to tell the deputies much of anything. One of them took out a notebook and began to ask her questions about how long James had been gone, whether or not she'd just punished him or had a particularly bad argument or fight with him, whether there were relatives close by that the boy might have gone to. She would have hated them if she hadn't been in shock and so exhausted and eaten up with worry she hardly knew what she was doing. Even so, she wanted to slap the notebook and pen from the deputy's hands, only Edward came walking up just then and changed everyone's focus of attention.

"I think I've found which way the boy went," he told them in a voice that was calm, intense, and very tired all at the same time. "He slipped off into a gully at the end of the cow pasture and turned just about straight east, but we'll need to get dogs from the penitentiary."

"Well, Mr. . . . ." the deputy flipped back a page in his notebook with his clean, square, freckled hand, "Mr. Tally, we need to ask just a few questions here and gather some information." He smiled politely at Edward and then at her. "I'm afraid we don't have any authority over the penitentiary people; they're state and we're county. But we'll look at what you found in just a second."

"We need those dogs," Edward said. "I doubt my son weighs much more than eighty pounds, and the ground was frozen yesterday."

She heard what was in his voice, but apparently neither of the deputies did.

"Now," the deputy said to her, "you say you've checked with all his friends?"

But before she could answer, Edward was standing almost on top of the deputy and had closed his hand over the deputy's, crushing the notebook. "Do you know how goddamned cold it was last night?" Edward asked him.

The deputy looked taken aback and Madeline thought she saw anger flare behind his eyes.

"Look at the sky!" Edward was saying. "If it snows, the dogs can't . . ." But he didn't finish. "We need to get started quick. We don't have any time," he said and released the deputy's hand and the disfigured notebook.

Edward wasn't angry, Madeline realized, only urgent. Perhaps the deputy realized that too, but whatever Edward saw in the deputy's face didn't satisfy him because he turned, started back up the driveway, and said: "I'll call the damned penitentiary myself."

"Rafer," the second deputy said, "the warden's name is Rafer."

"Bill Rafer," the deputy with the notebook added. "We'll bring what pressure we can from the sheriff's office."

EDWARD:

But when he told the warden the circumstances, what he'd found, his dealings with the sheriff, how long James had been gone, and his fears about the weather, Bill Rafer seemed to listen. How old was this boy? he wanted to know. What was Edward's relationship to him? Where had the boy disappeared from, and what direction was he headed in again? Each time Edward answered, the warden went silent, as though to ponder. "Well," he said and sighed, "that will put him in Pisga National Forest pretty damn quick, and I've lost one or two in there." He paused again as though thinking it over. "I'll see that you get your dogs, Mr. Tally," he said, "but I fear it will take the better part of an hour." Once more the warden asked him where he was calling from, and when Edward told him, he said all right, he had the Marshall place under his finger on the map, he just wanted to be certain there was no mistake.

MADELINE:

Much of what went on around her, she was too exhausted to acknowledge. People had begun to come and go about her like figures appearing and disappearing in a dream, and even when they spoke to her about James or tried to offer comfort, the person they thought they were speaking to, this James they spoke about, seemed curiously and strangely removed and separate. Even the guilt she felt seemed thin, although she affirmed her culpability. One of the deputies stayed to help in the search and two men from the forestry service came to help, although she wasn't clear how they knew about it. Somehow she learned her father was also going to join the search party. And Edward seemed to be everywhere she looked. But for a long time only her mother seemed to come vivid and clear in her vision, as if everyone else were a bit out of focus; but even her mother seemed somehow dreamlike, as though she had been drawn across many years from Madeline's childhood memory of her.

"I want you to sit down and eat something before you fall," her mother said, so bright and clear there seemed to be light around her. She led Madeline to the table and set a plate in front of her. Oh Momma, she wanted to say, doesn't anyone ever own themselves? Do we always give ourselves away? And does it always cause such injury when one of us tries to get ourselves back again? Only she didn't say anything at all. Her mother had gone away to try and make Edward come and eat something. And just as her mother said, she realized she *was* close to fainting because even her plate had a halo around it. Still, she poked at her food listlessly, not even quite sure what it was; and she managed a few bites only after Edward was made to sit down and eat.

When they could get away, Edward led her off to the trailer, where, numb and wordless, they looked at each other for a long time.

"We'll find him now," Edward told her at last. "I'm pretty sure I got hold of which way he went." He took her hands in his and gave them both a squeeze. "I'm satisfied I did," he told her, "and we'll get him back."

Tears spilled over her eyelids without warning, broke in her throat, and she began to sob. There were so many things to say, but they were so tangled in disillusion and sadness, in vain hope and regret, they couldn't come out. He held her while she sobbed. "I promise I'll find him," he told her and held her and laid his cheek against the top of her head.

"Do you love me?" she asked him at last.

"I love you," he said.

"Do you love me?" she insisted.

"I love you," he told her.

She sat up and looked him in the eyes. "But do you love me?"

"Yes," he said.

It wasn't any of the things she'd wanted to say; it had nothing to do with what was so tangled up inside her. She considered his face while he looked back steadily, but outside someone was calling, "Mr. Tally? Mr. Tally?" and in the next minute began knocking on the door.

Men were standing about the pasture, their breath steaming in the damp cold, the tall, stooped figure of her father among them. Two more men were trying to get dogs on long leads through the fence by the stile. "Do you have some dirty clothes your boy has worn recently, missus?" the man who had knocked on the door was asking her. In the hamper back at the house, she started to say, but then she thought of James's blanket and tilted up the couch, only to see that it was gone.

Edward saw it too, and deep, deep in his eyes, almost too faint to notice, the missing blanket seemed to light a spark, as though of confirmation. "Get the sheet," he told her; "the dogs can take a scent from that."

Two of the dogs, although large, had slithered under the bottom strand of wire, and their handler, wiry, bow-legged, and not young, had managed to slip through the fence and pass their leashes from hand to hand under the bottom strand, so that man and dogs were free. But one of the other two dogs had gone through the fence while the second went under, and one of them had hurt itself or was tangled because she heard impatient yelps and some of the other men had gone off to help.

The dogs were big and rawboned and clumsy looking and didn't seem to pay as much attention to the sheet she offered them as they might have, except to smear it with their muddy noses, but then Edward was beside her with James's Sunday jacket, which he'd turned wrong side out to offer them too, and then the second pair of dogs was there, the four of them filling each other with excitement and impatience, going from sheet to jacket, inquiring of each other's presence and the presence of the gathered men, tangling their leads, plodding about. And then Edward had handed her James's wrong-side-out jacket, given her a long, fierce, wordless hug, with his cheek pressed hard against the top of her head and her arms crushed awkwardly against her. And the next thing she knew, she was watching men and dogs negotiate the fence at the end of the pasture; and some indeterminable time after that, she was all alone and very cold, stooping to gather up her son's good Sunday jacket, lying wrong side out on the trodden earth, where she didn't know she had dropped it.

EDWARD:

Seeing that his son's blanket was missing allowed him to know absolutely what he knew already, and he didn't need the firm tracking of the dogs for further proof. But he feared the weather, and he wanted the handlers to turn them loose. The old one, Miles, had told him that it was raining already to the northeast at the penitentiary; but he wouldn't let the dogs off their leashes. They were ordinarily gentle creatures, these half Plott, half bloodhounds of his; but prisoners didn't like being run down by dogs and often tried to kill them, had killed some; and the best dog of the four, an eight-year-old bitch, had turned right vicious. So the dogs scrambled up the gully on their leads, occasionally talking James over among themselves in their baying, croupy voices, while the men, seven of them in all, labored behind. But just as they came up on the highway, a cold rain started to fall.

"Shit," Miles said, "hit don't *never* fail." He turned up the collar of his jacket and zipped it shut. "But don't you worry," he said to Edward. "Trust ole Sal. It'll take more than this here to wash a trail so clean, she can't follow."

At first he thought it was squirrels cutting something high up in the trees and letting the debris fall, pattering, through the leaves. He was only partly awake, and he could almost see the squirrels rolling hickory nuts between their nimble claws while tiny pieces of the outer green hull rained down. Perhaps in a little while, when he'd rested more, he'd take up his slingshot and try for one. His stomach was an empty space, and its lining was spiced with hunger. But he was tired and quite stiff and cold, and he didn't wish to stir from his blanket just then.

Yet after a while, when the pattering had reached such a volume it pressed against his ears, he raised his head and looked dumbly about, but he didn't see anything that would account for it. The only strange thing in sight was a hemlock off to his left and not as tall as he, which was jittering. There wasn't any wind, but the little tree trembled and danced as though a hand had taken hold of its roots beneath the ground and was shaking it. He watched, fascinated.

Even after he smelled rain, it took him another moment to connect the small, dancing tree and the din of pattering with what he smelled. Of course, it was raining. He was lucky to have built his lean-to under a wonderfully big, thick hemlock, and he was smart to have covered his roof well. The woods were so dim, he still couldn't see the rain fall, but it pleased him somehow that squirrels weren't making all that racket, because there was no need now to take up his slingshot and try to kill one for food. He could worry about food later, and he could worry about gathering firewood later too. It would be a silly thing to try and do in the rain, and he'd been bothering himself on and off about it. He could go back to his dreams, which seemed pleasant, if he could remember where he'd put them.

But while he was searching around for his dreams, he came across Earl Carpenter, who was trying to look as goofy and sad as Lester. He'd got himself one of Lester's ridiculous haircuts, and his shirt was too small and out at the elbow, like some of Lester's. Also the smirking cruelty was gone from his face, as though he were no longer the heartless bully James knew. "You're not fooling me any," James told him. But he could tell Earl was trying to be invisible and watching his chance to jump out the schoolroom window and make his escape. It was just an evil trick, this transformation, and James resented it. Who would have thought that Earl was clever enough to imitate someone who was better than he himself could ever be?

But then, wrapped in his blanket with something cold crawling through the roots of his hair, he saw the matter inside out and was even more astonished to realize that Lester and Earl were built of exactly the same stuff. Fear and failure and trouble. The only difference was that Lester kept all the bad things he'd been given to himself, while Earl gave them a cruel twist and tried to pass them on to everyone else.

Earl must have spit on him while he was considering this. The spit was icy, but weak, since he didn't fear Earl quite so much anymore.

No, he'd walked out in the rain after all to pick up firewood, never mind that he'd already decided he wouldn't bother.

No, the rain had worked its way through the tree and his roof and found him even though he hadn't gotten up. He knew he hadn't because his hip and back were still aching and stiff, and the cold had tightened its vices on his feet again. He could feel the rain, broken and tiny, on his face and in his hair, and he pulled the blanket up to cover his head. He would wait for it to go away. Also he needed to remember where he'd mislaid those good dreams he'd had so he could remember what they were. He didn't want any more silly things to bother him.

EDWARD:

"Well," Miles said when they crossed the wood's road, "we're in by God Pisga." He waited until everyone caught up. "We're gonna hafta hump," he said. "We got forty-five minutes or less of daylight, and the trail's beginning to wash, so them that can't keep up will get left. Stay where you're at if I lose you, so we can pick you up on the way back. If I have to give up and come hunt this boy tomorrow, I don't want to be huntin nobody else too." He brought a small round tin out of his hip pocket and tucked a pinch of snuff behind his lower lip. "Sal!" he said.

"Sally girl!" And he gave the bitch's leash a jerk and started off behind her and the other dog in a bow-legged trot.

Up the steep ridge they went. Miles and his dogs in the lead. Edward second with his breathing ragged and husky and his knees burning. The other brace of dogs and their handler trotting behind him. One of the forest rangers came next. Then Harley Marshall with his steady long stride. The second forest ranger. The deputy.

By the time they went over the crest, they were all soaked, and the rain was beginning to freeze on the ground, and still the old man's bitch seemed pretty sure of herself, although she didn't strain against her leash as much and seemed to work closer to the ground and move her head from side to side much more than she had been. The hound next to her seemed content merely to imitate her from time to time, but the second brace of dogs seldom bothered to put their noses to the ground.

Going down the steep far side, even the bitch got confused and stopped and tried to back up in order to smell under her own forepaws. She tangled herself for a moment with the other dog, whom she tried, without seeming to notice him, to shoulder out of the way or root under or climb over. After a moment Miles passed the leash of the second dog to Edward and, against her will, dragged the bitch around an outcropping and down the slope. "Come on. Come on. Sal! Come on," he told her. At the foot of the drop he said, "All right, she's got him again. He musta jumped or fell, I reckon."

By the time Edward got around and down, Miles was out of sight in the thick woods below. Edward let his dog lead him, more on the trail of the bitch and Miles, he figured, than James. He was soaked as much with sweat as rain, the woods were growing darker each moment, and a panic was building in him that they were going to be too late. It afflicted his stomach and made his heart ache in some far-off way, as though he might be yearning for something as unapproachable as a star.

By the time he struck the river, it wasn't raining anymore or even snowing exactly. Slender needles of ice were falling and hissing against the trees and the dead leaves on the ground, and

Miles and the bitch were coming back down the riverbank. He had a flashlight on.

Miles spat out his snuff when he stopped in front of Edward, spat two or three times extra and shook his head. "I'm sorry, son," he said. "I was hopin we'd catch up to him before now." He gazed through the driving needles of ice across the river. "If I had to guess, I'd say he crossed over, but even this old bitch can't track him now. The scent was already gettin froze down and sealed up before this shit started comin. Sal can run it till it's gone, but hell, she started casting around up river, didn't even have enough scent left to backtrack herself."

"I'm not going to quit," Edward said.

"If it thaws, the chances are good she can pick him up tomorrow. Sal's the best I ever followed, and anyhow, we'll be able to see. You could walk right by him tonight and not know it."

"He's my son," Edward said, "and it might not thaw."

"Well then, if he moves and we cut his trail, we'll find him. With or without the dogs, we'll find him then."

"He may not move either, goddamn it!" Edward said.

Miles looked away across the river. "I been doin this all my life," he said almost apologetically. "You're gonna tromp around and mess everything up over there, and chances are we'll be lookin for you."

"I'd like to borrow your flashlight," Edward said.

The second handler and his dogs came up then and, a moment later, Harley Marshall and one of the forest rangers. The second handler had produced a poncho from somewhere, which he was wearing, and all three men had flashlights. For a moment no one spoke, and the whole tired company merely gazed at the ice passing like slivers of broken glass through the beams of their flashlights and listened to it hissing around them and rattling against the young man's poncho.

"Well," Miles said, "looks like we lost a couple."

"Your partner took a little fall a ways back," Harley Marshall told the forester; "put his back out someway, so I don't expect him. I can't say as to the deputy," he told the rest of them. "Haven't seen him since we topped the ridge."

"Clarke," Miles said to the young handler, "you take Sally home, dry her good, use some of that salve under my bunk on her off front foot, and give her a good feed. Use a boot on her tomorrow if she needs it. I want her back here in the mornin ready to go. And I want your flashlight and that goddamned tarp you're a-wearin. Me and Mr. Tally are gonna stay with it awhile."

MADELINE:

She couldn't wait in the house, even though that was where the phone was. She felt in exile somehow, even if she was too tired and afraid to consider if it was through fault or circumstances. Her mother would come and get her if there was a call, just as she had automatically taken over Harley's duties at the post office. No one was accusatory any longer, not even her nieces. This wretchedness was hers alone, and she understood that, and so, at last, did everyone else. Only Lily presumed to come to the trailer and wait with her; but even Lily had the good manners not to speak. Without a word she made coffee for herself and Madeline and sat across the little fold-down table, while Madeline, rigid and scarcely breathing, found herself consecrated to something so awful and pitiless, she would never have guessed it. How could she have known that her own feelings could be so treacherous and that there was no end to wretchedness, no bottom to it? She would never have guessed she'd want to bargain away everything she'd wished and hoped for, if only things could be back the way they were, if her sweet son could be brought back to her alive and well, if her family could be restored in just the way that, not so many months before, she had found intolerable.

EDWARD:

He was grateful the older dog handler had understood him. He couldn't say aloud or even think what he dreaded most. And so the young handler, the forester, and three dogs had been sent back to collect the other two men; and Harley had been persuaded to search the near side of the river.

The nice thing about the dogs, Miles told them, was they followed their noses and didn't think; he did all the thinking and guessing and therefore made ninety percent of the mistakes. He was guessing that James had crossed over because Sal had hesitated for a beat or two at the edge of the water before she went on up the bank and then lost the trail altogether. He unzipped his jacket, reached around toward the small of his back, and gave Harley his pistol.

"Turns out I'm wrong and you find that boy," he told Harley, "point the muzzle in our direction and fire a shot. Fire another every twenty minutes till we find you."

When they had stripped to the waist, waded the river, and re-dressed, they separated and began to climb, Miles with the remaining dog, which he claimed was only a little bit better than no dog at all, and Edward with a borrowed light and poncho, since he hadn't given a thought to how he was dressed or what he might need. "James!" he called every fifty yards or so; "James!" although it didn't help tame the fear that had hollowed out his chest whether he chose to acknowledge it or not.

"Whooee!" Miles called off to the north, his voice made thin and faint by the ice hissing down between them. They were no more than a hundred yards apart, but Edward seldom saw a glimmer of the other man's light, as though the curtain of ice between them not only sliced voices thin, but turned light back nearly altogether.

His stiff back; his pelvis, which felt perversely twisted where it hooked to his spine; his hips and legs, which felt as though they'd been beaten; his feet pressed tightly in their separate vices—all these he came to regard with a sort of distant, fond pity as though they were former friends he'd learned were unhappy, or poor countries he'd studied in a geography lesson. But he had retreated toward the center of himself where he was more or less all right and able to take the long view of things. He'd left a lot of things so far behind, he had trouble recalling what they were. He had a remote memory of waiting for a vision and a new name, such as Indian boys were supposed to receive, but he'd mostly given up now. It would have been nice, but perhaps a vision and a name weren't going to visit. No matter. Anyway it wasn't so hard to be alone once he'd learned that pride couldn't help. Like guilt or fear or courage, pride wasn't made of such sturdy stuff, and he'd left them all nearly as far behind as his feet. There was about the same amount of conceit in any one of them as there was in any other, and that was the head and tail of it.

Finally he'd realized that the *it, itself*, was the most interesting thing of all. *It* was raining was not conceited, but very important. *It* was snowing. And perhaps *it* was too late. The most comforting part of all was that he had become a part of *it*, at last.

EDWARD:

Even when he went athwart the grade of the mountain to the north, he no longer heard Miles whoop or saw any light, although they had agreed to zigzag toward and away from each other so as to cover more ground and stay in touch. Perhaps he'd let himself slide too far south. Perhaps when he was moving north, so was Miles, and vice versa. "James!" he shouted.

A hundred times a bush, a log, an outcropping of granite, sometimes nothing at all, had made his heart jump. But at least for the last hour the ice had quit coming down, and his flashlight, though weaker, revealed more. "James!" he called.

When he played the light over the lean-to, he didn't know what it was and swept the beam on past. Not until the second time he washed the lean-to with his brassy light did he see the two forked corner posts and realize what he was looking at. In the next instant he saw the cut boughs inside and the humped blanket, frosted over and completely still.

There were filaments of ice in the boy's hair, and a faint rim of ice in his eyelashes sealed his eyes. Gently he cleaned all this away with a hand that seemed obscenely warm against his son's icy flesh before he tried to gather the small, stiff, terrible body against his chest as though to rock it and beg its forgiveness.

But the boy moved and groaned. He was certain of it. "James! James!" he croaked and rubbed the boy's small back savagely. "Son! Son?" he shouted and put his face against James's lips. He wasn't sure he felt any breath at all. He felt the boy's icy neck, digging his fingers under the jawbone for the carotid artery until, at last, he felt the faint, slow jog of blood. "I gotcha," he said, laughing and crying at the same time and holding James against his chest, "I gotcha now!"

Fiercely, he ripped off his poncho, laid James on it, and rubbed the boy's chest and arms and legs. Without ceasing to work, he shouted, "I found him!" to the north so ferociously, it seemed to rip the lining of his throat. He shucked himself out of his light jacket and put it on James, fearful of the awful stiffness of the boy's limbs. Gathering him up, poncho and all, fumbling until he got hold of his flashlight, he started off down the mountain. "I found him!" he shouted again.

Once he fell to his knees, and once he lost his footing so completely that he fell flat of his back, but he was up again almost immediately. Twice more he cried out that he had found his son, but he was so winded, he didn't think his voice could have carried very far. Still, a few minutes later, he heard Miles whoop, and a few minutes after that he saw a light bobbing and jigging toward him.

Miles helped him get his son across his sweating back, tying James's wrists together around Edward's neck with a handkerchief and ripping out the hood of the poncho until it would accommodate both Edward's head and James's too, which rested against the nape of Edward's neck. Miles did the shouting after that, while Edward labored and breathed great ragged, snoring breaths like a winded horse.

They didn't stop at the river but waded directly in. Miles set his dog free and kept himself downstream to brace Edward at every step while they waded toward the light Harley Marshall shone toward them from the far side.

EPILOGUE

What she decided in the next days and weeks was this. Everyone had deep desires and strong yearnings of the heart. The important thing was to know which were to be acted upon and which were to be confined to the realm of dreams. It made her happier, although on some level sadder too, having grown so wise. It was a relief to define things in a way that didn't put herself and everyone else in such peril and allowed her to know, as much as anyone could, what was going to happen tomorrow and the day after. And it was true that Edward had changed as well, and whatever else could be said, she would never again doubt that he loved her.

As for James, he left the hospital diminished by three toes and part of his left heel but enhanced by the profound and pleasant aftermath of a dream he couldn't quite recall. Still, he could not be made to add anything to the cryptic note he'd left. He'd merely grow uncomfortable and inward and say he was very sorry and would never do it again. And that was partly true. He wasn't sorry, but he would never do it again because he'd lost all superstition, never mind that he'd gotten nearly everything he'd wished for.

Even to Lester—who had turned handsome in the hospital although his perfect white teeth made him look a little as if he might bite—James kept his peace.